Lost American Fiction

Edited by Matthew J. Bruccoli

The title for this series, Lost American Fiction, is unsatisfactory. A more accurate series title would be "Forgotten Works of American Fiction That Deserve a New Public"—which states the rationale for reprinting these titles. No claim is made that we are resuscitating lost masterpieces, although some of the titles may well qualify. We are reprinting works that merit re-reading because they are now social or literary documents—or just because they are good writing. It isn't quite that simple, for Southern Illinois University Press is a scholarly publisher; and we have serious ambitions for the series. We expect that "Lost American Fiction" will revive some books and authors from undeserved obscurity and that the series will therefore plug some of the holes in American literary history. Of course, we hope to find an occasional lost masterpiece.

Fourteen titles have been published in the series, with four more in production. The response has been encouraging. We are gratified that many readers share our conviction that one of the proper functions of a university press is to rescue good writing from oblivion.

M.J.B.

A First National and Vitaphone Production.   *The Last Flight—Movie of Single Lady.*
RICHARD BARTHELMESS AS CARY LOCKWOOD AND HELEN
CHANDLER AS NIKKI.

Single Lady

John Monk Saunders

Afterword by Stephen Longstreet

SOUTHERN ILLINOIS UNIVERSITY PRESS
Carbondale and Edwardsville

Feffer & Simons, Inc.
London and Amsterdam

Copyright, 1931 by John Monk Saunders
Reprinted by special arrangement with Harcourt
Brace Jovanovich, Inc.
Afterword for *Single Lady* by Stephen Longstreet; and
Textual Note by Matthew J. Bruccoli copyright © 1976 by Southern
    Illinois University Press
All rights reserved
This edition printed by offset lithography in the
United States of America
Designed by Gary Gore

Library of Congress Cataloging in Publication Data
Saunders, John Monk, 1897–1940.
    Single lady.
    (Lost American Fiction)
    Reprint of the 1931 ed. published by Brewer & Warren, New York;
with new afterword.
    I. Title.
PZ3.S2575Si6   [PS3537.A8834]   813'.5'2   75–37829
ISBN 0–8093–0761–8

FOR FAY

*From ghosties and ghoulies and things that go bump
in the night dear Lord protect us. . . .*

> . . . the Cornish Litany.

" Well, the old guerre is fini."

" That's right."

" What you going to do now ? "

" Get tight."

" Then what ? "

" Stay tight."

> . . . SHEPARD LAMBERT.   In conversation
> Nov. 11, 1918.   Fismes, France.

Single Lady
BOOK I

Single Lady

BOOK I

CHAPTER I

S HE was sitting on a high stool at the bar
at Claridge's. The labels on the bottles
on the shelves behind the bar swam mist-
ily before her eyes; Campari, Byrrh, Mari-
ani (Unique Aperitif), Rossi, Pernod Fils,
Malaga, Punsch, Grande Champagne, White
Horse Cellar, Porto Rouge.

Her hand was so unsteady that when she
raised her glass she spilled her drink on the
front of her dress.

"You see," Shep said, "she can't even hold
a glass."

"Well, *he* can't either," she said, pointing at
Cary. "Besides he has to use two hands."

Cary Lockwood turned away quickly, got
down from his stool and left the bar.

Shep looked at Nikki. "Of course he can't
hold a glass," he said savagely. "His hands
are burned."

"Burned? How burned?"

"You don't deserve to spill your drinks."

"How burned?"

"He brought a ship down on fire."

"In the war?"

"He held the stick until his hands began to slip and then he held it inside his arms."

Nikki sat very still.

"He was trying to bring his gunner down safe."

"Did he bring him down safe?"

"He brought him down," Shep said.

"So that's why——"

"Yes," said Shep, "that's why he can't hold a glass. And you, you little—you little——"

"I know," said Nikki, "I ought to be shot. Will he come back, do you think?"

"I don't know."

"I'm so ashamed," said Nikki.

"You ought to be. How about another drink?"

"Could I have another?"

"Anything you like."

Nikki said she would have another of the same. She kept looking over her left shoulder for Cary.

"*Jean,*" Shep said to the barman, "*champagne cocktail pour Mademoiselle et encore un Martini pour moi.*"

Jean had worked at the Claridge bar for a long time, but he did not speak English.

"Plaisir," said Jean.

"You see," said Shep, "you have to be very careful with other people's feelings——"

Cary was coming back to his place at the bar, so Shep stopped short. Nikki slipped off her stool and ran to him. She caught his hands in her hands and pressed her face down into them. "Oh, your poor hands," she wept, "your poor hands."

Scarlet with embarrassment, Cary stood and looked down at her.

"Oh, your poor hands—your poor, poor hands——"

Very gently Cary released his hands. Then he turned away again and left the bar.

"Come here," Shep called to Nikki. "Come back here. If you aren't the worst—if you aren't—first you insult his hands and make him mad, then you cry over them and make him self-conscious—for Christ's sweet sake, what do you think you are trying to prove? He'll never come back now."

Nikki suddenly stopped crying.

"Then we'll have to find him."

"What do you want to find him for?"

"I want to tell him."

"You want to tell him what?"

"How ashamed I am."

It looked as if Nikki was about to have another *crise des larmes.*

"Well, anyway," Shep said, "you don't have to get emotional about it."

"Who's getting emotional?"

"You are. You're coming all apart."

"Encore pour Mademoiselle," he said to the barman. "Take a few more drinks and get yourself organized," Shep advised her, "and then we'll go look for him—and listen, if you don't stop weeping I'll leave you, too. Here, drink this. Make you laugh and play."

Bill Talbot turned around and asked what she was crying about.

Nikki was making up her tear-wet face with the aid of a lip-stick and two small mirrors which she held up so that she could see her profile.

"She's crying on account of they didn't wash her strawberries this morning," Shep explained.

"They didn't wash her strawberries?"

"No," said Shep, "they weren't washed."

"Well," said Bill, "I don't suppose there is a whole hell of a lot we can do about it now."

Shep paid for the drinks. He got down from his stool and so did Nikki.

"Where are you going?" Bill demanded suspiciously.

"Oh, out——"

"Out where?"

"Out to get a drink."

6

"I suppose you couldn't arrange that here?" Bill asked.

"Come on, Nikki," Shep said.

"I suppose you couldn't arrange about a drink here?" Bill persisted.

"No," Shep said firmly, "we got to go somewheres else."

"Suits us," Bill said. "Come on, Johnny. Come on, Francis. We got to go somewheres for a drink."

The Avenue des Champs Élysées was wet and glistening under the street lamps with early April drizzle. When they got in the cab there were five: Shep, Nikki, Bill Bronko Talbot, Johnny Swann and Francis, The Washout.

Shep made Bill and Johnny Swann sit on the jump seats in the cab. It was his cab and his driver so he distributed the occupants the way he pleased. He made Bill sit on one of the jump seats on account of his displacement. Bill Talbot's shoulders were a mile wide and he had a high specific gravity.

Shep made Johnny Swann sit on the other jump seat on account of, he said, Johnny was a licentious old man. Therefore he couldn't sit beside Nikki. Johnny was young and pink-cheeked and he used fixative on his hair. He protested fiercely about being described as a licentious old man. Shep and The Washout occupied the rear seat with Nikki sitting between them. Shep and The Washout were both slender and besides Francis wasn't interested.

On their way across town Shep suddenly shouted to his driver to stop.

"There he is." He was pointing at a semi-solitary figure seated at a table at a sidewalk café near the Madeleine, reading a paper backed book.

"Who?"

"Cary."

Cary looked up without surprise as the cabload of passengers got down in front of him.

"What the hell?" Shep demanded. "Trying to disown us?"

Cary said that he wasn't and politely invited them all to sit down and have a drink.

Shep accepted for the lot and looked into Cary's glass to see what he was drinking.

"Martinis? We'll all have Martinis."

They disposed themselves in chairs about Cary's table. Nikki sat down beside Cary.

"Could I have something else?" she asked timidly.

"I think she's going to be a problem," Shep said severely.

She wanted another champagne cocktail.

"That's what I started on," she explained.

Shep got a waiter over and ordered the drink.

"She's got so many things wrong with her," Shep proceeded, "so many things."

"I know," said Nikki, "I know. But what, for example?"

"Well, drinking, for one."

"What's the matter with my drinking?"

"You're a sissy drinker."

"Well," said Nikki defensively, "I've got the shakes."

"You should only have those in the morning."

"Maybe I can improve," she said hopefully.

"What were you doing sitting at the bar at Claridge's anyway? Didn't you know you're not supposed to sit there? There's a sign says ladies must sit at the back."

"But I can't read that far," she said.

The drinks came and Shep paid for them.

"We'll just have to take care of her, I guess," he said. "Do you think she's good-looking enough?"

"I know I'm not good-looking," said Nikki quickly, "but——"

"But what?"

"But when I went to parties when I was a little girl, my mother always said I had the nicest hair-ribbon."

They all stared at her. They were trying to imagine Nikki as a little girl with a big pink bow.

9

"Then there's your teeth now," Shep pursued, "one of them is turned sidewise——"

"You mean this one?"

"That's the one. Why don't you have it turned around?"

"Well, I would, only——"

"Only what?"

"Only it's kind of a help."

"In what respeck? In what respeck is it a kind of a help?"

"Well—when anyone kisses me too hard it splits my lip. And you could tell whenever I was kissed too hard on account of my lip would bleed. So now I don't let anyone kiss me."

"We'll let that pass," Shep said. "But how about those stains——"

"On my teeth?"

"Yes, the nicotine stains—why don't you have them ground off or something?"

"They won't come off," said Nikki, "and anyway they aren't nicotine stains. When I was a little girl——"

"A little girl where?"

"— a little girl in Honolulu. I was very ill once and those are fever stains."

"What was the matter with you?"

"I don't know. My mother was a Christian Scientist and she wouldn't tell me."

Bill looked around, got up and went off.

"Where's he gone?" Nikki asked.

"Went off to tame a alligator," Shep informed her. "He'll be right back. Now about your nose——"

"What about my nose?" Nikki said, running the tips of her fingers along the slender bridge of her nose.

"It doesn't run quite straight. It kind of fades off to the right."

"Well," said Nikki, "when I was a little girl——"

"—in Honolulu."

"—in Honolulu—I got bumped by a swing."

"Were there people in the swing?"

"Yes, standing up—pumping."

"How did you happen to get bumped?"

"I just walked right through the gate. I was only seven."

"Didn't you see them?"

"I can't see very far," Nikki reminded him.

About her neck, on a slender platinum chain, Nikki carried a diamond-and-platinum lorgnon. It opened with a spring and had small rectangular lenses. She used it frequently, peering at unfamiliar objects and people in a helpless, near-sighted way.

Nikki's eyes were unnaturally large and black and blind; like the eyes in the heads of girls painted by Marie Laurencin. They

11

looked as though they had been treated with belladonna; the pupils were so dilated as to blot out the irises almost.

"Did it hurt?" Shep asked her.

"Yes . . . it made me dizzy all day."

"Well," Shep said to the others, "I guess we can't hold that against her."

"Everybody makes mistakes," said Johnny Swann.

"Sure," said Shep, "Michelangelo painted Adam with a navel."

Nikki looked shocked for a minute and then gave a quick little burst of laughter. Shep wanted to know what she was laughing about.

"Even so," Nikki said, "even so, I think he would look funny the other way."

That's right, the others thought, he would look funny. You couldn't really imagine anyone without a navel. No sense to it.

Pretty soon Bill came back and then Johnny Swann left.

"Where's he going?" Nikki asked, looking after him.

"Off to shave a horse," Shep explained. "Have you got a husband or anything?"

Nikki shook her head.

"Father?"

"No."

"Mother?"

"Yes—but we haven't met for a long time."

"Why not for a long time?"

"Oh, on account of lots of things. My mother's name was Beulah and you can't have a mother named Beulah, so I changed it to Jane and that's how it all began."

"How old are you, Nikki?"

"Who, me?"

"She's younger than us," Bill said.

"Well, let's see," Shep ruminated. "I'll bet she belongs to the Oh-You-Beautiful-Doll period. Late, very late Oh-You-Beautiful-Doll."

"One-of-These-Days-You'll-Miss-Your-Baby," Nikki said.

"What kind of a girl do you think Nikki is?" Shep asked Bill.

Bill said he knew the kind of girl Nikki was *not*. He asked did you ever see the type that reported at the proper station on board ship for lifesaving drill—when the bugle was blown? With those Boddy Finch preservers on?

"Oh boy," said Bill, "there's where you see conservative females. Conservative and lumpy. No garter-snappers there, my boy."

Nobody could imagine Nikki in a cork lifepreserver.

"Well, I think she's the kind of girl that elderly gentlemen retrieve ping pong balls for."

"Don't play ping pong," Nikki said.

"Well then," said Shep, "I think she's the kind of a girl that sits down on Victrola records."

"—and always the favorite one," Bill agreed.

"Oh sure, nothing but Red Seal. She wouldn't put that aristocratic—I mean to say she wouldn't relax on anything less than the Hungarian Rhapsody Part Four."

"People shouldn't leave their records lying about," said Nikki.

"You see," said Shep, "you see, you *have* sat on records, haven't you, Nikki?"

Nikki crossed her legs and said, "The Nut Cracker Suite."

Anyway, Shep said, he bet she wasn't the kind of a girl that pearls grow dingy on. Bill said he thought probably she was the kind of girl that pearls grow dingy off.

Cary Lockwood didn't present any theories in regard to Nikki. He sat and listened. Nikki stole oblique glances at his hands.

Johnny Swann came back and pretty soon The Washout left the table.

"Got to sharpen my skates," he said apologetically.

"Who's he anyhow?" growled Bill. Nobody seemed to know.

"How the hell should I know?" Shep said. "He was in the Ninety-fourth. Used to fly

14

with some chap. Damn good team until the chap got killed. He's lonesome is all."

"He gets in your hair," Bill said.

"I like him on account of his watch," Shep said.

What about his watch, Nikki wanted to know.

"Don't you *know?* Haven't you *heard?*" Shep queried with profound concern.

Nikki shook her head blankly.

"Well," said Shep, "Francis carries a chiming watch. On account of he's always falling asleep in the daytime. It wakes him up every fifteen minutes."

"What kind of chimes?" Nikki asked.

"Three kind of chimes," Shep said, "Westminster, Canterbury, and Whittington; what kind you like?"

"Vanilla," said Nikki promptly.

"I think he's kind of a Miss Nancy," Bill said.

"Listen," said Shep, "listen. Just because you're a big bombardier. . . ."

"Don't rub it in," Bill said.

"—and an all-American," said Johnny Swann.

"All-American what?" Shep demanded.

"Half-back," said Johnny.

"Where?"

"Montana State or somewheres. Idaho or

something. Didn't you never read about Bill?
Bronko Bill?"

"Tell us about some of your s'periences on
the gridiron, Mister Talbot," Shep pleaded.

"Never had no experiences on the gridiron,"
Bill said. "Just played football."

"I think it's a forgery," Shep said.

"What do you want me to do? Bill said,
"tackle a horse or something?"

"Sure," said Shep, "go tackle a horse. Here
comes one now. Go tackle a horse."

Bill eyed the approaching horse expertly.

"Not that one," he said.

"Why not that one?"

"He's on the wrong side of the street and
beside he's got that high knee action. He runs
like Milton Gee. I might miss him and anyway there's somebody in the hack."

The waiter was setting down some more
drinks when Bill stood up and said, "Here
comes my horse."

He slipped in between the tables, crossed
the sidewalk and balanced on the curb.

"Hey, Bill," Shep called. "Bill! Come
back here! What the hell . . ."

As the horse came on, Bill took a couple of
mincing steps, opened up his stride and swung
alongside. He made a peculiar sliding tackle,
dropping down along the horse's fore legs,
locking them in his big arms and tripping him

up. The horse went down like a hunter over a
hedge; at the same time Bill contrived to throw
his one hundred and ninety pounds against the
horse so as to upset him, so that the horse fell,
not on his knees, but half on his shoulder, sliding along the wet pavement.

For an instant they lay together, Bill and the
horse, then Bill was up and helping the horse
to his feet, holding his head so powerfully that
the animal could not struggle. The hack had
not overturned. A crowd was gathering on
the sidewalk. Shep broke through and ran
to the coachman.

"You shouldn't drive so fast," he cried at the
coachman in French. "You nearly killed my
friend who was just trying to cross the street."

The hackman opened up his mouth wide to
let go a flood of expletives and Shep pressed
fifty francs into his hand.

"Nice horsie," Bill was saying to the horse,
stroking the shoulder on which he had fallen.

"Come back here!" Shep commanded, pulling him away.

As the horse trotted off, Shep watched him
to see if he was lame. He wasn't.

"Listen," said Shep, as he led Bill back to
the table, "you're an all-American—you're
two all-Americans—you're the whole bloody
team. Now you don't have to tackle any more
horses, see. Nor run back any Bugattis, nor

throw any gendarmes for a loss. You are the twelve greatest all-Americans in my estimation. Now come and finish your drink."

"O.K.," said Bill, grinning all over the place. "But wasn't that a sweet spill?"

"Sure was a sweet one," Shep agreed. But the muscle under Shep's left eye was flickering. Shep had a spasmodic tic. It jumped whenever he was excited—or sober.

The boys stood up to welcome Bill back to the table, but Nikki sat still and pale as anything.

Finally she stood up, a little unsteadily.

"Where are you going?" Shep asked.

"Will you excuse me for a moment?" she said.

"Where you going?"

"To take a Chinese singing lesson."

"Par ici, madame," said the waiter at the door.

The low throaty tones of Nikki's voice remained on their ears for some moments after she left. Shep was trying to remember who else had a voice like that and suddenly he remembered Tallulah Bankhead. Nikki's voice had the same husky, throbbing quality.

Shep ordered some more drinks and they all waited for Nikki to come back.

"Could we go to Montmartre, do you think?" Nikki said when she sat down again.

They all looked at her speculatively.

"She hasn't been in Paris long, I guess," Shep said.

"That's right," Nikki admitted.

"You want to go to Montmartre?"

"I want to go dancing."

"To the Florida or Perroquet, I s'pose."

"Anywhere," said Nikki.

"We *could* take her to the Florida," Shep said eyeing her critically.

Nikki was dressed for the evening. Under her mink wrap she was wearing black chiffon over gold metal cloth, with a wide, golden sash draped in the oriental manner. She had on a gold metal cloth turban disposed in soft, exact folds about her head.

"Only," said Shep, "it's too early."

Nikki was disappointed.

"What about the Moulin Rouge?" Johnny Swann suggested.

"Well——"

"Or the Monaco? Le Rat Mort? Bal Tabarin?"

"Bal Tabarin."

"How about it, lads?" Shep inquired of the others. "Shall we break down and take Nikki up on the hill?"

"Anything to please a lady," said Johnny.

"We're off in a billizzard of horse-radish," Shep announced. "Somebody pay for the drinks, and Cary, you're coming along too."

Shep signalled his driver and they all piled in. Shep told him where to go and the driver turned his cab into the Boulevard de la Madeleine.

"I wonder did anyone ever tackle a horse before?" said Johnny.

"I knew a boy once who swallowed a goldfish," Nikki volunteered.

"Swallered a goldfish, did he? Well—well. How come he to do that?" Shep was interested.

"It was at a party. He just reached in the bowl and fished out a goldfish and swallowed it."

"Land sakes," said Shep, "what happened?"

"Nothing. Just the end of the goldfish. We all stood around waiting for something to happen, but nothing happened. He took a couple of drinks and cut in on the first couple that came along."

"What was he drinking?"

"I don't know—it was out of a flask."

"Why did he swallow the goldfish?" Bill demanded.

"I asked him afterwards—and he said he didn't know. It seemed like a good idea at the time."

They all fell quiet, thinking about the boy who swallowed the goldfish. The cab rolled through the Place St. Georges, followed the Rue Fontaine for a couple of blocks and turned up a steep street leading to the Place Pigalle.

"You see," Bill told Nikki, pointing to a lettered bunting flung across the brilliantly lighted marquis in front of the Bal Tabarin, "it says *gala de soirée.*"

"What does that mean?"

"Well, it means a gay and lively celebration. It means there'll be a hot time in the old town tonight."

"The real idea is," Shep said, "that you can drink nothing but champagne inside. That's the point. On gala nights they add a special charge.

"So every night is gala night in Paris at special rates. Oh, the French they are a funny race, they fight with their feet——"

Bill gave Shep a sour look. Bill was already beginning to show symptoms of dignity in Nikki's presence.

Shep bought a handful of little red ten franc entrée tickets at the window on the right in the lobby. They passed through the swinging doors and down the steps into the ball room.

Nikki said she had never been in the place before. They left their things at the checkroom and went out on the floor. Bill signalled the captain and they found a roped-off table for six on the low balcony along the right by the mirrors.

The boys took the place as a matter of course, being interested only in the location of the table and the wine list.

Nikki, however, still had the quality of eagerness. She looked about her with bright interest, peering here, there and everywhere with her lorgnette.

Who does not know Le Bal Tabarin on the Rue Frochot? The dance floor, filled with a mongrel collection of Americans, Argentines, blacks and yellows dancing with red-lipped little French tarts, resembles a cabaret in the reserved quarter of a Mediterranean port. There is a bar at the left and the bowling alleys downstairs, and the artist who sketches your picture for ten francs or so.

"We'll order a bottle of champagne for our girl friend," Shep said, "and then we'll have to wangle some still wine."

"What's the matter with champagne?" Nikki asked. "I always thought——"

"You'll find out," Shep said, "if you stay with it long enough."

"It keeps coming up in your nose," Bill said.

"It turns sour on your tongue and gives you wambling of the insides."

"Hey," said Bill.

"It's only for Americans," Johnny said. "We French never touch."

"I like champagne," Nikki said.

"Give the gal some Cordon Rouge," Shep sighed.

"Who wants to dance with a girl?"

"Cary is the best," they told her. "He hasn't got so many feet and he practically never falls down."

"Don't you even care about dancing?"

"Do you tango?" Cary asked skeptically. The orchestra was playing only tango music.

"I don't know. I never tried."

They stepped out on the floor and Cary took her in his arms. Nikki shivered ever so slightly.

"Bring us back a parrot," Shep called.

"Bend your back a little more—when you come forward," Cary was saying. "My, but your back is tight—can't you let go a little?"

"Give me a minute," Nikki said, "I'm so nervous. My back always gets tight when I'm excited."

"What about?" Cary asked.

"Well, leave a lady a few secrets, won't you?"

Cary took her slowly through the first movements of the tango.

"How did you get so good anyway?" Nikki asked.

"A girl, and I'm not too good anyway."

"What girl?"

"I don't know her name."

"Don't know her name?"

"Shep calls her Kiss-Me-Quick."

When Nikki had overcome her original panic, she began to follow Cary nicely.

"Thank you so much," she said when the music stopped. "I enjoyed that."

"Thank you, I enjoyed it, too," Cary said simply.

"Your Mr. Lockwood is a wonderful dancer," Nikki announced when she returned to the table.

"Oh sure," Shep agreed without jealousy, "the Duke is a fast torpedo. You should see him run the high hurdles."

"Does he do that, too?"

"Fifteen flat on turf."

Nikki could see Cary, clean-limbed and fleet, skimming over the high hurdles.

"Really?" she said. She couldn't tell when any of them were serious. "Where?"

"Jolly old Oxford."

"Did he go to Oxford?" Nikki turned to look at Cary again.

"Ra-ther," said Shep, "he's up there now."

"You don't mean right now?"

"He's on his vacation, I mean."

"Vacation?" Nikki said. "Vacation in March?"

"It's like this," Shep said, "we got three terms at Oxford."

"That's nice for you," Nikki said.

"We got three kind of terms," Shep proceeded, "Michaelmas, Hilary and Trinity."

"I'll take vanilla," said Nikki promptly.

"And Cary is between Hilary and Trinity," Shep said, "for a month or so."

"Did you go to Oxford, too?"

"Ra-ther."

"Did you graduate or anything?"

"Ra-ther," Shep admitted amiably. "Magister Artium. Magna cum lousy."

"How about Bill and Johnny?"

"They came after. Just a couple of disabled war vetrians. Turned the place into an Old Sodger's Home."

"Well, well," said Nikki, "so that's how it is."

"Cary is a Rhodes Scholar."

Nikki didn't know what that was.

Shep explained that it was a kind of strange specimen of American that was unloaded upon poor Oxford every year under the eccentric terms of an old will.

"And now look at him," Bill said.

"Most high-powered chap ever went up to Oxford," Shep continued. "Runs the hurdles,

number two on the tennis, addresses the Union,
used to play the organ in chapel——"

"Doesn't he play any more—" Nikki began
and suddenly checked herself, remembering
Cary's fire-scarred hands.

Cary paid no attention to the discussion.
The lights went down; white and blue spot
lights were turned onto a large woman in white
tights who came out on the floor to dance the
cancan. She danced around holding one foot
in her hand over her head.

"French women never shave under the
arms," Shep observed. "Is that a good title
for anything?"

"Too long," said Johnny. " 'The Girl With
the Smoldering Armpits' is better."

When the billowy creature retired after doing the split, the spot lights were trained on a
transparent gauze curtain on the orchestra
dais behind which posed a tableau of nude
ladies.

"Why is it," Shep demanded, "that women
look much harder at nude women than men?"

"You mean than men look at nude women?"
Nikki asked.

"That's right."

"Well," said Nikki, not taking her eyes off
the nudes, "it's on account of comparison."

"I'll tell you something funny," Shep said.
"I was only four years old once——"

"What did he say?" Johnny inquired of The Washout.

"Tsaid he was four years old once."

"Amazing."

"—and my aunt had a very décolleté dinner dress——"

"What did he say?" Johnny inquired again. He was studying the nudes and didn't keep his mind on the conversation.

"Tsaid his aunt had a low-necked dress."

"Incredible," said Johnny.

"—and she sat right across the table from me and I said, 'Auntie, I can see your knees.'"

Shep looked very pleased with himself. Nobody changed their expressions.

"Maybe I better do my match tricks," Shep said.

"You do and I'll recite," Nikki said fiercely.

"What? Recite what?"

"Poetry."

"Whose?"

"My own."

"Do you write poetry?"

"Yes. I'll send you a photograph of it if you like. Would you like a photograph of my poetry?"

Shep picked up the Cordon Rouge bottle. "What the hell's in this anyhow?" he said, sighting along the neck. "Nothing intoxicating, I hope."

"And if you do card tricks, I'll sing," Nikki threatened.

"You sing," Shep warned, "and Bill is liable to do nip-ups."

"All hands to repel boarders," Bill said. "Here comes Johnny's friend."

"Who?"

"Little Kiss-Me-Quick."

"For God's sake where?" Johnny said.

"She goes for Johnny," Shep explained. "Isn't she cute?"

"She looks like something that ought to be tattooed on a sailor," Nikki observed.

"In red ink," Shep agreed.

Kiss-Me-Quick, smiling saucily through her red lips, spied Johnny and came over.

"*Viens* dance wiz me, Zhonny," she said. "Be my comrade. *Hola,*" she said looking at Nikki, "zat is zee mos' pretty girl what I 'ave seen." She regarded Nikki still more closely. "*L'amour n'avait pas passé par la,*" she concluded.

Nikki smiled happily. "She's cute."

"'E is so naughty, zis one. 'E run away from Renée. Come on, bébé. Dance wiz Renée."

Reluctantly Johnny went off with her. She took him over to the bar and made him buy her a side-car. He did not come back for a long time.

"What did she say about Nikki?" Bill asked Shep in a whisper.

"She said," Shep replied, "she said love has not yet passed that way."

"Well, I'm a son-of-a-gun," said Bill and regarded Nikki's pure profile for some time.

Le Bal Tabarin opens early and closes early. Around midnight Shep suggested going to the Monaco around the corner. He sent Bill over to collect Johnny. He brought him back by the ear.

The group left the table and arrived unexpectedly upon a little tableau in the coat room. One of the hat-check girls had thrown Nikki's dark mink coat over her shoulders and was posing for the others. At the sight of the owner, she shrieked and burst into profuse apologies.

Nikki smiled at her.

"If I am not too bold, Madame, what did the coat cost, perhaps?" the girls asked.

"Cinq minutes de folie," Nikki said brightly.

The girls in the coat-room laughed and chattered like magpies. *"Cinq minutes de folie,"* they repeated, *"cinq minutes de folie, oh, la la."*

"I read that in a book once," Nikki explained to Shep.

"I don't think so," Shep said.

Bill wanted to know what it was Nikki had

said that made the coat room girls laugh so much.

"Well," Shep said, "one of them asked her how much her coat cost and Nikki said five minutes of folly."

Bill looked startled.

"But she didn't mean it. She said she got that out of a book."

A dark furtive little youth came up to them as they came out on the sidewalk.

"Would you care to see the exhibitions," he invited. *"Très original—tres amusant—vrai Parisien——"*

"Get the hell out of here," Bill growled at him.

La Monaco was a later, noiser place and very crowded. The floor was smaller and there were any number of attractive, unattached young ladies about. Nikki asked about one of the men dancing on the floor. His chin was disfigured by a long deep scar. Nikki said she thought he had an interesting face. Shep said it was Eugene Criqui, the French prize fighter. He had his jaw shot away in the war and French plastic surgeons made a new one for him out of sheep bone. He was going over to America soon to fight for the championship. Nikki said she hoped he would win.

They drank some more wine and danced a few dances and then because no one had thought of anything to eat, Shep suggested taking Nikki down to *La Père Tranquille* for onion soup.

"Onion soup?" Nikki queried. "Onion soup? Who ever heard of such a thing?"

"Fine for the hips," Shep told her. "Make you laugh and play."

Nikki was dubious, but she came along. It was four o'clock in the morning. Bill brushed aside the authorized guides, who clustered about them on the sidewalk outside the Monaco and they all piled into Shep's cab.

"There's someone in this outfit that attracts guides," Shep said sternly looking at Johnny Swann, "and I'm not sure yet who it is."

Johnny looked as innocent as possible.

On the way Shep asked Nikki if she'd ever seen the dawn crack over Notre Dame and Nikki said no, so he told the driver to drive to the Isle de la Cité.

"We got to show this gal the town," he said, "being as she's not been here so long."

"She's been here long enough to get the shakes," Johnny said.

"That doesn't take long," Shep said, "if you apply yourself to the job."

It was still dark when they got there. They drove across the Island in front of the cathedral and got out on the Petit Pont, the little bridge across the Seine that connects the Island with the left bank.

Shep stopped the cab and they all got out and sat on the wide stone railing of the bridge and waited for the dawn to crack.

The dawn came up all purple. First you could make out the dim outlines of the twin towers of the church. Then you could see the early morning figures hastening through the mist across the square. Then suddenly you could see the whole thing, the church and the river and the trees and the carts.

Nikki was enchanted. "You have such fine ideas, Shep," she said.

"Now we can go for our soup," Shep said.

They slipped down off the railing and climbed back into the cab. As soon as they entered the market district around Les Halles, Nikki felt excited again. The clean intoxicating smell of fresh vegetables filled the morning air. The cab made its way through the wooden carts piled high with carrots, celery, watercress, onions, garlic buds and cabbages.

They alighted in front of a little restaurant on a corner in the very heart of the market. Shep led the way up some stairs and as soon as he entered the room he was swept into the majestic bosom of the proprietress.

"*Mon enfant!*" she cried and embraced him. She was a splendid healthy creature, in close-fitting black sateen, was Madame, the proprietress. She radiated high spirits and peasant vitality. She combed her black hair straight back from her forehead and she had a faint dark moustache on her upper lip. Shep said it was the moustache that won the madame to his heart. It was one of the Madame's chiefest charms. He said he found it irresistible.

The Madame embraced the others, especially Johnny Swann, and led them off to a large table at the far side of the room. Shep said they all wanted onion soup, so she went off herself to attend to the matter.

"There goes the real love of my life," Shep explained to Nikki as he watched her fine figure disappear through a doorway. "She parts her teeth in the middle. In fact, come to think of it, she parts everything in the middle."

Nikki said she thought she was charming.

"She's my extra special darling," Shep said. "My sweetheart de luxe."

"She likes you," Nikki said.

"Boy, what a bosom," Johnny murmured, "if that bosom were placed end to end. . . ."

". . . . it would require five hours to pass a given point, *I* know," Shep said. "There goes that licentious old man again. You ought to be ashamed of yourself, Johnny."

The Madame came back in a minute bear-

ing a ukelele in her hands. She said she had
ordered the soup. She said what was she to do
with the little *violon?* The young gentleman
who was with them the last time left the *violon.*
She kept it in her office, but he never came
back for it. Was he coming back ever, or
what was she to do with it?

"Play it," Johnny Swann suggested.

The ukelele belonged to Joe Sayles, of
Queens College, Oxford. Joe always started
off with a ukelele, but he seldom came home
with one. His ukeleles were scattered all over
the place. He only played when the mood
was on him, and he never knew when the mood
might seize him, so he carried a ukelele along
just in case. He was pretty sure to get hot in
low company, in places like, say, the Lamb
and Flag at Oxford or Le Pere Tranquille,
places where his genius for ribald ditties found
full expression.

Once the mood was past, he abandoned the
ukelele. He said he couldn't bear the thought
of carrying a cold instrument about in his
hand. He felt kind of ashamed of it.

Johnny Swann took the ukelele from the
Madame and handed it to Nikki. "You're
from Honolulu," he said.

Nikki tuned it, strummed a few chords.

"Il marche?" demanded the Madame eagerly.

"But yes," Shep said, "it marches like anything."

Nikki said it was quite a good ukelele. She leaned back against the wall and began to sing a native song of the islands. Heads came up all around the room. Something in the tone of the instrument and the husky quality of Nikki's voice made them attentive.

Nikki sang in such a low voice that the girls across the floor leaned forward, straining to hear the words. Mischievously, Shep signalled them to come over.

In a minute they had a party. The Madame, seeing how things were going, ordered the tables put end to end along Nikki's side of the room, so that it made one long picnic table.

The new arrivals, girls who came in mostly in twos, came over to the table. The hat-check girls came out of the check room and stood listening. Shep was delighted. The Madame beamed. Nikki played and sang without the slightest trace of self-consciousness.

The strange, poignant quality of her voice, coupled with the haunting note of the island songs, had a devastating effect upon one of the girls across the table. She began to weep gently into her handkerchief. All the other girls nodded compassionately at each other. Poor Yvonne, she had the blues again.

Shep told Johnny to go over and comfort

the poor child. So Johnny went over and sat down beside her and she wept on his shoulder. It was very touching. Yvonne poked blindly about in her bag and brought forth a snapshot of an American army Captain and showed it to Johnny. Le Capitaine had said he would send for her, but he never even wrote.

Johnny was doing a fine job of comforting the girl when Kiss-Me-Quick came in. She separated the two and turned loose a flood of French upon Yvonne. Yvonne tearfully held up the picture as a kind of defensive explanation. Kiss-Me-Quick regarded the photograph and then sat down and began to comfort Yvonne herself. Yvonne burst into fresh tears.

Nikki sang *China Lady,* and *Southern Rose,* and *Show Me the Way to Go Home.* It was all very splendid indeed.

Half way through the last song, another voice came into Nikki's, a clear nicely-pitched tenor, following in perfect harmony. The Washout was sitting back against the wall, his eyes half-closed, singing along with Nikki. He sang so easily and with such absence of effort that for a moment no one knew quite where the voice came from.

One of the girls clapped her hands and cried: *"Bravo le negre-blanc!"* The girl beside her gave her a slap on the mouth and told her to shut up. A startled, hurt expression came upon the face of the slapped one. She had not meant to be insulting; she only wished to applaud the albino, of which Francis was a pure type. No one knew this better than Francis himself. Besides, he did not, at this time, take offense easily. He merely blinked at her and continued to harmonize.

Shep looked pleadingly across at Cary sitting abstractedly with his elbows on the table and his chin cupped in his hands. Cary knew that Shep wanted him to join in, too, so more in order to please Shep than any desire to sing, Cary added his baritone to the mixed duet. Shep sang tenor, and when he came in, Francis, with no apparent effort, lifted his own voice into a counter tenor and then they had a fine blending of voices.

". . . . *well, I've been drunk for the last six months, show me the way to go home."*

Then they sang, a little uncertainly to be sure, two current song hits, *My Sweet Little Alice Blue Gown* and *Whispering,* and then the onion soup came. Shep said that he didn't know there was such talent in the outfit. He said he was going to organize an *à capella* choir and tour the capitals of Europe. He asked Francis how come he to have such a voice, and Francis said, unblushingly, that he used to sing in a choir.

Single Lady

Shep looked at him in astonishment. "A choir boy? A choir boy? Whoever heard of such a thing?"

Yet when Shep stopped to think about it, it wasn't at all incongruous that Francis should have been a choir boy. In fact, come to think of it, Francis couldn't have been anything else but a fair-haired choir boy with a sweet soprano voice. Shep wondered why he never thought of it before.

Nikki was enchanted with the onion soup, hot and pungent and nourishing as it was. She said it had a fine bouquet, too. When she had finished, she gave back Madame the ukelele and said suddenly that she wanted to go home. Shep paid the account for the long table of guests.

"I'll take you home, Nikki," Shep said. "Where do you live?"

"Carlton."

"The Carlton? The *Carlton?*"

"I'll take her home, too," Bill offered generously.

"Let's all take Nikki home," said Johnny Swann.

Shep looked at Nikki again. The Carlton. The Carlton was a sort of rendezvous of racing people. A bit on the sporting side. Not many Americans stopped there. What was Nikki doing there?

They all said goodbye to the Madame and went downstairs and out into the fresh morning air. Shep's cab was standing at the curb; the poor driver asleep at the wheel. It was five in the morning. Shep woke him up and they all clambered into the cab.

There was no one at the porter's desk or at the lift at the Carlton when they came in. The Carlton seemed an empty, deserted place at this hour. The electric lights in the lobby were burning pale and feeble in the watery half-light of the early morning. Shep fished Nikki's key out of her box and they decided to run the *ascenseur* themselves.

"I'll run it," Bill said.

"The hell you will," Shep retorted, "you'd try to do tricks with it. You'd run us all right through the blinking roof. You'd——"

It was agreed that Bill could close the gates, but Nikki should operate the car.

She slid back the handle and the car jerked a couple of times, but refused to rise.

"Pull out the wheel-chocks," said Bill.

"Maybe they's too many of us," said Shep. "Somebody ought to get out and run up." But they all pretended to be sound asleep.

Nikki tried the handle again and the car began to rise smoothly.

"Do you know how to stop her, Nikki?" Shep asked.

"I think so."

As they were passing the third floor Bill looked at his wrist watch. "Don't we change time here or something? Lose an hour or gain an hour or anything? Rocky mountain time or something?"

"There's not any up-and-down time," Shep said, "only crosswise. You won't have to change your watch when you go to heaven."

"My ears are popping," Bill said.

Nikki stopped the car at the fifth floor. Shep had her key so he went on ahead to open her door. He unlocked it and switched on the light inside.

"Well, I'll be—well for—why she's got a whole apartment," he said when they streamed into her room. The magic of the night still existed in the room, the drawn curtains held out the early morning light.

"And a gramophone."

"Why, Nikki!"

Shep walked over and opened the connecting door. It opened into her bedroom.

"Hi!" he exclaimed, "look at all the bottles! Come and look at all Nikki's bottles!"

Nikki's bedroom, enormous, wide, and high-ceilinged, glowed mysteriously in the half-light of the red shaded lamp on her night table. Red and gold. Red and gold. Red and gold. The room might be gold in the mornings, but at night it was red, deep rich red, raspberry red. The carpet was red and the leather screen by the fireplace was red and the drapes were red. The walls were gold with brocaded figures. The brass rails of the twin beds shone bravely.

The counterpanes were red. Only one bed had been opened. Across it lay a flowered chiffon night gown, sheer and transparent as gauze, but with a belt and a tiny lace handkerchief folded in the pocket.

Beside it lay a kimono splashed with Hawaiian birds and flowers and fishes. Two huge steamer trunks beplastered with stickers gaped open near the foot of the bed. Silk stockings and silk underthings and pink tissue wrappings peeped from the half-pulled-out drawers; the only disorder in the room.

But the bottles. Nikki's glass-topped dressing table in the corner by the French windows was loaded with scent bottles; tall and long and narrow crystal bottles and squat and round and square and fantastic bottles, black bottles and pearl bottles; bottles with tall green stoppers in them and red stoppers; bottles filled with pale, clear amber liquor that caught and imprisoned the rose-colored light from the lamp.

"Can you imagine so many bottles?" Shep inquired breathlessly.

Single Lady

Besides the bottles there were boxes, leather boxes with tassels—red and green leather cases with pale pink and blue linings. In and around the bottles and boxes crept long strings of pearls. A watersnake skin bag and a gold cigarette case and a gold lighter lay among the bottles.

A tall glass vase filled with cut roses balanced on a side table and there were a lot of books with painted jackets lying about.

Johnny Swann picked up a scent bottle and cried, "Ylang! Ylang!"

"Hey," Bill growled at him, "don't be handling her things. Put that down."

"Chichi," said Johnny.

"Leave 'em alone."

"Salammbo," said Johnny.

Bill started over toward Johnny.

"Caprice," Johnny cried. "Jinko, Chypre, Borgia, Mea Culpa, Reve de Vestale, Lys Noir . . . " he ducked behind a chair.

On the night table beside Nikki's bed was a magnum of mineral water and a glass and a red leather traveling clock with an octagonal face. On the little shelf underneath stood a tiny pair of red satin mules with gold pompoms. The pompoms looked kind of lonely.

"See," said Shep, picking up the clock, "she never winds her clock. It says eleven and I've never been anywheres at eleven o'clock in my life."

"What time are you anywhere?" Bill asked.

"Two o'clock. It's always two o'clock in my life. Listen," he said, "besides never having any matches and spilling her drinks, she doesn't wind her clock. I'm going in the bathroom and see if she leaves the cap off her tooth paste. Is it all right?" he asked, looking at Nikki.

"Help yourself," said Nikki.

Shep went into the bathroom and they heard him exclaiming again. They all peered in and saw him standing in front of a table, gazing reverently at a bewildering assortment of bottles, face lotions, hand lotions, astringents, a great round bottle of green crystals, and a huge square bottle of eau de Cologne, as big as your head.

On the table, too, was a long vial of bromide tablets, effervescent, a gold safety razor, a bundle of orange sticks, a great bottle of bath salts, a jar of healing cream, a glass cylinder of red liquid dentifrice, a nail brush, a chamois buffer, and cakes of green and yellow soap.

In a shallow pool of water in the bottom of the wash basin two turtles paddled solemnly about after a green lettuce leaf. The shells of the turtles were inlayed with brilliants.

"Well, strike me pink," said Shep. "She's a turtle fancier."

On the white tile floor of the bathroom, like stepping stones across a shallow pond, lay orange and rose and blue berets. Snoozing softly on a pile of colored berets in the far corner of the bathroom was a white and black wire-haired puppy with a red collar with brass studs. He lifted his head, blinked in the light, and came trotting over.

"Look at that thing," Shep said, "what's he doing here?"

"He lives here," Nikki said.

"What's his name?"

"Eighty-Eight Carlton."

Shep said he was a noble animal and patted his head.

Nikki said indeed he was a noble animal, only it was hard to tie the bows on your slippers when he was around. He thought it was a game and poked his nozzle into your hands and nipped your fingers and got in the way generally. Nikki picked him up and put him back in his beret bed and switched off the light in the bathroom.

They went back to her bedroom. Shep opened the door to her wardrobe and peered in at a long row of gowns neatly hung on hangers and at tier upon tier of shoes and slippers.

"Do you s'pose you could excuse me?" Nikki asked, "because I'd like to go to bed."

"Certainly," said Bill Talbot, "I'll clear us all out of here. Say good night to Nikki," he commanded. They all said good night to Nikki and Bill steered them toward the door.

He lifted up Johnny Swann who had gone to sleep on the chaise longue at the foot of Nikki's bed, with his head buried in the dark, glossy fur of Nikki's coat, and carried him into the sitting room.

Shep went over and fixed a place for himself on the sofa. "This is a fine place," he said, "I like this place."

Johnny took off his dinner coat and rolled it under his head on the floor. "I like this place, too," he said.

"Well, I'm damned," Bill said. "You guys think you're going to stay here?"

"Sure," said Shep.

"Sure," said Johnny.

Both seemed to feel that they were happily situated.

The door to Nikki's bedroom opened. She stood in the doorway in her mules and a white Hawaiian kimono with red sunbursts.

"Will somebody scrub my back?" she inquired innocently. "My maid is gone." She held out a hand towel, crushed and soaked in eau de Cologne. Shep responded instantly.

45

He skipped over and took the towel from Nikki's hand. She turned around and slipped the kimono off her shoulders, holding it tight and high in front. The top of the garment hung in a graceful loop across the small of her back, exposing a wide area of dazzling white skin.

Bill Talbot stood transfixed.

Nikki looked back at Shep over her shoulder.

"Scrub *hard,*" she said.

"Did anyone ever see such a back in their life?" Shep murmured reverently. "Did . . . anyone . . . ever . . . hear . . . of such a thing? Look at that back. Just look at the beautiful, beautiful thing. *Look* at that thing."

Shep was practically speechless with admiration. He was exalted with the rare privilege of scrubbing Nikki's back.

"My, my," he said, "I could go on doing this for a long time."

Nikki reached around for the towel.

"Thank you, Shepard, that feels ever so cool and nice. Good night," she said again and closed the door softly behind her.

Shep retired to the sofa again.

Bill, who had returned to consciousness, glared at him and at Johnny Swann.

"Are you drunks parking here," he demanded.

"That's right," Shep agreed amiably.

"That's right," echoed Johnny Swann.

Bill regarded them scornfully.

The Washout had somehow disappeared.

"Well," he said, "it's all right with me." He stretched his great frame on the floor across the closed doorway leading into Nikki's bedroom.

Cary Lockwood switched off the lights as he went out.

CHAPTER II

THE Carlton Bar opens at nine in the morning. You'll find the stools stacked on top of each other with their legs spraddling into the air, the charlady scrubbing the floor, and Madame La Directrice deep in her accounts behind the grating at the far end of the bar; and the barman busy with his cloth, polishing glasses, but you can get a drink straight-off. Shep was wearing his dark glasses and had a theory about drinking.

"It's the sleep that upsets you," he said. "I was all right when I went to sleep. Now look how I feel."

"How do you feel?"

"Well, I feel so bad my teeth are numb." Behind the dark glasses the nervous tic under his left eye was working.

"You're sure it wasn't something you et no doubt?" Bill inquired.

"It's the sleep that does it," Shep insisted. "Sleep's poison. Got to invent some way out of sleep."

"You do pretty well," Bill pointed out.

"Yes, but I break down practically every night. Just a weak character is all."

48

Nikki came in some time after eleven in tow of that impatient pup, Eighty-eight Carlton, at the end of a red leather leash. She was looking trim and smart in a tan suit with a narrow skirt and short jacket with red facings. She was wearing a cardinal red hat with a black half-veil.

"Hi, Nikki," Shep welcomed her.

"Hi, Nikki."

"Hi, Nik!"

"H'lo," Nikki said in her low voice, "they told me you were down here."

"How you feel, baby?"

Nikki spread her fingers lightly over her shapely midriff and made a wry mouth.

"You don't look a day over ninety," Shep said comfortingly.

"Did you ever see those looping old monograms on the backs of watches?" Nikki inquired, describing the design in the air with her finger.

"No," said Shep, "but once I saw figure skaters on the Palace Rink at St. Moritz, and I get the idea."

"*My* stummick is hanging by its knees," Johnny Swann offered.

Nikki saw that they were all dressed for the street and that they were all dressed in the same fashion; full, high-waisted, gray flannel trousers and blue, single-breasted coats. Cary wore gray suede Oxfords. They all looked comfortable and easy in their street clothes. She remarked on Shep's necktie, which was a kind of mauve color sprinkled with vagrant blue dots.

"Very fruity," Shep admitted and then explained that it represented the Spirit of Indigestion.

"I didn't expect to see you all back here so early," Nikki said.

"Back here?" Shep said. "We never left."

"Haven't you been home?"

"No," said Shep, "we camped on your doorstep last night. We thought you might need some more help on account of your maid was gone. Anyway we arranged to move in here."

"Here? The Carlton? Whatever for?"

"On account of you. We want to be with you. Despite your practically innumerable faults, we like you."

Nikki thanked him.

"So we decided to adopt you," Shep said.

"But how did you all get dressed?"

"Shep sent his driver over this morning for his things," Bill explained, "he's got a cab driver who follows him around all over the place. So I said to get my things, too, and pretty soon everybody said to get their things."

"Where are you?"

"Fifth floor, same as you—down at the end.

Place is as empty as a barn. Nobody here but us horses. Cary didn't want to come but we sent for his things anyway."

"What kind of a thing is that?" Nikki asked, peering into Shep's glass.

"Oh, that there," said Shep, "why that there is a prairie oyster."

Nikki looked at the yellow yolk of an egg floating in a dark mixture in a shallow wine glass.

"What does it do to you?"

"Well, it picks you up for one thing."

"Is that what you're all drinking?" she said, looking at the other glasses.

"Well, no," said Shep, "most of us."

"Well," Nikki said a little uncertainly, "do you think I might have one?"

"Prairie oyster pour Madame?" said Charles, the barman, who had been paying attention.

"Are you sure that's what you want?" Shep asked.

"Well . . . something," said Nikki uncertainly.

"You won't be bored," Shep assured her.

Charles began to prepare the prairie oyster.

"What's that?" Nikki asked as he dashed a few drops of something into the glass.

"Worcestershire sauce."

"And that?"

"Brandy."

"And *that?*"

"Paprika. The genoowine Hungarian."

"Voici," said Charles, setting the glass before her.

Nikki picked it up a little hesitantly.

"Happy landing," Shep said as Nikki tilted back her head and poured the drink into her mouth. Almost instantly a startled look came into her eyes; she stiffened, her throat contracted, and the egg, bursting like a star shell, exploded in all directions. She fell into a violent paroxysm of coughing. The onlookers ducked, but it was too late.

"My, but you're careless," Shep said. "Look at me." His face, his hair, his blue coat, his shirt and tie were all stippled with yellow.

"Oh, Shep, I'm so sorry," Nikki said, when she could get her breath. She took the handkerchief from the breast-pocket of his coat and began to police him up. "But that—that thing—was so sudden."

Charles, the barman, was extremely concerned.

"Il ne descende, l'oeuf!" he explained to Madame, the manager. *"C'etait une bombe! Il poppait! Un accident triste!"* He hastily began to wipe the bar and the bottles and mirror back of the bar with his cloth.

Shep was looking admiringly at himself in

the mirror. "Not a bad effect," he said, "when sprayed on—by a lady."

"Certainly looks cute," Johnny Swann agreed.

"Now look," Shep said to Nikki.

"I'm so sorry," Nikki said. "I'm so terribly sorry—"

"Now look," Shep said. "This is the way to take a prairie oyster internally."

He put his head far back, lifted his glass and let the egg slide silently down his throat.

"Just one gulp, Nikki. It's only a swallow."

"Please may I try another?"

"Do you think you want one?"

"No, only I s'pose I should try to be a success."

"You're a big success, baby," Shep assured her. "You don't have to take any more prairie oysters."

"*Non, non,*" Charles, the barman, said sympathetically, "no prairie oyster for madame. I make her nize Porto Flip." He set to work on another drink.

"This will make you laugh and play," Shep assured her.

"Well—" said Nikki, raising the glass Charles set before her, "Happy land——"

"Don't point that at me," Shep said and ran behind a pillar.

"Wait till I get out of range," said Johnny.

"Take cover, men," Bill ordered.

Cary and Francis found shelter and Nikki put back her head. Charles looked on apprehensively. The drink slid down Nikki's throat without interruption. The others came out from back to their stations at the bar.

"How do you feel now?"

"All right, only will somebody light a cigarette for me?"

Shep lighted a cigarette for her. "Good ol' Nik," he said. "She never has any matches."

They talked for a while, and then Shep got restless. He never drank very long in the same place.

"Listen," he said, "we're going down to Claridge's."

"What for?" Nikki said.

"We're going down to Claridge's to drink side-cars before lunch. Jean builds the best side-cars. And we've got to hurry."

Nikki wanted to know what was the hurry all about so Shep explained. It was all on account of the little fellers who were follerin' him about. (It was one of Shep's notions that he was pursued by hordes of strange creatures; frilled lizards, hop-toads, weasels with fiery red eyes, pigmy elephants with no hind legs, troops of penguins in echelon formation, Striped Grunt that walked on their hands, blue sheep with curved horns who sang soundless music, and battalions of little visitors from Mars. These last were serious little hairless chaps with wide, flopping ears, and tall silk tiles who were constantly engaged in military drills and exercises under the command of Josie, the Little Red Howler.) When Shep got behind in his drinking he said that they came up and nipped at his heels and plucked at the cuffs of his trousers. You had to keep, well anyway, two drinks ahead, else they all might suddenly burst into tongue and leap upon you.

Shep explained all this to Nikki who saw the necessity for speed between drinks.

"Are you going to walk?" she asked.

"Oh sure, it's only a couple of blocks or so."

Nikki looked down at her black patent leather pumps. "Well then," she said with sudden decision, "I've got to go change my shoes."

"Change your shoes? Why?"

"Because I can walk faster in red shoes."

Shep meditated over the statement for some minutes. "I think she's right," he announced finally.

When Nikki came back down they were ready to go. They all left the Carlton together and turned to the right along the Champs Élysées.

Single Lady

Nikki was flirt-footing along the sidewalk in her red shoes with Bill; the others walked ahead. They came to the corner crossing at the Avenue d'Alma, and stood waiting. Bill stepped off the curb in a momentary lull of traffic expecting Nikki to keep step with him. But Nikki, because of her near-sightedness was timid about crossing streets and hesitated on the curb. The traffic closed in behind Bill and he found himself on the opposite side of the street. He looked back and saw Nikki standing helplessly alone. A couple of men came up and stood behind her.

Bill was half-way across the street on his way back to fetch Nikki when he heard her utter a faint, startled cry. She had turned and was looking bewilderedly at a man retreating hastily down the street. Bill rushed to her side.

"What's the matter?"

"He—he pinched me," Nikki said.

"Who?'

"That man," Nikki pointed at the figure of a man fast disappearing out of her short range of vision.

Bill turned and dashed after him.

"Hey you!" he shouted.

The man halted immediately and turned.

"What the hell's the idea!" Bill demanded ablaze with righteous anger. Without waiting for an answer Bill slapped him. He didn't

hit him; he slapped him with his open hand.
You could hear the sound across the street.
The man spun about, poised for a second like
a dying top and sat down on the sidewalk,
his back resting against one of the circular
iron tree fences. His hat was cocked over his
left eye and his collar was sprung loose from
his neck band and stood open at the throat.
His attaché case lay spilled beside him on the
pavement. His face assumed a pleasantly
astounded expression.

Some passers-by closed in between Bill and
his fallen victim and stood staring down at
him with stupid wordless concentrations of the
curious. Bill found himself on the outside
fringe of an ever-thickening semi-circle, so he
turned and went back to Nikki.

"Where did he pinch you?" Bill demanded.

"Right here," said Nikki, putting her hand
on the place.

"The son-of-a-gun," Bill said. He was all
for going back and administering further
chastisement, but Nikki took him by the arm
and said could they please go.

They found the others in the Claridge Bar.
Shep noticed Bill's flushed face and angry expression.

"What happened to you two?" he demanded.

"Somebody pinched Nikki."

"When you were walking with her?"

"No. We started to cross the street and she turned back. I was on the other side."

"You shouldn't leave her alone."

"It was just a mistake," Bill said, "I thought she was with me."

Shep turned to Nikki. "So you got pinched, did you, young lady?" he said and roared with laughter.

Nikki nodded gravely.

"Ain't you never been pinched before, baby?"

Nikki shook her head.

"What? You never been pinched? That tells me how long you been in Paris. It's a national pastime. The place is full of Frenchmen who go about pinching young ladies on their tender little bottoms."

"What for?"

"For a thrill, what did you expect."

Nikki refused to believe it.

"You got pinched right on your little sitdown, didn't you?" Shep accused.

Nikki wouldn't say.

"Well," said Shep, "I don't see how you escape being pinched every time you go out. That skirt and the way you wave that thing around. . . ."

"Hey . . ." said Bill sharply.

" . . . I'd pinch you myself," Shep said, "if I knew you well enough."

"How about not getting so personal," Bill said.

"So you caught the dirty rascal and swatted him, did you, Bill?"

"I didn't really give him what was coming to him," Bill said.

"Did you knock the man down?" Nikki inquired.

"I only slapped him once."

Nikki sat thinking earnestly for a moment.

"Bill," she said presently, "I don't think that was the right man."

"What do you mean?"

"The one you hit. I don't think he was the right one."

Shep began to laugh again.

"But that's the one you pointed at," Bill protested.

"I was pointing at the one ahead of him," Nikki said.

Shep became convulsed and nearly fell off his stool.

"Great lord," he said, "but that's funny. Nikki get's her back side pinched and Bill gallops up and swats the wrong man. By gosh, if that isn't just like Bill. Good ol' Bill, the Bombardier. Good ol' Bill."

Bill, mollified, began to blush furiously.

"Gosh," he said, "I didn't know."

"It was my fault," Nikki said, "and I'm dreadfully sorry."

Shep took command of the bar and ordered side-cars and asked Jean where were all the potato chips and olives and eggs and things? Jean promptly produced them from behind the bar.

Bill warned Nikki about the side-cars. "Don't try to keep up with Shep," he told her privately. "You can't drink more than five side-cars. One, two, three, four, five, and out, see?"

"What's in 'em?" Nikki asked.

"Oh, I don't know, Cointreau, lemon juice, brandy and heavens knows what."

"Where is my boy friend," Shep said, turning around on his stool, "Oh, there he is, the little dahlink."

He pointed out to Nikki a man sitting at a wall table at the far end of Claridge's Bar. His skin was sun-and-wind burnt to the color of an Arab. He had an intense, interesting face, with a three-pointed scar on his left cheekbone. He looked like what you would imagine an ex-officer of the Foreign Legion would look like in gray tweeds.

"He's got a swell history," Shep said, "I don't know what it is. He's here every day, isn't he, Jean? That's right. And

he drinks himself blind every night. Brandy.
But he always leaves here under his own power.
He's trying to talk himself in or out of some-
thing. Look at him."

The man was addressing an imaginary
figure across the table from him and making
slight, imperative gestures with his hand.

"My theory is that he left his little baby
lambrequin and he knows he was right, but
anyway he wants to go back to her. He's right
but he knows he's wrong."

"Shep is a great guy for theories," Bill said,
"titles and histories and theories."

"Now look at him," Shep said, "he's spoken
his piece. See now he's finished. He has a
drink. That's the period. Now he's listening. He's surprised. Why he's angry. Now
he argues. He argues harder. Now he *is*
sore. Take it or leave it. All right. He's
through. Well, just one more last chance. Before he goes out into the night. No? Well,
he gave her a chance anyhow. This is good-
bye."

"Why Shep," said Nikki, clapping her
hands, "that's really quite good."

"Look," said Shep, "there be begins all over
again, the discovery, the speech, the argument,
the challenge, the exit. He goes over it a
thousand times a day in his mind."

"Shep sure has some powerful theories," Bill said airily.

"And I got a powerful theory about you too," Shep said.

"What kind of a theory've you got about me?"

"I got a theory you better get your hair cut."

"Who, me?" said Bill.

"Who, you." said Shep.

"Do I need a hair cut?"

"Get your hair cut or buy a violin, one. I swear I saw a bat fly out of all that broccoli last night."

But Bill was obstinate. He said you'd never trap him in one of those French barber chairs. They locked you in a night gown and *anything* could happen to you, he said, and besides it was too far away from the bar.

"But look, Bill, it's just around the hall to your right."

Bill said nothing doing.

"Well, all right, only we won't be seen out with you any more."

"Ashamed of me, hey?"

"You're a disgrace."

Bill finally broke down and went off in the direction of the barber shop.

A long young man in an unpressed top-

coat and a gray turn down hat came into the
bar.

"Hi, Wiffy!" Shep called.

Shep was glad to see Wiffy. So were the
others. They all liked Wiffy. He was a
gentle soul with a sweet disposition.

"Come have a drink," Shep said. "What
are you doing up-town?"

Wiffy said he would be very happy to have
a drink. Shep presented him to Nikki and
gave him Bill's place beside her at the bar.
Shep said to look out for Wiffy on account of
he was a ball-of-fire.

Nikki turned and leveled her lorgnon at
Wiffy.

"How do you do," she said. "I'm not sure I
heard your name."

"Wiffy Crouch," Shep said.

"Beg pardon?"

"Wiffy Crouch, Wiffy Crouch, Wiffy
Crouch."

"Sounds like *Wiffy Crouch*," Nikki said.

"That's how it is," Shep assured her.

Nikki looked uncertainly from one to the
other. "I knew a girl once named Hattie
Dozier," she declared finally.

"Did you?" Shep said, "I knew a boy in
the fourth grade once named Joe Speewack."

"This girl got married right away."

"Sensible idea," Shep said.

"Listen," said Nikki, "did you ever know anybody named Fred you liked?"

"Nope."

"Wilbur?"

"Nope."

"Me neither."

"How about Herman?"

"I had a turtle once named Herman," Nikki said.

"You know the name I like the best?" Shep said, "Pete. Pete is the honestest name they is. Captain Pete Hudgins is my favorite name."

"Did you know someone of that name?"

"No, but it just occurred to me."

"Well, Minnie Haskins is my favorite."

"How are you on people like T. Arthur Aspinwall?"

"Not so good," said Nikki, "not so good. But just pay no attention and sometimes they go away."

Wiffy sat and listened to the two with an expression of mild concern.

Wiffy's full name was Willard Frink Crouch. He had taken a terrible beating under that name. First he tried Willard F. Crouch in the hopes that somebody would call him Bill. Nobody did. Then he tested out signing himself W. Frink Crouch and that didn't work either. He finally resigned himself to W. F. Crouch and some serene soul called him Wiffy and that did it. Wiffy Crouch. No one knew better than Wiffy what a disaster that was to your personal dignity. No one named Wiffy would ever turn the tide of empire.

Wiffy had gone to Princeton. Afterwards he worked on the New York *Tribune* and was sent abroad to fill a vacancy in the Paris office. He got sixty dollars a week and a living allowance. He liked to drink and went about with all sorts of strange people. He had written a highly unpublished novel. Wiffy described it afterwards as an Early Work. He predicted that it would be included among his Juvenilia. He sometimes forgot to button all his buttons. He knew he wasn't going to last long in the Paris Bureau because his stomach was troubling him. All those Martinis. He said he dassn't go back to New York because he had only just been sent over. He said he thought the best thing he could do would be to go to Italy and write a book. He said he didn't think it would be a success because he was too pornographic.

"Who is your swell friend?" he asked Shep.

"Oh her," Shep said, "I don't know. Just an old hussy we found scattered around."

Wiffy said he wisht to God he'd seen her first.

"How're tricks?" Shep inquired of Wiffy. And when was he going to write that pornographic novel?

Wiffy said as soon as his stomach gave out, which ought to be pretty soon now.

"When are you going to go to work?" Wiffy asked, in turn.

"Work?" said Shep. "Work? Work? What kind of work?"

"Oh, any kind of work."

"Where?"

"Oh, anywhere. Why don't you go home and go to work?"

"What would I do?" Shep inquired. "Sell washing machines? Rake up lawns? Tend furnaces? Read meters? Mend old furniture? Raise artichokes? Drive a milkwagon?"

"How about aviation?" Wiffy wanted to know. Why didn't Shep go back to flying? Be a commercial pilot or fly the mails or something?

Shep thought of himself, with his shattered nervous organization, sitting at the controls of an airplane.

"Hell," he said wryly, "I couldn't even pass the litmus test."

"Well, there ought to be *something*," Wiffy said vaguely.

"Maybe I could put an ad in the paper,"

Shep speculated. "I know what I could do if
I was in London. I could play a barrel or-
gan, or I could draw pictures on the sidewalk.
I could play *'Where Do Flies Go in the
Wintertime'* on a barrel organ, and be a big
success in London. It's a favorite tune of the
English."

"What kind of pictures would you draw?"
Wiffy asked.

"Still life," said Shep, "fruit and fish. Fish
mostly. The English are very sentimental
about fish. I would draw a bloater with sad,
stupid eyes, and be a big success. Bloaters
have such sad eyes. Have you ever noticed?"

Wiffy said he'd never noticed, but he told
Shep he'd ought to make up his mind about
something.

"I'm trying to make up my mind," Shep
said. "I don't know whether to go to work or
take up drinking. Drinking and polite conversation."

"I know the answer to that one," Wiffy
said. "Don't you ever get outside of a bar?"

"No," said Shep, "I have to tend to my
drinking. I don't get much opportunity."

"All kinds of things going on outside,"
Wiffy said. "Trees growing and the sun
shining, and people walkin' around and all
kinds of things happening."

Shep's eyes grew big with wonder. "Right

now, you mean? While we're a-settin' here?"

"Sure," said Wiffy, "right now. Babies being born."

"Nurse girls being ruined, too, I bet," Shep said. "It all sounds pretty pre-war to me." .

"Well," said Wiffy, "you ought to get out once in a while and go places and see things. Improve yourself, old boy, improve yourself."

"Not a bad idea," Shep admitted and ordered a couple of side-cars for their mutual improvement.

"Where do you get all these lofty notions?" Shep inquired further. "What are you doing that makes you so noble?"

Wiffy said he was writing a Sunday feature. He said he was supposed to hand in two a month for the second news section of the New York *Sunday Tribune,* but he found it hard going. He guessed he didn't have any nose for second-news-section subjects.

"What's the one you're doing now?"

"It's all about the treasure on the bottom of the sea," Wiffy said, and burst into a gale of laughter. It sounded so silly when you said it out loud.

You got that way from working on a newspaper, Wiffy said; Treasure on the Bottom of the Sea.

Shep asked him why he bothered about the treasure on the bottom of the sea anyhow.

Wiffy said they expected a couple of pieces from him every month besides the cables, and anyway he got seven dollars and a half a column for it. The way things were, he said, he could use the money. Wiffy was generally broke.

"What about all this treasure anyway?" Shep wanted to know. "We're all practically dying to hear about it."

"Don't you know there's over four billion dollars worth of shipping lying at the bottom of the sea?"

"Hadn't heard a thing about it," Shep assured him. "Not a thing. Nobody breathed a word of it to us. And say," he demanded, "what's the idea of the newspapers playing up this homo-sexual affair between Ignatz and Krazy Kat?"

"All sunk by unrestricted German submarine warfare," Wiffy continued.

Shep said, "Can you imagine?"

"Take the *Laurentic*," Wiffy said academically, "she went down with twenty-five million when she was torpedoed off Malin Head in nineteen seventeen."

Shep made a great show of alarm and Nikki said it sounded scandalous.

"Take the *Lusitania*," Wiffy said.

"Oh, tell us about that."

"She had six million in her strong room when she foundered. Take the German War Fleet; there's millions in costly metals lying at the bottom of Scapa Flow."

"Who ever heard of such a thing. Somebody ought to write about that."

"That's what I'm doing," Wiffy insisted. "Didn't I tell you?" He looked from one face to another.

"Oh, that's right," Shep admitted. "I forgot. Well, what else?"

"Well, there's the *Egypt*——"

"The *Egypt*," Shep repeated.

"And the *Belleville*——"

"Regular mine of information," Shep commented. "What about the ol' *Belleville?*"

"Well, she's the biggest prize of all. She went down with the largest shipment of diamonds ever sent out of South Africa."

"Listen to that, Cary," Shep said, "isn't that fantastic?"

"Torpedoed?" Cary inquired, turning around.

"Yep."

"Where?"

"Somewhere off the Coast of Portugal, nobody knows exactly."

"How much were the diamonds worth?"

"About six million sterling. The insurance companies took an awful loss."

"The *Belleville*," Cary repeated. "How big was she?"

"Twenty thousand tons."

"What line?"

"Cape or something. Belgian registration."

"No survivors?"

"Lost with all on board. At least that's the way she's listed at Lloyd's."

"Lemme give you a good title for your piece," Shep said.

Wiffy looked at him suspiciously.

"Call it 'The Flute Player's Revenge.'" Shep laughed so hard at his own title that he nearly fell off his perch. Nobody else thought it was particularly funny, or funny at all, but Shep was enormously pleased about it.

Pretty soon Wiffy said he had to go back to the shop. He was still puzzled about Nikki's status.

"So pleased to have met you," he said.

"Thank you," Nikki said.

"May I—may I call you up sometime?"

Nikki thanked him again.

"Where can I find you?"

Nikki regarded him uncertainly for a moment. "In the Almanach de Gotha," she replied finally.

Wiffy blushed a deep red, but quickly recovered himself and by way of showing his respect for one of the nobility of Europe, kissed her hand when he left. Unexpectedly Cary Lockwood went along with Wiffy.

Shep thought it was perfectly swell the way Nikki had refused to give out her telephone number.

Nikki gazed silently after the two as they departed.

"Tell me about Cary Lockwood," she said to Shep.

"You like Cary?"

"Yes," said Nikki simply, "I like Cary."

"Well," Shep said, "you'll think I'm trying to be funny. The first time I ever saw him was in the baths at Cardinal."

"Cardinal?"

"Cardinal College at Oxford."

"Oh, that's right, you both went to Oxford."

"Rather. Him and me both. That's where I met him. He had a locker next mine, but one, in the baths, and the first time I saw him stripped he had a great, angry bruise on his shoulder. Right up here by his throat, blue and yellow and purple and all the ruddy colors of the rainbow. Like a Hawaiian sunset or a peacock's tail or a aurora borealis or something." Shep was strong on simile. "It ran half way down his side and clear across his chest. I told him he bruised easily."

" 'Well,' he said, 'under the circumstances.' "

" 'What happened to you?' I said. I thought

he'd been kicked by a horse or fallen down an elevator shaft or been run over by a char-a-banc or something.

" 'A lady bit me,' he said.

"Aren't you surprised?" Shep demanded of Nikki.

"No."

"Well *I* was. I thought he was pulling my leg. But a lady did bite him. She bit him coming over on the boat. He told me about it afterwards."

"Must have been interesting," Nikki murmured.

"She was an actress; a blonde actress, you'd know her name, and she was going to London to open a new play. Cary danced with her on board ship and afterwards they went up on the boat deck. They talked a while, Cary said, and it was about three o'clock in the morning and all of a sudden she just bent down for no reason at all and bit him. She bit him so hard his knees buckled and he fell down on the deck.

"Then the next thing he knew she had his head in her lap and she said, 'Oh, baby, baby, did I hurt you . . . did I hurt you, baby?'

"Now," said Shep enthusiastically, "isn't that a terrible thing to happen to a young man from Seattle?"

"From Seattle!" Nikki exclaimed. "Certainly not! It was probably all for the best."

"I never thought of that," Shep said. "But tell me, why did the girl bite Cary?"

Nikki looked at Shep and burst out laughing.

"What's the matter?" Shep said.

"You're funny."

"How so?"

"Well, I asked you why the man pinched me. And now you ask me why the girl bit Cary."

"That's right." Shep admitted. "Looks like people just go around pinching and biting each other. But tell me why did the lady bite Cary?"

"Because."

"Because why?"

"Well, it probably seemed like a good idea at the time."

Shep studied her for a moment. "How sweet the moonlight sleeps on yonder bank," he said finally, "and how about another drink."

"A pleasure," said Nikki.

Bill came out of the barber shop in an uproarious state, grinning all over the place.

"What the hell," Shep said looking at him.

"I'm a bull-fighter," Bill explained. Bill's hair was parted just a little off-center. It was slicked down flat on the left side, with a slight frisky up-turn at the ends, like an old-time bartender's. He had a wave on the right side and a spit-curl, curving like a scimitar, tight against his forehead. And somehow the barber had contrived to fashion a miniature coleta in the thick, curly thatch of hair at the back of Bill's head.

"I'm a bull-fighter," Bill repeated, "and if you don't stop looking so superior I'll stick you with an armadillo."

"Peccadillo, is the word," Shep said.

"Pussy willow," Nikki suggested.

"You can't go around with us like that," said Shep.

"The hell I can't. Try and lose me. Now listen," he said, "and I'll tell you how it happened. The barber wanted to know if I was a Suedois. And I told him no that I was an Irishman with the heart of a Turk—"

"Well, that's pretty good for you," Shep said. "I never knew you had any imagination."

"So he said I must have a lot of little ones. And I said yes, fourteen, and they were all in school in Switzerland."

"You see what happens when Bill strays away from us like that," Shep told Nikki.

"And so he wanted to know the names of my p'tits, and I said their names were all Hortense. He couldn't understand about that until I told him all the mules in Mexico were named Jesus."

"That cleared up the whole thing?"

"Right."

"You didn't tell him you were a Saint Bernard, did you?" Shep was unkind enough to ask. "Was you ever in the fourth grade?" he turned to Nikki.

Nikki said, "Oh, sure, everybody's been in the fourth grade somewhere."

"Well," said Shep, "didn't they have a fine big picture of a Saint Bernard in a blizzard? On the Alps?"

"Yes," Nikki said, "with a barrel or something tied around its neck—looking for lost travelers or something."

"And looking unhappy as anything," Shep said. "I bet if you tied one of those casks around Bill's neck and sent him up in the mountains he'd save thousands of people."

"He has the eye for it all right," Nikki agreed.

"And the hair," Shep said.

Bill paid no attention to them and went right on with his story.

"And then I broke down and told him I was really a bull-fighter and that I was traveling anonymous. So he fixed me up. And they'll send drinks in from the bar and the name of the manicurist is Suzanne and she has blue ear-tabs."

"Well," Shep said, "that's all very fine indeed, but you better get your hair combed decent else you can't be with us."

"I don't want to go back," Bill protested, "I was a big success."

"Well, go jump in the piscine. It's just around the corner to your left. You can be a big success there, too."

"That's a powerful thought," Bill admitted. "Give me a drink and lemme dwell on that thought for a while."

Bill had another side-car and went off in the direction of the baths.

When he came back he was very thirsty and started drinking beer and developed hiccups.

"Man," said Shep admiringly, "those certainly are powerful hiccups."

"Aren't they fierce?" Bill said.

"I wisht I could find somebody to match you with," Shep said, "I bet you could hiccup anybody bow-legged. You ought to take some brandy and sugar," he added, "because we're going out."

"Why?"

"Well, you see," Shep explained, "you've been in Paris all this time and all you know is the bars. You ought to go places and see things. Improve yourself, old boy, improve yourself!"

"All right," said Bill promptly. "Let's go and take a look at Napoleon's tomb."

They argued back and forth as to where they should go. Eventually they put it up to Nikki.

"Well," Nikki ventured, "how about Versailles?"

They all considered the idea for a while.

"Anyone been to Versailles?" Shep asked suspiciously.

They all shook their heads. "Well," said Shep, "how far out is it do you think?"

Nobody had any idea. Jean, the barman, told them it was only a case of forty minutes or so.

"We can stop at places along the way for drinks," Shep mused. "How about lunch?" he asked Jean, was there any place out there for lunch?

Oh sure, Jean told them, lots of nice places.

"Well," said Shep, "everybody better drink their drink because we're going to Versailles."

Three men came into the bar and sat down at a table along the side. The waiter brought them coffee. No one took any particular notice of them except Francis, The Washout. Suddenly he got down off his stool and went over. He moved like a modiste, swinging his long legs gracefully from the hips.

He tapped one of the trio lightly on the shoulder. The fellow turned his head around and looked up. "Oh hello," he said without enthusiasm.

"Tsay," said Francis, "you didn't come."

"No," the fellow said, "I couldn't make it."

"But I waited for you."

"I got tied up." He turned back to the others.

"You didn't send any message."

The other turned to him. "I couldn't make it, I tell you!" Anyone could see that he was embarrassed and angry and that he wanted Francis to go away.

But Francis wouldn't go away. He stood at the man's shoulder looking down at him.

"Well, I waited for you," he repeated in his high insistent voice.

One of the other men at the table snickered.

The man suddenly got loud.

"Listen, *you*," he shouted at Francis, "I don't have to explain anything to you. *See,* I told you I couldn't get there. That's sufficient." He turned his back.

"No," said Francis, "that's not tsufficient."

"Get away from me," the other cried, "or I'll slap you down." He brought up his left hand.

Francis' clear pale skin turned sheet-white with scorn. He began to quiver as if he had been lashed by a knout.

Single Lady

Bending over ever so slightly, he swept the hot coffee into the other's lap.

"Oh my God!" the man howled, leaping to his feet. He doubled over, trying to back away from the burning liquid that saturated his trousers. With his finger tips he tried to separate the steaming cloth from his skin.

Francis flew at him like an unloosed fury. Shep said afterwards that he swarmed over the man like Harry Greb. The man went down under the fusillade of slaps and cuffs. Francis was on top of him instantly; he drew up his foot to stamp out the face beneath with his heel.

The other two jumped up and caught Francis by the arms. It was as if they had seized a high tension cable; they were flung off so quickly.

But the momentary interference had given the fallen one a chance to get to his feet. He held his arms in front of his face, backing away. "Don't!" he cried, "Don't! Don't!"

Shep slipped over and took Francis by the elbow. Francis whirled about. In his pale yellow eyes Shep saw the insane rage of a killer.

"Come along," Shep said easily. "He's had enough."

Suddenly Francis buried his face in his hands and fell into an hysterical burst of weep-

ing. Shep put his arm about his shoulder and
walked him out of the place.

Bill Talbot sat perched upon his stool, sau-
cer-eyed with astonishment.

"Can you imagine that?" he demanded of
Nikki. "S-a-ay——!"

When Shep came back down he was smiling.
"He's all right," he said, "I put him in a cab."

The three men at the side table had disappeared.

The others, Johnny Swann, Bill, and Nikki,
were strangely affected by the whole affair.
They had seen beneath the gentle, sleepy de-
meanor of The Washout for the first time, and
what they saw there was murder. Johnny
Swann shivered. Bill was shocked. Nikki
was pale. Only Shep was elated.

"Wasn't that fantastic?" he demanded. "Did
you ever see anything so fast in your life? He
went into action, didn't he? Boy, he's meaner
than a Posen Pole. I told you to lay off
that guy, Bill."

Shep was simply bubbling over with en-
thusiasm. Life was very fine and exciting.
Life was filled with strange bitter excitements.
How about another drink before we go.

CHAPTER III

SHEP'S broken-down Russian was waiting faithfully outside Claridge's in his broken-down cab. He was a big moon-faced Muscovite, who sensed Shep's tender-heartedness and followed him around like a whipped puppy. He didn't know Paris very well and his speaking-French was pretty terrible and other taxi-drivers grimaced at him and he had a large, dog-eared folding, colored map of Paris. Shep borrowed the map once and left it somewhere and that did it. Helpless without his map, Serge attached himself to the man who last had his map. When he showed Shep a picture of himself and his good wife and fine daughter, Shep's resistance broke down completely and he had a cab-driver and a cab on his hands.

In time Shep had become fond of both the cab and its driver. He was very happy about the cab; it was a great, roomy, wheezy old vehicle, with a bend in the middle like an old sway-backed mare. The number on the license plate of the cab was 1-4-9-2, so Shep called it obviously the Santa Maria. Shep said that once he gave three Jews a lift and the sea gulls deserted the cab at the Place Vendôme.

"What are Versailles anyway?" Bill demanded as they got into Shep's cab. "And let's pull down the top, so we can catch a lot of breeze."

"If we had Cary along he could tell us," Shep said, "and look out for your fingers, here she comes."

"Where is Cary?" Nikki asked.

"Went off with Wiffy. I think he's got ideas. He gets ideas."

Settled in the Santa Maria, none could get his mind away from the scene he had just witnessed.

"Tsay," said Shep, imitating Francis' manner of speech, "didn't he tsusprise you though?"

Nikki wanted to know if it was really true that Francis had been an aviator in the war.

"Tsure," said Shep.

"Now, tShepard."

"Tsweetheart!" exclaimed Shep. It was very easy to fall into that way of talking once you got it on your tongue. Shep told Nikki that Fwancis had really been one of the tsweetest pilots at the front; that he had been tsuperb marksman, that he had half a dozen official and unofficial victories to his credit and that he had abruptly lost interest after his team-mate had been killed.

"And him so harmless looking," said Johnny Swann.

"Oh, he's a rare tsoul," Shep said. "You all don't appreciate him; especially Bill here."

Nikki wanted to know what a Posen Pole was.

"Ask any Russian," Shep said.

"What does Francis hang around for?" Bill said. "Why doesn't he stick to the others?"

Shep tried to explain to Bill with very indifferent success why Francis hung about. "He's trying to be normal," Shep said, "he is cultivating the society of normal people in order to keep his balance."

Bill snorted with derision. It seemed damn funny to him; Francis trying to find a balance amongst their strange, disordered lives. Normal people!

But Shep assured him that that was the case. The Washout was lonely and all he wanted was a little normal association.

But Bill suspected him of some sinister design. "Where does he go at night?" Bill wanted to know.

Francis had a strange habit of disappearing without explanation, at night. He was always on hand in the mornings. Once he had come back pretty well scratched and torn up.

Shep said he could explain that, too. There was a strange group of people, men and women who met secretly at night somewhere in the Bois de Boulogne. The exact spot and the hour remained a secret until the last minute when the word was passed around. It was something like the mysterious floating dice game on Broadway. Only these ones did not convene for the purpose of gambling.

Shortly before the appointed time, taxi cabs could be seen to leave various of the smart hotel's headed in a mutual direction. The cabs would arrive almost simultaneously at the prearranged spot in the Bois. Lights were turned off. Mysterious figures debouched from the tonneaus and flitted into the darkness.

Bill wanted to know what happened then.

"Brother," said Shep, "it ain't no Church Social."

It was understood that whoever embarked upon these midnight excursions was morally emancipated and committed to any consequences.

"You can choose or be chosen," Shep said.

Nikki burst out laughing. "It all sounds so silly," she said.

"Would you like to go?" Shep said.

"Thank you," said Nikki.

"Do you mean to say that Francis goes on those things every night?" Bill demanded.

"I don't know," Shep said.

Shep thought it was a sly idea to make out Francis as mysterious a creature as possible if only to intimidate Bill. To Shep's way of thinking, Francis was an emotional defective, likely to become violent under the stress of anger, fear or passion. Potent forces lurked behind his pale yellow eyes.

So that was why Francis was always so sleepy during the day, Bill reflected. That was why Francis carried that little chiming watch to wake him up at odd moments.

"How does he keep awake at all?" Bill asked.

"Sleeping tablets," Shep said. He knew they would think that he was joking, when, as a matter of fact, he was telling the truth. Shep had once seen Francis privily drop a tablet in a glass of carbonated water at the Claridge Bar and that told him the whole story. It was probably allonel or luminol or, anyhow, some derivative of barbituric acid. Taken in charged water it had quite the opposite of its intended effect. It made you spin.

So Francis and his chiming watch went spinning, light-headed through his days, spinning, spinning, spinning, faster and faster. But Shep did not attempt to explain all this to the others. Maybe he was wrong anyway; and

A First National and Vitaphone Production.   The Last Flight—Movie of Single Lady.

"DON'T YOU KNOW THAT LADIES ARE NOT SUPPOSED TO SIT AT THE BAR IN CLARIDGE'S?"

whose business was it if you went in for a little
light drug-using?

They stopped at several side-walk cafés on
the way out for drinks, so it was after two before they arrived at the Esplanade. Shep
espied a little open air café with clean white
tables under a white and green awning and
with garden boxes of red geraniums. He
steered for that. It was cool and nice under
the awning out of the sun. The name of the
place was the *Café Restaurant de Londres
(Place d'Armes)*.

"Now let's have some good food," Shep
said, "and sort of get in training for this here
excursion."

They all settled about a long table for eight.
It gave them room to sit sidewise and put their
feet on the rungs of the other chairs.

"You know," Shep complained, "I've
noticed that when people go places they have
books. We haven't any books."

That's right they agreed, and they thought
it would be a splendid idea to send Johnny
over to get a guide-book or something. Shep
said he would order for him.

Johnny went off and came back after a
while with a book. The others were still drinking cocktails, but were getting ready for some
assorted hors d'œuvres.

Single Lady

Shep took the book from Johnny, opened it at random and began to read:

" 'Other rooms afforded discreet refuges for certain persons of the fair sex.' Hey, what is this anyway?" he demanded of Johnny. " 'Madame de Mailly, who used to constellate her head with diamonds as a preparation for sleep, had sometimes a logis there, and so had one afterwards, her sister, Madame de la Tournelle and Madame de Pompadour in the early period of her favor. A lot of the lesser mistresses, grisettes and common girls were also put up in the Little Closets. Indefatigable Le Bel would hunt out the creatures, bathe and scrub them, if required, inspect their teeth and neatly dress them before introducing them to the King.' "

Shep began to shake his head sadly and looked up at Johnny. "Look what kind of a book that licentious old man brought us."

Johnny blushed and protested about that. He said he wasn't a licentious old man.

"Have you got references?" Shep demanded, "no two of whom are relatives?"

Johnny said he got the book at the book stall at the gate.

"You're an old lecher," Shep accused him sternly, and went on reading.

" 'One of the King's greatest delights was to get the Post Office to bring him his sub-

jects' private mails which he would seal and re-seal after having enjoyed the love affairs they disclosed, and ascertain what people thought and wrote of him.' "

Bill wanted to know how about a bottle of wine?

" *'His favorite cat, a huge white angora, used to sleep every evening in front of the fireplace on a crimson satin cushion.' "*

Shep said to give him the wine card.

"Gimme that there book," said Bill.

"Vins de Champagne," Shep read, "nope, nothing gassy. *Vins de Bordeaux Rouges,* who wants red Bordeaux? No? Good, no Bordeaux Rouge.

"Do you know what they call a lady from Bordeaux," he inquired as an afterthought. "A Bordelaise. And do you know what they call a man? A Bordello. That's very naughty, Nikki, you aren't supposed to know about that."

Nikki never seemed to be paying attention when things like that were said.

"Rhine wines and Moselles," Shep continued, "could anybody go for some Rudesheimer nineteen twenty-one at thirty-eight francs the one-half Bout? No? Chablis? Graves? Barsac? Sauterne? Sauterne? Oh, here is a beautiful wine. *Château Yquem.* That's the best wine they is going. Not too sweet. Not too dry. Make you laugh and play. How about it . . . for a hundred and eighty francs the bouteille? Sold? Sold. Make you laugh and play. Gimme back that book." He took the book away from Bill.

Bill was nervous about letting Shep go on with the book. He kept eyeing Nikki to see if she minded.

" '*It was to this room,*' " Shep read, " '*where through flitted numberless mistresses of passage that Louis Fifteenth, aged sixty-four, was carried back. He had been suddenly stricken down by infectious small-pox communicated by a joiner's daughter who had had intercourse with him on the preceding day.*' "

"That's what you get for opening other people's mail," Johnny pointed out. "Maybe we might go take a look at that room."

"It says these rooms are of no admittance to the public. That's always the way it is," Shep lamented. " '*Like the building of palaces, a King's amours add to his fame.*' Why only a King? '*Francis I, the Roi Chevalier, could not count the number of his mistresses, scattered about everywhere.*' Here comes the soup. '*A year had scarcely passed since his marriage when Louis the Fourteenth began to notice one of the maids of honor. . . .*' Hey, this is good soup. '*Sweet seventeen, a native of Touraine, petite and slender, with no figure to speak of——*' No figure to speak of—well, we'll let that pass for a minute. *'Teeth not so pearly, a somewhat thick-tipped nose and a slight limp.'* . . . Outside of that," Shep said, "the gal was a knockout, *'the girl was yet extremely winsome due to an abundance of silvery fair hair, and blue eyes from the limpid depths of which shone Love Expectant.'* Love Expectant," Shep repeated, "how's that for a Title?"

"How about pouring out some more of that Château Yquem?" Bill inquired.

"Right-ho. Fling you lip over that."

Shep went on with his reading. " *'Anne of Austria attempted to check her son's growing passion; at which he wept, but declared that he neither had the strength nor the wish to overcome his attachment or resist his feelings.'* That's the way to express yourself, isn't it? How's the fish?

" . . . . *'as for Mlle de La Valliere, who was attracted quite as much by the man as by the Monarch, she glided of herself into his arms . . . . the King gave a carousel in her honour. . .* ' Well, I didn't s'pose she had any by now."

"Not after that glide," Bill said.

" . . . *'which took place in the inner court of the Tuileries. . . . .'* "

"Now look—Little La Vallière can no longer suffice the increasing pride of the old

Single Lady

boy, so he begins to look sidewise at Madame de Montespan. She is blonde but of a fiercer hue. A fierce blonde, can you beat that? It says her shape is perfect and listen, *'like all other persons both men and women, she made use of strongly scented rouge, powder and perfumes to disguise a neglect of personal cleanliness, a common failing in those days, of which the King himself was not guiltless.'*"

Nikki made a face.

"That's not like our little girl-friend," Shep said.

"I'll bet the King gave the blonde a carous*el* too," Johnny said. "That's how you pronounce it; carous*el.*

"Oh sure. He gave her a carous*el* that cost eighty thousand dollars. It says here they had *'an artificial hill with caves full of cold meat and ham. On a second stood tiers upon tiers of cups, and goblets of sherbet, wine and brandy.'* Those were the days, eh, Johnny? *'The other buffet supported a pyramid of preserved fruits, a miniature castle built of almond paste and a rock of caramel. Between these sideboards stood, in silver or china flower-pot holders, small trees covered with other kinds of preserved fruits tied to their branches with ribbons. Rows of melons and jars of jam were arranged alternately on grassy banks all around the grove. Oranges, cherries, apricots,*

*peaches, currants and pears had, by the skill of
gardeners, been forced to ripen at the same
time. . . .'"*

"Read about the mistresses," said Johnny
Swann, "that's more exciting."

Nikki wanted to know what time it was.
She was getting a little worried about the time.

It was after one when they left Claridge's
and they'd been an hour and a half getting out
there. The midday sun had long gone, and
the shadows were beginning to lengthen under
the elm trees.

Each time they were ready to make a start,
however, they discovered that one of the party
was missing. Whereupon Shep would order
another bottle of wine and launch into further
conversation. Nikki was afraid they might
not start before it was too late.

Finally the party was complete and Shep
paid the account and they started for the
palace gates.

A cab driver standing by the entrance
waved to them.

"*Fermé!*" he called.

Shep stopped short. "He says it's closed,"
he said hopefully.

"Well, let's go see anyway," Nikki said.
"We've come this far."

"I'm sure it's closed," Shep said. "See,
everybody is coming out."

"Well, let's make sure."

They finally compromised on sending Johnny over to investigate while the rest of them sat on the curb. Shep sent Bill to fetch the Grand Duke and his cab, so they wouldn't have to walk back. Nikki was glad to sit down on the curbstone. She was a little dizzy with all that Château Yquem.

Johnny came back just as Bill arrived on the running board of the cab. "Closed for the day," Johnny said.

"Well," said Shep, "we made a noble effort, didn't we?"

Nikki saw that there was nothing to do now but go home. Maybe they could start earlier next time.

"It certainly was a good effort," Shep said over and over again on the way back, reminiscing over the Versailles excursion.

"Jolly good effort," Bill agreed.

"We damn near made it."

"Missed it by a pig's whisker."

"But it was a good effort," Shep told the others, "a jolly good effort."

They all agreed that it was a jolly good effort to visit Versailles. They had read all about it in a book anyway.

When they got back to the Carlton Nikki said she wanted to take a bath and change.

"How about tonight?" Bill asked.

"Take me dancing?"

"Sure," said Bill.

They left her at her door and went off down the corridor.

A moment later the telephone rang in Shep's room. Shep picked up the transmitter.

"Allô," he said in his best French manner.

Nikki's voice came floating uncertainly over the wire. "Shep?"

"Yes, darlin'."

"Was there anything intoxicating in those drinks this afternoon?"

"Certainly not. Why?"

"I tried to unlock my door with a pocket comb is all. Thanks."

At seven Shep collected Bill and Johnny and Cary and Francis and went back to Nikki's room.

Nikki looked very mysterious and alluring in a Venetian dress with a tight silver bodice and swelling skirt of silver-tipped black tulle. At her waist she wore a little bouquet of flowers with multicolored ribbons. She was wearing tulle wristlets and a green jade bracelet about her upper arm. She had on a black hat fitted closely to her head and with a sheer black veil that fell below her chin. Slender jade pendants hung from her ears. She carried herself like a princess on her high pointed heels.

Single Lady

"Gosh," said Shep when he saw her. "You look like something out of the Tales of Hoffmann."

"Yessir," said Johnny Swann, "she looks just like the Barcarolle sounds."

Nikki looked so lovely they decided to take her to the Ritz for cocktails.

At the Ritz they had a lot of dry Martinis and smoked any number of cigarettes. While Shep was talking, Nikki interrupted to inquire of Johnny, who was sitting beside her on the wall seat: "Just what are your plans?"

Johnny blushed and withdrew his hand from beneath the table.

They all looked at him severely.

"You have to watch that lad," Shep said, "he's head of The Wandering Hand Society and he has a groping good time. You wouldn't begrudge him a few free feels, would you, Nikki?"

But Bill was sore. "You know better than that," he told Johnny.

Shep said that besides being a licentious old man Johnny Swann was some kind of a burrowing animal.

"Your behavior, sir," Shep announced, "is unseemly, unethical, indelicate and lousy. Have I made myself clear?"

Johnny Swann said that it was all a mistake; he felt like a brother to Nikki.

"Sure *I* know," Shep said, "a slightly incestuous brother."

A boy was sitting all alone along the wall beside Johnny. He was quite young and pale and handsome in his dinner clothes. He bent his glance on people with the stern fixity of the very drunk. Everybody avoided his eyes. He had spoken to Shep when they first came and Nikki asked who he was.

Shep said he was a drinking acquaintance.

"Somebody gave him a case of absinthe," Shep said, "and he's drinking his way through it all by himself. He won't give anyone else a drink."

"Well," said Bill, "I hope he makes it."

"He sees everything green by now," Shep said. "He looks at things through a green mist. He's living in a green dream."

The boy finally managed to fix Johnny with his eyes.

"*I'm* all right," he said as if Johnny had accused him, "but *you've* got a green parrot on *your* shoulder." He snicked the parrot off Johnny's shoulder.

Johnny thanked him and said, "Be careful. Don't knock the parrot's hat off."

"Where are we going for dinner?" Nikki asked.

"Château Madrid," Shep said. "Ever been?"

"No."

They had some more cocktails and then climbed back into the Santa Maria.

It was a long cool ride out to the Château Madrid. They found a table under the colored lights in the trees beside the out-of-door dance floor. Nikki was enchanted with the place. She liked the food and the music and the wine.

A lot of gigolos were there, and Kiss-Me-Quick was there and came over and dragged Johnny out on the floor.

Cary and Bill and even Shep danced with Nikki during the cool April evening. They strayed away, though, one by one, on vague errands. Finally Nikki, herself, went for a stroll.

When Shep and Bill came upon her she was standing beside a great flowering hydrangea bush at the far end of the garden with a glass in her hand—as usual.

She made a lovely picture in her black and silver dress against the giant blooms.

"Hi, Nikki," Shep said, "what are you doing all by yourself? Where's everybody?"

"They all kind of wandered off," Nikki said.

"Well, that's no way to treat a lady. What've you got in that glass?"

"Teeth."

"Teeth?"

Nikki held out the glass for them to see.

"Can you imagine that," Shep said, "it's teeth."

"Full set," said Bill, "upper and lower."

"What a beautiful smile," said Shep. "Nikki, how come you to win those teeth?"

"Well," said Nikki, "I was just standing here and a young gentleman came up and begged my pardon and asked would I mind holding his teeth for a minute."

"What did he want you to hold his teeth for?"

"Said there was somebody he wanted to biff."

"And?" said Bill.

"And I said, 'no not at all. There isn't anything particular doing at the moment,' I said, and it seemed like a good idea."

"Good ole Nik."

"He said thank you and he took out his teeth and put them in my glass and then he went off."

"Yeah?" said Bill, his face lighting up, "which way did he go?"

"Around to the right," said Nikki, pointing.

"Come on, Shep," Bill said. They left Nikki standing wistfully by the hydrangeas.

The orchestra was playing tango music and people were dancing on the floor in the center of the garden.

Cary and The Washout came along. "What's that?" The Washout asked, looking curiously at Nikki's glass.

"Teeth," said Nikki.

"Whose teeth?"

"I don't know," Nikki said, "somebody came along and asked me would I hold his teeth a minute."

"What did he want you to hold his teeth for?"

"Said he was going to biff somebody."

"Which way did he go?" Cary said.

Nikki pointed.

The Washout and Cary started off in the direction indicated by Nikki's finger. "Come along, Nikki."

"No," said Nikki, "I have to stay here and mind the man's teeth."

After a while Shep and Bill came back. Nikki was standing in the same place by the hydrangeas. Her glass was empty.

"We missed it," Bill said.

"Did something happen?"

"They carried somebody out. What did you do with the teeth?" Shep said, looking at the empty glass.

"Oh, the man came and got his teeth."

Shep and Bill looked at her interestedly.

"He looked just the same—only a little happier."

"What did he say?"

"He said could he have his teeth back now."

"Was that all he said?"

"Well, he said he thought I was kind of sweet to help him out like that."

"What did he look like?" Shep wanted to know.

"Oh, he was very nice looking," Nikki assured them.

"Was he old?"

"No—he wasn't very old."

"How old do you think?"

"Oh, about twenty."

"Twenty?"

"I think he fell in an airplane in the war and got his teeth knocked out."

"Why do you think that?"

"Well, his jaw was kind of cut up—like it had been smashed."

Shep was interested.

"Why do you think he was in the war?"

"Well," Nikki defended, "he had a kind of little striped ribbon in his button hole."

"Well, what makes you think he was a flier?"

"His eyes," she said simply.

"His eyes?"

"He had the same kind of look in his eyes that you all have—and Francis."

They all laughed at her. "You can tell
fliers better by their ears," Shep said.

"He had the nicest lisp," Nikki said dreamily.

When it was time to go home they couldn't
find Johnny. They hunted all over the place
for him and finally left without him.

Going back in the cab, Bill pointed off to
the right.

"That certainly is a beautiful lake," he said.

"Lake," said Shep, "that there's a palm
tree."

"Palm tree," Bill repeated stubbornly.

"Lake."

"Palm tree."

"La—a—ake."

"Palm tree-e-e-e."

"All right," said Bill, "stop the cab. I'm
going to jump into it. And if it splashes it's
a palm tree."

"O.K.," said Shep. They stopped the cab
and got out.

"It isn't a palm tree nor it isn't a lake," The
Washout confided to Nikki.

"I know," said Nikki quickly.

Back at the Carlton, they all took Nikki to
her apartment and said good night to her.
Half an hour later The Washout came back
down the corridor and knocked at Nikki's
door. Nikki opened the door and came out,

closing the door behind her. She was wearing a fur wrap and a black hat with a half-veil. The two descended the elevator and left the hotel. It was two o'clock in the morning.

CHAPTER IV

THERE was a note on Shep's tray when the waiter brought in his coffee and brandy in the morning.

"I have a dreadful attack of the plain and fancy shakes and please bring back my kimono and Eighty-Eight's nose is hot and one of my turtles is missing."

There's a damsel in distress if there ever was one, Shep told himself as he prepared to go to the rescue. It was eleven o'clock, however, before Shep appeared in Nikki's sitting room with Bill and Cary.

Nikki was in a chair by the French windows in an Hawaiian kimono, her flowered night gown rucked up over her knees. The morning sunlight was streaming into the room. Eighty-Eight Carlton was nosing aimlessly about. The turtles were somewhere around on the floor. Nikki's bare feet rested on a red hassock. She looked as fruity as a Clara Tice color plate. A little agate-eyed Oriental knelt in front of her. He was painting her toenails with a tiny brush.

"Hi, Nik!"

"H'lo Shepard. H'lo, Bill."

"How's th' ol' gal this morning? Well look at Nikki!"

They all stood still and gazed at Nikki.

"Nikki's having her toenails painted," Bill observed. "Can you imagine that? What's the idea, Nikki?"

"An old Turkish custom," Nikki explained, "and how about something to pick up a chap?"

"Are you dying, Egypt, dying?"

"Simply dying, Egypt."

"Well, we certainly ought to do something about that," said Shep, and went to the telephone to order some drinks sent up.

"No prairie oysters," Nikki said.

"Picon citron," Shep said, "will make you laugh and play." He came back and took his place in the half circle about Nikki.

"You don't mind a gallery, does you?" he asked.

"Love galleries."

"What you having your toenails painted for?"

"Well," began Nikki vaguely, "seems like a good idea."

"That there," Shep told Bill, "is practically the loveliest pair of laigs I ever clapped a eye on."

"Like my legs?" Nikki inquired, bending forward to look at them.

"Look at those legs, Bill. Why they practically match. Did you ever see sich a set of legs!"

"Very bracing," Bill agreed.

"What can we do about it?"

"Burst into tears is all I know."

Seated as she was, Nikki presented a dazzling pair of legs. She had the small knees and the almond-shaped, well-set knee caps of a runner. The skin of her well rounded calves just kissed each other. She had slim, tapering ankles and a small high-arched foot. Cary thought she had legs like Atlanta, the huntress. But all Shep could think of was Swinburne's voluptuous description of Dolores, Our Lady of Pain.

"Would it embarrass you, if we burst into tears, Nikki?"

"On account of my legs?" Nikki said, "I think that would be sweet."

"Well, on account of her feet, too, Bill. Don't you think? Look at those feet. Aren't they too divine?"

"Too divine," Bill agreed.

"Those are the highest arches in the world, I bet."

"You could practically walk under Nikki's arches in a high dudgeon or something," Shep said. "You know, I think outside of her legs, Nikki's arches are her best feature. I'd marry the gal on account of her arches. Here come the drinks."

A waiter was coming in with a tray of drinks in tall glasses. Shep told Bill to go into action with the syphon.

"I'd marry the gal anyways," Shep was saying, "she's a mighty fine type of architecture."

"You like grenadine in yours, don't you, Nik?" Bill inquired.

"Just a dash."

Bill squirted the soda water bravely into a glass and handed it over to Nikki.

"What color you having your toenails painted?" Shep inquired, peering over the Chinaman's shoulder.

"Rose," said Nikki.

"Rose, hey? Why not green or lavender or something?"

"Rose," said Nikki, "is my choice."

"And very nice too," Shep agreed, "And here's to Nikki's dainty leg," he proposed, raising his glass, "as smooth and hairless as an egg."

"Happy landing," said Nikki.

Bill told Shep not to get vulgar.

"Vulgar?" said Shep, "vulgar. Why that's Shakespeare, my boy. Shakespeare."

"Nikki's dainty leg?" Bill queried. "That's not Shakespeare."

"Well Julia's dainty leg, then," Shep admitted. "if you're going to get academic about it. Nikki, that certainly is a cute way you've got your toenails trimmed. What is that? Square cut or something?"

"Emerald, and they have to be done like that," Nikki said.

"A cause de quoi?"

"A cause de mon grand-père."

"On account of your grandfather?"

"On account of my grandfather died of an ingrown toenail. It's in our family."

"How could anyone die of an ingrowing toenail?"

"Blood poisoning or something."

"Pore ol' Gramp. Well, Bill, you'll never die like that."

"Not me."

"Bill is certainly out of luck," Shep said, "if he'd of got killed in the war, they'd of named a landing field after him. How do you like Nikki's toesies?"

"Pretty supreme," said Bill.

Nikki suddenly became shy and covered her toes with her hands.

"My poor toes," Nikki said, "I'm afraid they're ruined."

"How so?"

"Can't you see anything the matter with them?"

"Not from here, I can't."

"Well, they're kind of red and rough on top."

"They look all right to me. What's the matter with 'em?"

"Well, when I was a little girl——"

"——in Honolulu, H. I."

"——in Honolulu, my mother bought me a pair of shoes. And they were too short, way too short. And I had to walk all the way to Sunday School and back. Down the road. And it was very hot and dusty——"

Shep and Bill could see a little girl in a bright hair-ribbon trudging down a hot, dusty road to Sunday School in a pair of shoes that were too short for her.

"——and when I got home my toes were spoiled."

"Take her away," said Shep, "she's breaking my heart."

"Listen, where did you go last night?"

"You mean after?"

"Yes, after the Château Madrid."

"How did you know I went any place?"

"Oh, your Uncle Shepard knows everything. Come on now, break down and tell us where you went."

"Oh, to a place."

"What was the name of the place?"

"The Star of Venus or something——"

"*The Star of Venus,*" Shep repeated incredulously.

"That's right," Nikki said, "*Installation Ultra-Moderne, Bain de Luxe, Ecran Artistique. . . .*"

"What!" Bill roared out. "Do you mean to say you went there?"

"Now, Bill——"

"What did you go for?"

"Well, not for the ride."

"I know, but what for?"

"To see the flagellations, if you must know."

"The——! Well, for gosh sakes! Who took you?"

"Francis."

"That twirp! I'll snap his spine!" Bill was sore as six goats.

"Well, will you please listen to Desperate Ambrose," Nikki appealed to Shep.

"He knows better than that!" Bill said. "What the hell does he mean anyway, taking you to places like that!"

"Well, it was my idea," Nikki said.

"Even so," said Bill, "he had no right to do it."

Bill was stalking up and down the room.

Cary and Shep looked at him. They could see that Bill was in love with Nikki. Jealously, protectively, possessively in love with her.

"Well," Bill snapped out, "what did you do there?"

"It turned out kind of badly," Nikki admitted.

"I should hope so."

"I couldn't stand it. One wretched woman beating another. I got hysterical and Francis had to take me out into the street."

"The snake."

"What I remember best was a sign in the hall. It said 'No Singing.' I thought that was kind of cute—in a place like that."

"If I could—" Bill began.

"Listen," Shep advised, "lay off him. It wasn't his fault. Nikki wanted to go."

"Yes, but no decent——"

"Oh zut," said Shep roughly, "since when did you start to move in polite society. And besides I told you before—I don't think you better cross that baby."

"Hell——"

"He's poison."

"Well, what does he keep hanging around Nikki for?"

Shep burst out laughing. "Well, what do *you* hang about Nikki for?"

Pr-r-ring! Pr-r-ring! Pr-r-ring! Pr-r-ring! Pr-r-ring! The shrill little French telephone was ringing.

Nikki reached over to the table beside her and lifted off the receiver.

"It's Johnny Swann," she informed them. There was a long pause.

"He's at the Château Madrid," she said, "he stayed there last night, and he wants somebody to come out and find out what name he registered under. . . ."

"What room's he in?" Shep inquired, "ask him what's his room number."

"What's your room number, Johnny?" Nikki asked. "Johnny, what's your room number? He doesn't know," she told the others.

"Tell him to go look over the door," Shep advised.

"Go look on your door, Johnny. Shep says to look on your door. He seems kind of agitated," Nikki said. "He says he's going to look. One twenty-two? He says his room number is one twenty-two and bring him a hat."

Shep went to the telephone and called the Château Madrid.

"What is the name of the gentleman in one twenty-two?" he demanded.

There was a brief silence while Shep stood smoking.

A voice came over the telephone.

"Doctor Krausmeyer?" Shep repeated. "Thanks. Well, Johnny's imagination is im-

proving," Shep told the others. "He's registered as Herr Doktor Krausmeyer and family.
I'll go and fetch him home."

"Finish," said the little Chinaman, gathering up his instruments.

"Oh, I forgot," Nikki said. "This is—"
She reached for a card on the table. "This is
Yu-Azim, Pedicure Chinois, English Spoken,
Face au Casino."

Yu-Azim grinned brightly.

"Paris lice?"

"Lousy," Shep agreed.

Nikki asked to be excused now, on account
of, she said, she had to get dressed.

Shep departed in search of Johnny Swann
and Bill and Cary went back to their rooms.

Cary went downstairs to exchange some
money at the desk and found a sheaf of letters
in his box. Colby, the Cardinal College porter,
had sent them on to the Washington Inn, St.
James Square, in London, Cary's first for-
warding address. They had been, in turn, for-
warded to the Hotel Observatoire, the quiet
little pension which Cary had occupied at the
edge of the Luxembourg Gardens, before
Shep had moved him to the Carlton. Cary
took them to his room to read.

The topmost letter was addressed to Cary
Lockwood, Esqre, Cardinal College, Oxford,
England, and was postmarked London—

Single Lady

2 P.M.—March 10. The handwriting on the
stiff, square envelope was small, regular and
English. The envelope was embossed in the
upper left-hand corner with a blue five-
pointed coronet. Cary broke the blue wax
seal and read the following message, written
on a card:

Tower House

*Saturday. Bakerloo Tube. Trains leave Piccadilly
Circus at five minutes before the hour and every
fifteen minutes thereafter. If you take the six:ten
the motor will be at the station to meet you. Viens.*

"*S.*"

The second letter bore a Lombard Street
return address in London, and was written in
a small wandering, uncertain hand. " . . .
*you are coming to London this week-end,
aren't you? I will stay in Saturday until you
call . . . please destroy this letter. . . .*"

A third was from 51 Victoria Road, Ken-
sington, W. I., and was inscribed in an even,
readable hand on light blue note-paper, yield-
ing a faint scent. (Shep Lambert used to say
that it was a pleasure to smell Cary's mail.)

A fourth was sheathed in a large, long, blue
envelope. It carried, in addition to the green,
five centime stamp showing the head of Albert,
King of the Belgians, a red fifty centime ex-

114

press stamp. The legends "Speed-bestelling Express" and "Express Fee Paid 3d" were stamped in black across the face of the envelope. The flap was sealed with red wax and impressed with the initials Y. L. It was scented with Chypre. The letter was dated "Anvers le 12 au soir," and began, *"Mon adoré: I suffer cruelly from your indifference . . . not one tiny word of consolation. My spirit and my imagination are too small to conceive my future life otherwise than with you. Perhaps you suspect me to be like most girls of this age, incapable of a veritable love. . . . I love you with all the plenitude of my soul . . . my love for you is sincere as it is profound and nothing in the world can change it . . . all the days of my life I consecrate to you. I am very triste and demoralized . . . all the world asks me if I am not ill. . . . I embrace you with all my strength. Mille caresses les plus tendres. Votre Yvonne pour toujours. Cela qui pense a vous."*

The next letter from Southampton was written in a girls' finishing-school script. *"Oh, Cary, I couldn't go . . . my heart failed me before I got to the boat . . . I'm coming back to London. Will you come to London when you receive this, or shall I come up to Oxford? Will you telegraph me at the Savoy?"*

Another letter contained the sentence:

Single Lady

"Why this *devasting* silence?" Still another said: "I washed my hair this morning and prayed for you," and in another was written: "Every tick of the clock brings me nearer to you."

Davis wanted to know if he would be on hand for tea at Balliol on Thursday; there was a notice that Dr. Wellington Koo would address the American Club; a reminder from the secretary of the Gridiron Club that he had not yet paid his dues; an announcement that the Rt. Hon'ble The Viscount Curzon would speak at the Union . . .

Dolbear & Goodall, Chymists of 180 High Street, respectfully sent notice that there was a matter of £5–6–10 owing.

The Slatter & Rose Booksellers & News Agents dr.—Acct. Rendered £2–9–6.

H. R. Hedderly, Athletic and Sports Outfitter, Tobacconist and Cigar Importer, submitted a respectful account of four pounds, eight shillings and sixpence.

Elliston & Cavell, Ltd., the Leading Linen Drapers, Silk Mercers, etc., would like a settlement on Cary Lockwood, Esqre's account of £8–2–6, past due.

There was a matter—past due, it was respectfully called to his attention—of £10–5–5 at Castell & Son (Established 1846), Suitings and Homespuns, Academic Robes, Shirt

Makers, Hatters and Hosiers, Athletic Out-
fits including our well-known Oxford Rowing
Shorts.

J. W. Piper of Ship Street, Oxford,
Breeches Maker (Hunting - Polo - Cycling -
Walking), wished to remind Cary Lockwood,
Esqre, that his account of five guineas was of
long standing.

Ducker & Son, Bootmakers on the Turl,
Genuine Handsewn Work,—£3–6–6.

To the Junior Common Room—for wine,
fruit, cakes, cigarettes, writing paper, sub-
scriptions and fees: twenty-five pounds.

To college Batells—for Platemen and
Waiters, College Charges, University Dues,
Tuition, College Library, Argent, Poor Rate,
Bedmakers, Buttery and Kitchen, Table-
cloths and Napkins, Porter's Note, Mes-
senger, Room Rent, Furniture, Rent, Electric
Light, Coal and Faggots, Laundress, Care of
Bicycle, Baths, Telephone, Luggage Porter
. . . £72–6–2.

Boul's Restaurant (Tea Baskets and Picnic
Hampers) invited attention respectfully to an
amount of £7–10–0.

Cary put down the tradesmen's bills, walked
to the window and surveyed the sunlit inner
court of the Carlton Hotel thoughtfully. He
turned away from the window, fingering the
gold pencil in his hand. He contemplated the

bronze figurines on the mantel; curled a loose loop of the telephone connection about his finger; went back to the window. The telephone bell rang.

"Come over here, will you, Cary," Shep said.

Cary went down the hall.

Johnny was sitting on his bed and Shep was standing by the window when Cary came in.

"Dr. Krausmeyer is troubled in his mind," Shep said. "I thought maybe you could cheer him up."

"What's the trouble, Johnny boy?"

"You tell him," Johnny said miserably to Shep.

"Well," said Shep, "Johnny thinks something's wrong."

"Wrong? Well," said Cary soberly, "why does he think that?"

"Well, on account of little Kiss-Me-Quick. He suspects the worst."

Cary looked at Johnny.

"Oh, I know it! I know it!" Johnny burst out. "I tell you I know it."

"But how can you, Johnny?"

"I tell you I know."

Shep and Cary were unconvinced. They looked at each other. Johnny was in a state.

"When I think that I got through school

118

and the war and everything and then do this, when I know better!"

"But Johnny," Cary said, "you're already accepting it as an actual fact. You might be wasting a lot of heroics. Just because you've been exposed doesn't mean——"

"I tell you I'm sure!"

They could see that Johnny was on the verge of hysteria. It would embarrass them if Johnny should weep, and the recollection would be embarrassing afterwards to Johnny. So Cary brought him up short.

"Well, after all, Johnny, however it turns out I think you ought to take it standing up. You have only yourself to blame."

"I know it," said Johnny quickly. "I know that. But it's such a hell of a hard thing to accept right away——"

"Lord," said Shep, "you shouldn't take it so big. Everybody I know has had it at one time or another."

"Yes," said Johnny, "but you never have."

"The hell I haven't," Shep lied. "I've had it twice!"

Johnny looked at him incredulously.

"It's no Sunday School picnic," Shep continued, "but you get over it. You get over everything."

"But I don't want to get over it. I don't want ever to have to get over it."

"What's so terrible about it?" Shep demanded. "If you've got it, you've got it. Then the thing to do is get rid of it."

"Oh, yes," said Johnny bitterly.

"Listen, it's only a matter of treatment . . ."

Johnny flinched. "Oh, I suppose so. But it's the idea——"

"The idea of what?"

"The idea of having it—when you never had it before."

Shep laughed. "You'll soon get over that. As a matter of fact I'm surprised at you, Johnny—carrying on like this——"

Johnny began to walk up and down the floor.

"If you were going to take it so big," Shep said, "why did you let yourself in for it?"

Johnny smiled wanly. "I don't know," he said, "it seemed like a good idea at the time.

"Oh, God," he went on. "I don't know. I don't know. I don't *know*. It's so easy to think now how it might have been different. I wish to God I had last night over again. I was tight . . . and we got in a cab . . . and she . . . Oh, hell . . . I don't remember much about it except this morning . . ."

"Did you ask her about it?"

"Yes."

"What did she say?"

"She just began to cry."

"Listen, Johnny," Shep said, "there were twenty-six in the flier's quarters at Avord and twenty-four of them had it."

"I suppose so."

"And nobody whimpered."

"Well, they all thought they were going to get knocked off anyway so it didn't matter. I wouldn't care either. But now it's different. I won't go through with it. I know what I'll do."

"Aw, Johnny," Shep said, "that's pretty cheap. Where is the old fight?"

"Didn't you have anything with you?" Cary said.

"No," said Johnny.

"Well, how long is it since——"

"It's too late. It's six hours—nothing will do any good now. I'm in for it."

"Johnny," said Shep severely. "I don't think you've grown up yet. I don't think there's a thing the matter with you."

Johnny was looking out of the open window at the streams of cars passing and repassing along the street below.

"Isn't it funny," he said, "yesterday everything was all right. A lot of fun. Now everything's different."

"I've seen that little Kiss-Me-Quick," Shep said, "and she always looked pretty choosy to

121

me. I don't think there's anything wrong with her. Maybe she was just afraid, too."

"I know what I'll do." Johnny was saying.

"You ought to be a little bit ashamed, Johnny," Cary said, "when you think of all the terrific things that happened to people in the war. All the mutilations and amputations and things. Things they can never get away from."

"It doesn't do any good," Johnny said, "to think about that. The only thing that counts is yourself. You two can talk because you're safe. But I'm the one. I've seen it happen all around me before, too, just as you have. But I always told myself that if it ever happened to me——"

"Good ol' Johnny Swann," Shep said, putting his arm about Johnny's shoulder. "He's in a state. I'll bet you a thousand francs there's nothing wrong. Pull up your socks, Johnny."

Johnny looked out of the window and said nothing.

"Hell," said Shep. "Come on down to the bar, Johnny, and have a drink."

"No thanks. I don't want a drink."

"Make you laugh and play," Shep encouraged.

"Oh, God," Johnny flashed out, "I don't want to drink! I'm tired of drinking! I'm

122

tired of just lifting glasses! I hate it! I don't
want another drink as long as I live. This is
the worst punishment I ever took in my life.
I swear to God I'll never drink again. I want
to go away. I want to do something else. I
want to get a hell of a long ways from here."

"All you need is a drink," Shep said.

Johnny had become fanatically obstinate.

"I guess I'm just not up to it," Johnny
went on. "You all can keep going and going
but I can't do it. I've got to get away."

"You really ought to have a drink, Johnny,"
Shep repeated.

"No thanks."

Shep and Cary tried to persuade Johnny
to come out with them, but he refused to leave
his room.

"Don't bother with me," he said, "you two
go on."

They didn't want to leave him by himself.

"Let's go down to Nikki's room," Shep suggested. "She ought to be ready by now."

Johnny finally agreed to come. As they
were going out the door he clutched Shep's
shoulder. "You won't say anything to the
others, will you?"

"Hell, no," Shep said.

"Thanks."

Shep and Cary collected Bill and Francis on
their way down to Nikki's room.

Single Lady

The door to Nikki's bedroom was half open when they came in, and they could see her seated at her dressing-table. She had on a straight, narrow frock of blue serge with red panels. It was fastened high and close about her throat with red buttons. She was knotting a kerchief of blue silk about her head.

"Hi, Nik," Shep called. "We brung home Doctor Krausmeyer."

"Good-morning, Johnny," Nikki said.

"Hello, Nikki."

"Johnny's in a state," Shep informed her. "He's all non compos bananas."

"Well, ring for a drink."

"He won't drink."

"Won't drink? Won't drink? Well, whoever heard of such a thing?"

"Nope," said Shep, "the good doktor refuses the sacrament."

"Well, well," Nikki murmured, "what's the cause of this strange manifestation?"

"Says he's tired of lifting glasses even. Says he's just tired is all. Come on out here, Nikki, and engage a fellow in polite conversation."

Nikki appeared in the doorway.

"Did you ever see such a dressy wench?" Shep said enthusiastically. "Look at that thing, Cary. Isn't that marvelous? Isn't that a fine piece of work?"

"Oh, Shepard," Nikki said advancing into

the room, "you make my heart melt when you say things like that."

"Let's not move from this place for a while," Shep said, "let's have some drinks sent up and sit here and look at Nikki."

"Help yourself," Nikki said, "I've got to compose a cable anyway."

"Hey, somebody," Shep said, "give the child a pencil and something to scribble on. Anything to keep her amused."

Nikki said she wanted colored crayons.

"Push the bell, somebody," Shep said, "us chaps has got to get to drinking."

Nikki pushed the bell. She sat down at the little table at the far end of the room, pulled out a drawer and selected a cable form. She swung halfway around in her chair and crossed her legs, tapping the pen holder reflectively against her teeth.

Shep drew in his breath sharply at the sight of Nikki's legs.

"Every time I see Nikki's legs," he said, "I want to go and sock somebody on the jaw. I don't know quite why."

Shep was sitting on the sofa with Cary. Bill was sprawled out in the big chair. The Washout was sitting on the floor and Johnny was wandering about the room like a lost soul, stopping occasionally to stare at objects as if he had never in his life seen them before.

Single Lady

"Light somewhere won't you, Johnny," Bill invited, "you're making us all weavy."

Shep was still thinking about Nikki's legs. "Let's not abandon that idear for a moment," he said. "Let me investigate it in my mind."

"Sure," said Bill, "go ahead and pursue it. Chase it up a tree or down a rabbit hole."

"Why do I want to punch somebody on the nose when I see Nikki's legs?"

"They're so stimulating," Bill said.

"How about it, Cary?" Shep demanded. "You've got answers for everything."

"You're excitant agents," Cary said.

Nikki was writing out her cable and paying no attention.

Bill Talbot could not divert his eyes from Nikki's legs.

"Give Bill a pair of skates now," Shep said maliciously, "and I bet he could jump over ten barrels."

"I wisht I had my ocarina," Bill said wistfully. "I'd play Beautiful Ohio, with variations."

Somebody rapped on the door. Shep went and opened it and it was the valet. Shep turned and looked mournfully at Nikki.

"Won't you ever learn?" He complained. "*Once* is for the waiter, *twice* for the chambermaid and *three times* for the valet de chambre. Look, it's all written out for you over the bell."

"Well," said Nikki, defensively, "I only pushed once."

"And it rung sixteen times," Shep said. "Nikki's got the jitters," he told the others. "Don't let her ring any more bells. Here, let an expert push that button." He told the valet it was a mistake and rang for the sommelier.

Johnny Swann continued his aimless wandering about the sitting room. Every once in a while he could cock his head to one side in a listening attitude and shout "Entrez!" Everyone would turn and look expectantly at the door, but nobody came in.

"Didn't you hear someone knocking?" he demanded.

"Poor Johnny," Shep said. "He hears things."

Johnny went to the door and pulled it open. He looked up and down the empty hallway. He turned around grinning foolishly. "Honest," he demanded, "didn't anyone knock?"

"Poor Johnny," Shep repeated. "He's got such a long ways to go yet. All he hears now is people knocking. Pretty soon the telephone will be ringing. . . ."

"It's ringing now," Johnny said.

"It's only your head ringing, Johnny boy," Shep said. "Now listen to your Uncle Shepard, Johnny. You better take a drink when they come up else you'll be hearing sleigh bells. Then pretty soon you'll hear whistles blowing and guns going off, and babies crying and horns tooting and dogs barking and wolves howling."

"And whispers," Bill added.

"Now that *is* somebody," Johnny said and ran over and opened the door. The hall was empty.

"Then after you get done hearing things, you'll begin to *see* things. First," Shep said, stretching his legs and settling down to an elaborate disquisition, "the patterns on the wall will begin to come to life and start creeping around. Did you ever see a big, black, hairy spider with red and yellow . . ."

"Say, Shep, what's that behind you?" Bill interrupted him.

Shep sat up, stiffened, but did not turn around.

"Has he got fur all over him?"

"Yep."

"And an orange tokus?"

"That's right, and he looks like he's going to jump."

"Well, that's my little Red Howler," Shep said. "Where's the waiter? Hey, Francis, you run down to the bar and tell Charles to send up a tray full of Martinis right away!"

The Washout got up obediently and went out.

When the cocktails came up, clear and clean and cold, Johnny obstinately refused to drink.

"You know," he said, "I think the French Cavalry is the place for a man."

"Listen to Johnny," Shep said, "he is took violently sober and he's full of ideas. He'll be inquiring about the Foreign Legion next. Listen, Johnny, don't try to run away from yourself."

They drank two trays of cocktails and sent down for another. Nikki had finished her cable and turned around in her chair.

"Nikki," said Shep, "are you rich?"

Nikki nodded.

"How rich?"

"Forty-eight thousand dollars," Nikki said.

"Is that all?"

"That's all."

"And then what?"

"And then there's an Argentine with forty-seven emeralds and a faint smell of decadence . . . and a college professor."

"What do they think about it?"

"Well, it's their idea."

"Good ol' Nikki. Where did they have the idea?"

"Up on the boat deck."

"You know, Nikki," Shep reflected, "I thought you were rich." He picked up one of Nikki's turtles.

129

"I think I am."

"I think you're just a gamey gal. Bill, one of us has got to save her from that there Argentine with the emeralds."

"Damn decent of you, old man," Nikki said.

"You know," said Johnny Swann, "I think the ideal life for a man would be in the French Cavalry."

"I'm afraid we're going to lose our Doktor Krausmeyer," Shep said with some misgivings. "He thinks the only thing left in the world to tie to is horses."

"He may be right," Nikki said, "and what are the plans for the day?"

"Plans?" Shep queried, "Plans? Plans? Whoever had any plans? You sound like Cary. He's always got a headful of plans. Do we have to have plans?"

"I'm sure I don't know," Nikki said. "You seem to get along without them."

Shep had drunk a dozen Martinis and he was feeling quite content. His tic had subsided so he took off his dark glasses and relaxed back in his chair. It was fine being here with Nikki and the others. He wasn't quite ready to leave yet.

"Loosen your stays and let down your back hair and set awhile," he told Nikki. "We're having a fine time."

But Nikki said they ought to go.

"Hey," Shep said suddenly, holding up the turtle, "her nose is hot."

"What?" said Nikki.

"Her nose is warm. I think she's got a fever."

"Better call the house physician," Nikki said.

Shep thought that was kind of a quaint idea to call the hotel doctor so he went to the telephone.

"*Attendez,*" he said to the operator, "I want the doctor . . . there's a sick turtle up here . . . *oui, une tortue de la terre* . . . send up the *médicin d'hôtel.*"

A muffled voice came floating over the telephone and Shep hung up the receiver.

"I guess it's no good," he reported sadly. "She said mineral water or ginger ale. I bet if I told her somebody was murdered up here she'd want to know mineral water or ginger ale."

Nikki took her turtle and set it under the cold water tap in the bathroom.

"I wonder," Shep said, when Nikki came back, "if the grunion are running."

Nikki looked puzzled.

"Shep's trying to be funny," Cary explained.

"In what way?" Nikki inquired.

"Grunion," Cary began, "grunion are kind

131

of little candle fish or something, that come up on the beach by the light of a full moon."

Nikki continued to look puzzled.

"Well, Shep you know is full of quaint conceits."

"That's right," Shep agreed.

"And one of them is that anchovies are grunion. Shep likes to eat anchovies with his cocktails, so he pretends to go grunion hunting at the Claridge bar?"

"Would you like to go grunion hunting?" Shep invited Nikki.

"At the Claridge?"

"Or would you druther go on a Weenie Roast? What would you druther if you had your druthers? Would you druther go on a Hay Ride or a Quilting Party or a Strawberry Festival or a Fish Fry or a Husking Bee? You know," he said with a loud wink, "if you find a red ear at a Husking Bee you can kiss your best girl."

"I'd druther go for grunions," Nikki said.

"What do you ketch 'em with?" Bill inquired.

"Oh, anything, dish pans, clothes tubs, wash boilers, commodes, anything."

"I was in a department store once," Nikki said, "and a lady was standing beside me, and she had a little boy, and somehow he managed to get one over his head."

"Ho, ho," said Shep, who was kind of a vulgarian, "that's funny."

"And he could't get it off, and his mother couldn't get it off, and the salesman couldn't get it off."

"I can see the whole thing," Shep said.

"And I suggested tapping it with a hammer——"

"Capital idea!"

"But the boy's mother got indignant. Said she wouldn't think of it—injure her little Wesley. She took him by the hand and led him off. I was only trying to be helpful."

"Ho, ho, ho."

"He did look a little unusual," she reflected. "It was quite a nice one—porcelain—with a border of maiden hair fern and red geraniums —in a very chaste design. Kind of a Dresden effect."

They all got ready to leave. All except Johnny who said he was going back to his room. Nikki slipped on a little jacket that matched her dress and picked up a long-handled umbrella.

"You all go on ahead," Johnny said, "and I'll find you later." But they knew that he wouldn't join them later.

"Good-bye, Johnny boy," said Nikki.

"Good-bye, Nikki. Be a good girl."

"What's the trouble with Johnny?" Nikki asked when they were in the hallway.

"He's ascared," Shep said.

"Ascared of what?"

"Ascared that he'll see pluses instead of minuses."

They all got in the cage and the boy took them directly down to the bar.

They ranged themselves along the bar on high stools and drank cocktails while they ate olives and potato chips, anchovies and cheese-straws.

"Tell me," Nikki said, "tell me what you are really thinking of doing this afternoon because I'd like to get a water wave. . . ."

"Well," said Shep, "here's the idea. Bill and Francis and I are going over to the Cluny and play billiards and drink beer. You've no idea what fun that is on a rainy afternoon. How about coming along?"

"What about Cary? Is Cary going, too?"

"Cary here has a funny notion," Shep said. "He wants to go to Père Lachaise."

"What's that?"

"That's a *cimitière*," Shep said, "do you know what is a *cimitière?*"

"Cemetery?" Nikki hazarded.

"Right. But can you imagine a chap spending Saturday afternoon in a cemetery?"

"Must be something," Nikki speculated.

"Well," said Shep, "we sort of figgered to take you along with us."

"No," said Nikki firmly, "I'm going with Cary."

CHAPTER V

"*Père Lachaise,*" Cary told the cab driver.
"*Père Lachaise,*" he repeated, "*Cimitière?
Oui.*"

"Is it very far out?" Nikki inquired, as she
got into the car.

"Twentieth Arrondissement," Cary said.

"Do you mind my coming along?"

"A pleasure."

A slight drizzle began to settle on the
streets. The cab slipped and slithered along
the wet pavement.

"If it rains do we go in anyway?" Nikki inquired.

"I think so," Cary said. He was looking at
her little red shoes with the high pointed heels.
"Can you walk in those shoes?"

"Do we have to walk far?"

"Well—an hour or so."

"I think I can manage it."

"The walking is a little uneven."

The cab swung past the Obélisque in the
Place de la Concorde, turned left into the Rue
Royale and right again along the Boulevard
de la Madeleine.

"Tell me," Nikki said, "have you got any

particular reason for going where you are going this afternoon?"

"Nothing very particular. There's some
thing by Epstein I wanted to look at."

They passed the Madeleine and entered the
Boulevard des Capucines.

"Are the others really going to the Cluny?"
Nikki asked.

"I think so."

"I wonder if they'll make it."

"Probably not."

Nikki was beginning to wonder if it made
any difference anyway. She had never known
anyone before to whom nothing really mat-
tered.

"How old were you when you went into the
war?" Nikki asked a little timidly.

"I'm twenty-five if that's what you want to
know."

What was it that Cary and Shep and Bill
and Johnny and The Washout were like? Nikki had come upon an expression in her mind
one night when she was thinking about them.
What was it now?

The cab was entering the Avenue de la Re-
publique.

"It's only a few blocks now," Cary said.

Spent bullets. That was it. They were
like spent bullets. Shaped for war and
hurled at the enemy. They had described a

beautiful high, arching trajectory. Now they were fallen back to the earth. Spent. Cooled off. Brittle.

It was still drizzling when they got down from the cab at the gate of the cemetery.

Nikki sniffed the air and looked up into the sky.

"I think it'll let up in a minute."

"Do you think so? Do you want to sit in the cab?"

Nikki was looking at a little sidewalk café on the left. "Could we sit down over there for a minute?"

"Restez ici," Cary told the driver.

"Oui, M'sieu."

They sat down at one of the little iron tables under the awning in the front of the sidewalk café on the Avenue Casimir-Perier.

Nikki was groping hopelessly in her bag.

"Have you got a cigarette?" she asked Cary. "Oh, that's right, you don't smoke. Why don't you smoke?"

"Do I have to say?"

"Yes, you have to say. You have to say why you don't smoke."

"Well," said Cary, "I don't feel keen."

"You like to feel keen?"

"Keen as ice."

"What about drinking?"

"It doesn't make any difference."

"That's funny."

"I think it has something to do with the chemistry of the blood. My blood accepts alcohol but refuses nicotine."

"How do you mean refuses?" Nikki was still searching for her cigarettes.

"Well, I get a reaction."

"Spots dancing before the eyes? Hot and cold flashes? Sensations of falling? Strange noises at night. . . ."

"I'm sorry," said Cary, "all I meant is a dull mouth in the morning, and a broken complexion."

Nikki looked at Cary's clear pale complexion.

"I can't imagine anything ever being wrong with your skin."

Cary leaned back in his chair and rapped on the window with a coin.

"So you don't smoke. You're just a strong character."

"That's right, I'm a strong character."

A waiter came out of the doorway of the café and stood beside their table.

"Ask him for some cigarettes, too."

"I'm afraid they'll be pretty bad. What do you think you'd like to drink?"

"I don't know," Nikki said. "What do you think would be nice for me? Some more Martinis?"

"No. I think an aperitif."

"Why that?"

"Très refrâichissant," Cary said.

"You order for me and remember about the cigarettes."

"Deux amer picons," Cary told the waiter, *"et de cigarettes."*

The waiter shrugged his shoulders and said he only had French cigarettes.

"Can you smoke French cigarettes?"

"I don't know," said Nikki, "I've never tried."

"Bring the best cigarettes you have," Cary told the waiter in French.

"So you don't smoke," Nikki mused.

"Don't give me any credit," Cary begged. "I have nothing to do with it."

"I'm not so sure."

"Listen," said Cary, "there was a Rhodes Scholar from the middle west at my college at Oxford. He was a minister's son and he was reading theology and he had a slight impediment in his speech. I was with him the first time he ever drank whiskey. I can remember how his face lighted up at the taste. He had kind of homely blunt features, and he began to smile. He lost his stammer after a few double Scotches. I never saw him sober again. He was tight for a year."

"What happened to him?"

"He was sent down."

"Because he was tight?"

"No. You never get sent down from Oxford for being tight. He pushed the dean's wheel chair into a bonfire one night. But the point is," Cary said, "the point is that he was a natural drunk. There was no escape for him once he had taken his first drink. He had nothing to do with it. He knew right away that all his happiness was going to come out of a bottle. And unhappiness."

The drinks came and Cary siphoned water into their glasses.

"This is refreshing," Nikki said, as she tried it. "Did you ask the boy for some matches?"

Cary stepped inside and came back with some matches. He lit Nikki's cigarette for her and she made a face.

"Don't say I didn't warn you," Cary said.

"Cary," Nikki said, "why doesn't Shepard Lambert go home?"

"I don't know. Why?"

"Well, it seems a pity just to go on drinking like that. He's such a sweet soul."

"One of the best," Cary agreed.

"Isn't he just sort of wasting himself?"

"Oh, no," Cary assured her, "he's doing the right thing."

Nikki looked at Cary in surprise.

"You mean you don't think it's a little—a little foolish for him to go on the way he is."

"No," said Cary, "I think he's a wise lad."

"Oh, Cary, how could he be wise?"

"I think Shep is wise to understand about himself."

"You mean you think he's hopeless?"

"It would be hopeless for him to go home."

"On account of his people, you mean?"

"On account of everything."

"I see," said Nikki, not quite convinced.

"Look," said Cary, "you may not know it, but Shep is terribly sensitive about that tic. He doesn't want to go home."

"Doesn't anybody know about it at home?"

"No. You see he was all right when he went away."

"But surely——"

"And then someone might be sorry for him. He'd never stand that. You see over here it doesn't matter. No one pays any attention."

"But isn't there some kind of treatment or something?"

"I suppose so. But Shep could never sustain a course of treatment. Side-cars is the best corrective so far as he's concerned. The tic doesn't work when he's tight, so he stays tight."

"It seems a shame," Nikki said. "He does

drink so desperately. How did he get the tic?"

"In the War," Cary said.

Nikki knew she was getting into tender territory. "I know," she said, "but——"

"Well, it's not very romantic."

"Don't tell me if you think you oughtn't."

"Well, as you probably know, a tic is a nervous habit."

"Yes."

"Lice under his bandages."

"Oh," said Nikki.

"He nearly lost his mind. So you must excuse him a little."

"Oh, I adore Shep," Nikki protested passionately. "Did you two fly together?"

"Yes," said Cary, "he was my rear gunner."

"Oh," said Nikki. She thought a minute. She remembered Shep's words: *He was trying to bring his gunner down alive.*

"So *Shep* was the one you saved," she exclaimed.

"I didn't save him much," Cary said briefly. "We crashed."

"Oh dear, oh dear," said Nikki. "I'm so sorry for Shep."

"Don't let him think so. He's had a pretty thin time."

"No, I won't," Nikki said.

Wasn't it strange, Nikki thought, the instinct they had to protect each other's feelings.

"But isn't he ever going home? Not ever?" Nikki asked.

"No," said Cary. "Not ever."

Nikki was ready to weep. "Poor Shepard," she said, "isn't it a shame? Can't anything be done for him?"

"He'd have to be reborn," Cary said.

Cary was right, Nikki thought, Shep would have to be reborn.

"But how is he going to end?" Nikki asked.

"How are you going to end? How am I going to end? How is anyone going to end?"

Nikki wanted so badly to hold Cary in conversation. Everything seemed so perfectly all right when you talked to Cary. It gave you a sense of security just to talk with him; you felt that everything would turn out all right even though the most dreadful things might happen. There was so much grave understanding behind his gray, indwelling eyes.

But you had to keep his attention, else he wandered off to remote, unreachable places in his own mind, or opened up one of those paperbacked books he was always carrying about. Besides you could find out a lot about Cary by asking him about someone else.

Nikki's questions were a little irregular, but they were enough to keep him going.

"What about money?" she asked. "How does Shep manage about money?"

Cary looked surprised. "Can you imagine Shep without money?"

No, Nikki said, come to think of it you couldn't imagine Shepard Lambert without money.

"He has money behind him," Cary said.

"How do you mean, money behind him?"

Cary shrugged his shoulders. "Oh, family money, I suppose. I don't know."

"Is his father rich?"

Cary said, indifferently, that he didn't know. "He has economic advantages."

"What does his father do?"

"Beef, Iron and Wine," Cary said, "or Blind, Sash and Window, or something. I don't know."

"Hay, Grain and Feed?" Nikki queried.

"You've got the general idea."

"Vegetables, Bulbs and Seed?" Nikki inquired. She thought it was a game. "Light, Heat and Power?"

"It's something like that," Cary said. "Shep always has a different one to offer. Anyway I know that they call Monsieur Lambert a valued client at the Equitable Trust Company."

The two sat at the little round iron table

under the green awning and drank their drinks and waited for the drizzle to let up.

"He has a house in Warsaw," Cary added absent-mindedly, "and a flat in Vienna and a boat down on the Mediterranean somewhere."

"What does he do about them?"

"Nothing. Tells his friends to go and occupy them whenever they're in the neighborhood. He's very generous-minded, you know."

"He's sweet," Nikki said, and then she inquired timidly, "Aren't you going home either, Cary?"

Cary shook his head.

"Never?"

"No," said Cary, "not unless I'm deported."

"What about Bill?" Nikki wanted to know.

"What about Bill?"

"Well, what about Bill? Is he a valued client and isn't he ever going home either?"

"Bill is studying music," Cary said soberly.

Nikki laughed outright.

"But does Bill do anything about music?"

"Oh, sure," said Cary cheerfully, "he's been to two concerts, and once he went to Carmen."

That appeared to satisfy Nikki.

"And you're a student, too?"

"That's right," Cary agreed. "I'm a poor student."

"Aren't you a Rhodes Scholar or something?"

"Don't hold it against me."

"Why should I?"

"We're a weird lot," Cary admitted.

"You have to be intelligent or something, don't you?"

"I don't think so."

"Well, you have to be *something*."

"Why?" Cary was interested.

"I don't know," Nikki said. "Weren't you excited when you won it?"

"I'm trying to think," Cary said.

"Don't you ever get excited about anything?"

"Is there anything to get excited about?"

"Don't you ever cry?"

"Cry? Cry? Weep, you mean?"

"Didn't you ever weep?"

Cary looked at Nikki thoughtfully.

"No," he said.

"But not ever? Didn't you ever cry?"

"Yes," he said, "I cried once."

"I would like to know when you cried once," Nikki said.

"It was a long time ago," Cary said.

"When you were a little boy?"

"When I was very little."

"Where were you little?"

"In Minnesota."

Single Lady

"Minnesota!" Nikki exclaimed, "whoever would have thought you came from Minnesota! Nobody comes from Minnesota. What place? Saint Paul or somewhere?"

"No," said Cary, "a little town about forty miles from Saint Paul—Pine City."

"Pine City. That sounds like a place where you throw away old safety razor blades. Is that where you cried? I don't blame you, poor sweet."

Cary eyed Nikki thoughtfully. "How does the vermouth go?"

"It goes fine," Nikki said. "I'm so glad you suggested it. It was a fine idea. Shep says you're full of ideas. You think I'm getting tight again, don't you? Tell me about when you cried in Minnesota when you were little. You must have been marvelous when you were little. I can see you just as quiet and looking at people. What kind of people did you look at in Minnesota? What were you doing in Minnesota anyway? You never belonged in Minnesota. Tell me about when you cried in Minnesota."

Cary told her that he was born in a big white house on a farm.

"On a farm!" Nikki said. "Think of that! On a farm! Who ever heard of such a thing! You were on a farm. But your father wasn't a farmer?"

No, Cary said, his father was a lawyer.

Nikki said that was better. "I have to imagine your father a kind of gentleman farmer," she pointed out. "Now tell me when you cried."

Cary said that he wasn't ashamed of the farm. He was happy on the farm.

"What is there to be happy about on a farm?" Nikki asked.

"Thorn-apple trees," Cary said, "thornapple trees in blossom."

"In blozzom?"

"Did you ever dig up an Indian mound?" Cary asked.

No, Nikki said, she never dug up an Indian mound. What an idea.

Had Nikki ever dug up an Indian mound and found a flint arrow head? Had she ever splashed in rain hollows in a pasture after a summer storm? Had she ever made dandelion chains, or drowned out gophers? Had she ever hunted eggs in the hay mow or found a tiger lily in the woods or uncovered a nest of baby field mice? Had she ever ridden bareback on a plow horse or coasted down a steep hill onto a frozen lake, or thrown stones at a hornets' nest or smelled burning leaves in the fall?

Well, yes, Nikki said, she remembered the smell of burning leaves in the fall.

Had Nikki ever felt hot dust squash up between her toes when she walked down a country road to school? Found a striped carnelian in a rain-washed ditch? Or drunk buttermilk out of a churn? Or heard the moaning of telephone wires in the winter wind? Or explored the old trunks in the attic?

Yes, Nikki said, and found some pictures of her mother in her wedding dress; very serious they were, too.

Had she ever read *Monarch, The Big Bear? Cudjo's Cave? Toby Tyler* or *Ten Weeks With a Circus? The Call of the Wild? Tom Sawyer? Hans Brinker and the Silver Skates? Treasure Island. To Have and To Hold? The Prisoner of Zenda? The Prodigal Judge?*

No, said Nikki, but she had read the Four Little Peppers or something.

Had Nikki ever seen a gypsy caravan? Once, looking out of the little four paned window of the attic, Cary had seen a caravan of covered wagons winding over the hill on the high road to town. To his excitement they had halted along the south pasture fence and one of the gypsy carts turned into the driveway. He had run down stairs and raced through the kitchen and found it standing by the windmill. Through the arched opening at the back of the wagon, a gypsy girl had appeared, a dark, lovely creature with ringleted hair, and dull gold circlets in her ears and an orange shawl about her shoulders. She talked fast and prettily. To Cary's terrible humiliation, his mother had displayed an aloof and disapproving attitude toward the garters, hairpins, soap, combs, pencils, buttons on blue cards, mouth organs, red glass beads, jews harps and flat boxes of lace which she daintily displayed with her quick brown hands. He was grateful when Anna, the hired girl, reached deep into her apron pocket and brought out a black leather, soft-bellied clasp purse and bought a strip of lace edging, blushing furiously. The gypsy eyes caught his just once and the two had stared at each other in startled recognition. He had never seen her before, and never saw her again, but they knew each other.

When he was ten years old, Cary said, his family moved from Minnesota.

"But when did you cry?" Nikki said, "when did you cry in Minnesota?"

"When we left Minnesota."

"The day you left Minnesota?" Nikki repeated. "You cried because you were leaving."

Cary nodded his head.

"On account of all the things you left," she demanded, "the blozzoms and the field mice and gopher holes, and the Indian mounds. . . ?"

"That's right."

151

"Not on account of anybody, but on account of things? Arrow heads and tiger lilies, and old trunks and red glass beads and things?"

"Not on account of the red glass beads," Cary corrected her. "The gypsy girl had the red glass beads."

"But anyway you cried?"

"Anyway I wept."

"When did you cry exactly?"

"I cried in the carriage when we were going over the top of the hill to the train, the last time I ever saw the farm."

"You never saw the farm again?" Nikki said slowly. "Well, you never will see it again."

"That's right."

"I'm so sorry," Nikki said.

The drizzle had let up, but the sky was slate gray and lowering. The cab driver was leaning against his cab smoking a cigarette.

"Do you think we might start now?" Cary said.

"Let's have some more vermouth." Nikki said, "and then I'll be all right."

Cary did not answer. He stepped inside and signalled the boy behind the bar. The boy brought out two vermouths.

"Do you like Paris?" Cary inquired.

"I like Paris," Nikki said, "only the view is

usually obscured by bottles and siphons and piles of saucers and things."

Cary saw that her mood had changed so he paid for the vermouths and the two left the table.

"I'm so excited," Nikki said, as they passed through the gate, "about visiting a cemetery with you. Who all is buried in here?"

"Lots of Frenchmen," Cary said, "except the ones that aren't in the Pantheon. Or Napoleon's tomb," he added.

"There's only one in Napoleon's tomb, isn't there?"

"Who knows?"

"Tell me some of the famous Frenchmen," Nikki demanded.

"Who would you like to hear about?"

"Who have you got?"

"Musicians, painters, poets. . . ."

"Cocoanut," said Nikki.

"No cocoanut," said Cary. "Musicians, poets, painters, philosophers."

"Cocoanut," said Nikki.

"No cocoanut," Cary said.

Nikki was picking her way daintily over the cobbles in her high heels.

"Why don't you walk along the gravel on the side," Cary suggested.

"Take my arm," Nikki said. "If I turn my ankle, will you carry me out?"

"A pleasure," Cary said. "There is somebody you know."

"Who?"

"Chopin."

"Oh yes," said Nikki, looking at the modest headstone. "I've practised him. Who else did you say was in here?"

"Well, let me see now," Cary said. "There's Balzac and Fabre and Delacroix and Alfred de Musset. . . ."

"De Musset," Nikki repeated, "who's that?"

"De Musset was George Sand's lover." Cary said.

"My, my," Nikki said mildly, "and so they buried him here."

"That's right."

"Is this where they bury George Sand's lovers?"

"He was a poet besides," Cary said.

"Who else?" Nikki queried.

"Well, there's Michelet and Ingres and La-Fontaine and Aubert and Héloïse and Abélard . . . ."

"Tell me about Abélise and Éloard," Nikki said.

"Abélise . . ." Cary stopped and looked sadly at Nikki. "Nikki," he said, "you ought to be ashamed of yourself."

"I really didn't do it on purpose," Nikki said. "It was on account of the vermouth."

"Do you really want to know about them?"

"Simply perishing."

"Well, they're buried here together—side by side—in the same sepulchre."

"I think that's nice," Nikki said. "Let's sit down."

They sat down on a low stone bench without a back at the side of the walk.

"Why are they buried together?" Nikki said.

"It's a long story," Cary said.

"Oh, tell me about it," Nikki pleaded. "I love to hear you talk, Cary. You never talk when you're with people. You never say a word. And you know so much about everything."

"Don't I just," Cary said.

"Tell me things, Cary, tell me things."

"Do you really want to know about Abélard and Héloïse?"

"Yes, I do. I want to know all about them. Is it all right to smoke in here?"

"I don't see why not," Cary said, absently reaching for a match. "Abélard was a scholastic philosopher."

Nikki evinced a mild astonishment.

"He used to live on the Isle Saint Louis, and he went to the great Cathedral School at Notre Dame."

"My, my, Notre Dame."

"He had a very cogent mind," Cary said. "Before he was twenty he had overcome all his teachers in dialectic. He upset the theory of Realism."

"Whatever that is," Nikki said.

"Whatever that is," Cary agreed. "Anyway, he set up a school of his own and thousands of students came from all parts of the world to hear him talk. He was of a distinguished figure and manner."

"Just like you," Nikki observed. "You say if I'm getting too fresh."

"He came to be the outstanding philosopher in the world."

"This was a long time ago, wasn't it?"

"Before you were born, even."

"I thought so."

"Now," said Cary, "to quote somebody or other, 'Within the precincts of Notre Dame, under the care of her uncle, there lived a young girl named Héloïse, of noble extraction.'"

"'Of noble extraction,'" Nikki repeated. "That sounds nice—'of noble extraction.'"

"Abélard gained a footing in the household as tutor to the maiden, and he employed his unlimited opportunities over her for the purpose of seduction. Not, however," Cary continued, "unmixed with real love. He carried her off to Brittany, where Héloïse gave birth to a son."

"Tell me more," Nikki said.

"Then Abélard proposed to Héloïse."

"That was nice of him," Nikki observed. "He couldn't have thought of that before, could he?"

"Héloïse refused him."

"Good for Héloïse."

"She didn't want to injure his prospects for advancement in the Church."

A gendarme in a blue cape sauntered by looking at them out of the corner of his eye.

"We aren't doing anything wrong, are we?" Nikki said apprehensively.

"I don't know about you," Cary said.

"Héloïse refused him?"

"Héloïse rejected his proposal but finally agreed to a secret marriage. When the news got out, she denied it. Her uncle was furious. Life became insupportable for her so she took refuge in a convent."

"You talk like a Britannica. Poor Héloïse."

"Her uncle blamed Abélard for the whole thing and conceived a terrible revenge."

"I'm afraid for Abélard. What was his first name?"

"Peter. Peter Abélard."

"Peter Abélard, I am afraid for you," Nikki said.

"Héloïse's uncle and some others broke into Abélard's apartment at night. . . ."

"Yes?" said Nikki.

"Do you want to hear the rest?"

"Well, we've gone this far."

"Héloïse's uncle and some others broke into Abélard's apartment one night and perpetrated on him the most brutal mutilation."

"Oh, dear. Poor, poor Abélard."

"There was left for him only the life of a monk."

"How can people do such things to each other," Nikki wondered. There she began to think about the war and about Shep's tic and Cary's burned hands.

"People do frightful things to each other all the time," Cary said.

"What happened to poor Héloïse?" Nikki said.

"She took the veil," Cary said. "She took the veil and she wasn't yet twenty years old."

Nikki was lost in thinking about young Héloïse taking the veil.

"This is a very sad story," she said.

"Afterwards Héloïse wrote a letter to Abélard—the most beautiful love letter there is going."

"Is she buried here, did you say?"

Cary nodded, "Both of them."

"Far? I mean is it far from where we are now?"

"No," said Cary, "just around to the right."

"Could you find it, do you think?"

"I think so. Do you want to see it?"

"Oh yes," said Nikki eagerly, "Oh yes, I do. Let's go and see it."

"All right," Cary said. They got up from the stone bench.

"There's a kind of a pretty legend about the tomb of Héloïse and Abélard," Cary said, as they walked along. "I'm sure I haven't got it straight. I don't know quite where I heard it."

Nikki said she would like to hear it.

"The story is that little heart-shaped stones are supposed to grow around the tomb."

"That's kind of nice, I think."

"And lovers come and find heart-shaped stones and exchange them with each other. And so long as you keep the heart-shaped stone from the grave of Héloïse and Abélard, no harm can come to your love."

"Why, I think that's beautiful," Nikki said.

"Isn't that a nice legend?" Cary said. "I'm sure I haven't got it right."

They turned into a little gravel path between tall memorial stones.

"There it is," Cary said.

"Straight ahead?" Nikki raised her lorgnette. "Why it's perfectly beautiful," she exclaimed.

"It's quite a famous one," Cary said.

159

Single Lady

"Matter of fact, it's probably the most famous one here."

Nikki was gazing at the tomb with the two stone figures on top lying side by side under the vaulted arch supported by fluted pillars. They came closer.

"Why, Cary, they seem so serene."

"There is a feeling of composure about it," Cary agreed.

Nikki stood and looked at the sepulcher of Abélard and Héloïse a long time. The late afternoon sun was beginning to fade and the drizzle began again. Nikki shivered slightly.

"I feel so lonely," she said.

Cary looked at her and he saw that her eyes, her nearsighted eyes with the enormous black pupils, were filled with tears.

"Poor Héloïse," she said. "Poor Héloïse."

They moved closer to the tomb, standing at the iron railing. Nikki peered through the palings. "There's an inscription, isn't there?"

"Yes," said Cary, "but you can't read it."

"Why not?"

"It's in Latin.

"Oh, but you can read it for me, Cary. You went to Oxford. You can read Latin. You read it for me. I want to know what is written on the tomb of Héloïse and Abélard."

Cary studied the design cut in the stone on the side of the sepulcher.

160

"Are you trying me out, or do you really want to know?" he said. Cary was a little suspicious of Nikki.

"Please translate it for me."

"It's kind of old Latin," Cary said, "I won't get it quite right, but I can give you the sense of it. Let me read it over first."

Nikki watched him in an awed way as he examined the lettering.

"Well, here goes for a sight reading," said Cary. "Here under the same stone, let's see, here under the same stone repose—repose— Here under the same stone repose Peter Abélard and Héloïse—alike in dispositions and in love; they were once united in the same pursuits, the same fatal marriage—the same fatal marriage and the same repentance; and now we hope they are joined in eternal happiness."

"How perfectly beautiful," Nikki said.

"Peter Abélard died the 21st of April, 1142; Héloïse the 17th of May, 1163."

Nikki was very moved.

"She lived twenty-one years after he died, didn't she? Isn't that tragic. That *is* tragic, isn't it? You don't think I'm sentimental do you, Cary?"

"Oh no," Cary assured her.

Nikki bent down and explored the glistening bed of stones about the tomb.

"Do you think we might find a heart-shaped

stone, Cary? Wouldn't it be lovely if we could. You look too, Cary. You help me find a heart-shaped stone."

Cary went round to the other side of the tomb. It was fast growing dark.

"We'll have to leave soon," he said, "they close up the place."

"Just as soon as we find our stones," Nikki said.

Cary came back with a handful of little white wet pebbles. "I found several; you pick the one you like best."

"So did I," Nikki said, "I found quite a few."

Cary held out his hand. Nikki peered into the palm and chose one. "Now you take one from me," she said, "isn't that right? Isn't that the way it goes?"

Nikki had found a tiny flat white stone fashioned almost in the perfect shape of a heart. Cary took it in his hand.

"Isn't that a splendid one?" Nikki said. "I found the very nicest one for you."

Cary gravely took out his wallet and slipped the stone into one of the small recesses. Nikki put hers into her bag.

"Cary, you're so sweet," Nikki said, "you're so sweet to tell me about Héloïse and Abélard and the legend. You're so sweet to let me come with you today. I've spoiled all your plans, haven't I? You were coming to see something else, weren't you?"

"It doesn't matter."

"It's too late now, isn't it? What did you want to see, darling?"

"Oh," said Cary absently, "someone who used to have my rooms at Oxford."

"And he's buried here? Was he very famous? What was he?"

"A writer," Cary said.

"What did he write?"

"He wrote some very charming children's stories. 'The Birthday of the Infanta.' 'The Star Child.'"

"Children's stories? What was his name, Cary?"

"His name was Sebastian Melmoth."

"And now it's too late," Nikki said. "Oh, I'm sorry. I'm so sorry."

Nikki began to weep softly.

"Don't pay any attention to me, Cary. I'm so ashamed. But I can't help it. You make me cry. Don't look so troubled, Cary. I'm all right. I want to cry for a minute. You can excuse me, can't you? You look so clean, Cary. You're the cleanest looking person. Your teeth are so white. I can't help crying. You're so civilized. I want to do something for you, Cary. I want to do something for you," she said wildly. "I want to help you."

Single Lady

She took his hand in her own. "Let me wash your ring, Cary; let me wash your ring."

Cary looked down at his ring. It was an emerald jade in a Cartier setting of a curious, proud design.

"It needs washing," Nikki said. "Give it to me and I'll wash it when I get home. I'll scrub it with a nail-brush."

Cary took off his ring and gave it to her. She slipped it over her thumb.

It was now quite dark in the cemetery and they left. The driver was waiting for them at the little gate by the Avenue de Repos.

CHAPTER VI

THE first thing that Shepard Lambert said when he found out that Nikki had left Paris was: "What's the use of anything?" Rooms 88 and 89 were as desolate and lifeless as a derelict ship.

Maria, Nikki's maid, had packed up everything neatly and followed her off, wherever she had gone, leaving Eighty-Eight Carlton, the noble pup, and the two turtles in the custody of a veterinary in the Place Perrier. It was all very casual, but poor Bill Talbot was devastated and went about with the sad, bewildered eyes of a lost camel.

Shep surmised that Cary Lockwood could throw some light on the secret of Nikki's disappearance, but Cary, too, had left Paris.

Shep and Bill Talbot and Francis resolutely refused to desert the Carlton and haunted the place in the hope that Nikki would reappear as casually as she had left and life would begin all over again.

Shep had a dim theory that Nikki and Cary might be together somewhere. In May, nearly a month later, a cable arrived at the Carlton

Single Lady

for Cary. It was from Dublin, Ireland. Shep opened it and read the message:

When you say your prayers please include bit from Cornish Litany quote from ghosties and ghoulies and things that go bump in the night dear Lord protect Nikki.

The cable was unsigned, and Shep knew then that Cary and Nikki were not together and did not know where the other was.

It was early in June when he came upon Nikki again. She was sitting at a side table in the Steam Room at the Ritz with a strange young man when Shepard came in. He went directly over.

"Hi, Nikki!"

"H'lo, *Shep!* How are you?"

"Charming," said Shep, "charming. I can truthfully say I've never been more magnetic in my life."

"How nice for you," Nikki said.

Shep saw at once that Nikki was changed. There were faint purple shadows under her eyes, and her skin was lustrous with hospital pallor. Her great black eyes were startlingly blind and luminous. Shep knew that a little suffering had passed that way. Nevertheless, she was the most interesting face and figure in the bar; she was bravely dressed in a copper

silk jersey frock and short white buckskin
gloves and a black, close-fitting hat.

"Where you been, baby?" Shep demanded.
"We been a-lookin' all over the shop for you."

"I been sick," Nikki announced, "and this is
Roger something, or something Roger, I forget which."

"Hello," said Shep, "my name is Lambert."

"How d'you do," said the other in a Cambridge accent, "my name is Stewart."

"Oh that's right," Nikki said. "This is the
Irish Earl."

The Irish Earl was quite young and thin
and handsome in an intelligent high-bred way.
He had a long straight nose and a fine forehead and a slight brown mustache. His gray
eyes had the far-away look of one who has been
drinking for a long time. His skin had the
telltale pale brick flush.

Shep scrutinized Stewart with interest. "Is
he really of the beerage?" he asked Nikki.

"Yep," said Nikki, "Stewart can actually
be found in Burp's Beerage, can't you, sweet?"

"No end of estates and retainers," agreed
the Irish Earl. When he spoke he gestured
jerkily. He was brittle as glass, ready to fly
into wild screaming pieces.

"He comes from a famous hunting country," Nikki explained. "He took me to the
Dublin Horse Show. He always carries a

hunting seat. Even on boats and things. Where is your hunting seat, darling? Didn't you bring your hunting seat? Aren't you afraid you'll catch cold without your hunting seat?"

"What will you have to drink?" the Irish Earl invited Shep.

"Thanks. A Martini."

"He followed me all the way from England," Nikki went on. "Didn't you darling?"

"Been follerin' her around all over the shop," Stewart said. "It's no use, apparently."

"Is that where you've been? England?" Shep asked. "Tell me, how did you ever get there?"

"Flew."

"What was the idea?"

"Regatta. Henly Regatta. We all flew over."

"What on earth did you do that for?"

"I don't know," Nikki said vaguely, "it seemed like a good idea at the time."

"Is that where you met his Grace?"

"On the Trinity Barge. He took me to a dinner at Cambridge."

"How was her behavior?" Shep asked Stewart.

"Splendid. She danced a hula in her barefeet. I helped skin off her stockings."

"It was better than the Dean's," Nikki defended her behavior. "I saw him sitting in the middle of the Quad under an umbrella, calling on God to witness that he was a mushroom."

"Good man," the Earl observed. And then as an afterthought, "but he'll never be a bishop."

The waiter came in with a loaded tray of cocktails. The Earl waved him to the table. "Bring six more," he said after the waiter had cleared off their glasses and left one for Shep. "It's best to order in series," he explained.

"Where's Bill," Nikki asked.

"He's knockin' about."

"Where's that licentious old man?"

"Doctor Krausmeyer? Oh, we lost the good doctor. He up and jined the French Cavalry."

"Honestly? What ever for?"

"Don't know. Probably seemed like a good idea."

"How about Francis?"

"He's still here."

"I missed you all."

"Thanks," said Shep. "We ain't been the same since you disappeared. Well," raising his glass to the Earl, "Slog Tabs."

Stewart's eyebrows went up in pleasant surprise. "You were up at Oxford?"

Shep nodded.

"What was your college?"

"Cardinal."

"Sporting chaps, Cardinal."

"Hearty," Shep agreed.

"I been sick," Nikki volunteered again.

"Poor darlin'," Shep said. "You really been sick?"

"Yes, I really been sick. In England. I thought it surely was ptomaine or something, but maybe I just forgot to stir out the bubbles."

"You should always have a swizzle stick handy about you," Shep reproved her. "A girl that drinks all that champagne. Doesn't she drink the bubbly, though?" Shep inquired of Stewart.

"Don't she just," Stewart agreed. "Downed all our chaps."

"I was sick as sick," Nikki said, "and I got in trouble, too. People got violent and I got hurt and I ran away. I dashed for home, but didn't quite make it. They had an ambulance out at the landing field for me. His Reverence arranged that."

"Jolly nice ride," agreed his grace.

"Did you ride in the ambulance, too?" Shep queried.

"Held my hand all the way," Nikki affirmed. "He *was* a lamb. It was the highliest decoratedest ambulance. Lots of floral marquetry and fancy woodwork and an elegant lace-covered pink satin quilt over the stretcher."

"Damned wagon had everything but springs," said the Earl.

"Did you go to a hospital?" Shep asked.

"Did I not! The American Hospital of Paris. Neuilly. I was a very special case. The first patient in months that didn't have the D.T.'s."

"Good girl!" Shep said, admiringly.

"I didn't have the screaming mimis or anything, so the coquettish French doctors called it appendicitis. I told them my appendix was gone. I let them see my scar, and they said it wasn't an appendix scar and how did I know it hadn't been overlooked in the operation, anyway. Then they went off leaving me feeling like Alice in Wonderland and hell."

Shep ordered more Martinis.

"I told the night nurse if she saw any frogs creeping upon me with a knife and a can of ether to bash 'em with a bed-pan.

"At a slight charge," Nikki continued, "at a slight extra charge, his Earlship got the best man in France for me. He said, acute colitis—at a slight extra charge."

"Were you in the hospital a long time?" Shep asked.

"Days and days and days. They said I

must never drink again," Nikki said, looking into her empty cocktail glass.

"Why didn't you let us know?"

Nikki said she had written a note to Cary.

"I don't think he got it," Shep said.

"Why not?"

"He went away. Whatever happened between you two, anyhow?"

"It was my fault," Nikki said.

"I'm sure it was," Shep agreed. "But what happened?"

"I said the wrong thing, I guess."

"You're marvelous that way," Shep said. "Put end to end to end—the wrong things you say would require seven hours to pass a given point."

"I didn't mean to. Tell me if you think it was very bad."

"All right," Shep agreed, "you present the facts of the matter and I'll hand down an expert opinion. The Earl here will sit on the bench with me. What say, Stewart?"

"Give me a wig," said the Earl, "and a drink."

"You remember the day you all went to the Cluny. And we went to Père Lachaise?"

"Yep," Shep said.

"It was raining and so we stopped at a place and had some drinks."

"Who is we?" the Earl inquired judicially.

"Cary Lockwood," Shep told him. "Cardinal man. Up before the war."

"The American runner chap?"

"Oh, do you know him?" Nikki said eagerly. "Where?"

"Saw him do the hurdles once. Stamford Bridge, Oxford-Cambridge sports."

"Did he win?" said Nikki eagerly.

"Win, my word! The fellow fairly flew over the things. None of our chaps near him. Is he about?"

"That's the point," said Nikki. "Leave me tell you. We had some drinks and it didn't stop raining, so we had some more."

"Good ol' Nik."

"When it stopped raining we went into the cemetery."

"My word," said the Earl. "Whatever for?"

"I can't remember," said Nikki, "only I remember that Cary started talking about Abélise and Héloard."

"Who?" inquired the Earl.

"Pyramus and Frisbe," Shep suggested.

"I get the idea," said the Earl.

"So then he told me the whole thing about them. And I wanted to see their tomb. You know the tomb of Abélise and Héloard. They're there together."

Neither of the other two looked particularly startled at the news.

"Well, maybe you're not interested," Nikki said.

"We're all ears, eyes, nose and throat," Shep assured her.

"So Cary took me to the tomb. It was a beautiful place. And Cary read the inscription for me. We were there a long time. Cary never did get to see what he went to see. They close the place up or something. So on the way out I said, anyway we'd found a name for my turtles."

"And then . . ." queried the Earl.

"He pulled down the iron curtain."

"Can't say as I blame the poor man," said the Earl promptly. "He didn't know you were looking for a name for your turtles? Has he a sense of humor, the runner chap?"

"Oh, sure," Shep explained, "but Nikki hasn't got a sense of moments."

"He didn't want to take her either," Shep remembered. "She just tagged along."

"I just tagged along," Nikki admitted. "Shepard," she said suddenly, "if I married an earl, what would I be?"

"You mean what kind of an oil-can, or what?"

"Oh, I say," objected the Earl.

"No, I mean what is an earl's wife?"

"A countess."

"Is that right?" she turned to the Earl.

"Quite."

"You'd be one under a marquise and one over a viscountess."

"Sounds like a good spot," Nikki ruminated. "What about a duchess?"

"She'd rank you."

"The servants would call you 'your Ladyship' and you'd have a coronet, a coronet with eight pearls and eight leaves."

"What kind of leaves?" Nikki wanted to know.

"Strawberry."

"I'll take vanilla," Nikki said promptly.

"No vanilla. Strawberry."

"Vadilla," Nikki repeated stubbornly.

"You see," Shep said to Stewart, "the girl is incoddigable."

"Where would I have the coronet?" Nikki wanted to know.

"Oh, on your note paper," Shep said airily, "and on your motor car and on your silver and on your turtles and bath towels and wash cloths and on your garter belt——"

"Hey there——" Nikki said.

"Beg pardon, milady," Shep subsided.

"I say but you two do rag each other," said Stewart.

175

"Every once in a while," Nikki said, "Shepard gets too fresh."

"That's right," Shep admitted, "I get fresh with Nikki."

"Shep," Nikki said, "what have you been doing anyway?"

"Research work."

"Are you interested in research?" inquired Stewart in mild surprise.

Shep said he was endeavoring to determine the effect of stimulants, in increasing doses, upon the human system. He said, he was conducting experiments along that line. "Just a martyr to science," he concluded. "Ole Martyr Lambert."

"Shep," said Nikki suddenly, "where is Cary?"

"Listen to that girl," Shep said, "whenever she mentions Cary her voice drops two registers."

"Don't be absurd," Nikki said, but she blushed a little.

"Ain't you seen him at all, darlin'?"

"No. I thought he was going back to Oxford. Wasn't he supposed to go back for Michaelmas or something?"

"Trinity," Shep corrected her. "How did you know he didn't?"

"Oh, I found out," Nikki said a little ashamedly.

"Did you go to Oxford," Shep accused her.

"Where did Cary go?" Nikki pleaded.

"He went off."

"I know—but where to?"

Shep began to tease her.

"Why?" he asked.

"Oh, Shep, don't be an idiot."

"All right," Shep said. "He went to Germany."

"Whatever for?"

"He went to Germany to find a submarine captain."

"There should be a lot of them lying around loose," said Stewart.

Nikki, suspecting a trick, refused to be drawn in any further.

"If you think Cary Lockwood isn't a big operator leave me tell you what he did."

"Who's holding you back," Nikki inquired.

"Now listen," Shep said, suddenly becoming enthusiastic, "now listen. Do you remember the day Wiffy Crouch came into the Claridge Bar?" he asked Nikki.

Nikki said she did.

"Do you remember him telling us all that nonsense about treasure on the bottom of the sea, sunk during the war?"

Nikki said she thought so.

"And about one ship in particular—the

Belleville? The one with the diamonds? From South Africa? Well, leave me tell you."

Here followed Shep's account of Cary Lockwood's movements since the fatal afternoon in the graveyard with Nikki.

The way that Cary had got into the thing was like this. If Nikki remembered, Cary had listened seriously to Wiffy that day and afterwards left the bar with him. They had gone to the *Tribune* office together and Cary had looked up the clippings.

Further, Cary had combed the files of the French journals and weeklies. Pieced together, here were the facts:

The name of the ship was the *Belleville*. She was a Belgian packet boat, a mixed steamer running between the Belgian Congo and the capital. One day early in September, she left the Colony with two hundred passengers in her cabin and in her hold rubber, ivory and palm nuts. Too, she carried the largest single consignment of rough-cut diamonds ever sent out of South Africa. They were blue brilliants, of perfect transparency and of the very finest water. They had been insured for the sum of thirty million francs.

"What's a palm nut?" Nikki inquired innocently.

"Cocoanut," Shep said.

"I'll take vanilla."

"But look," said Stewart, "I should've thought they wouldn't send all those diamonds out by steamer at that time. Weren't there a lot of submarines about?"

"No end," Shep agreed. "That's the silly part. They just did. That's all there is to it. They just did."

"Well, I shouldn't have thought any insurance company would take the risk."

"One did all the same. Or two or three or something. You see I don't know a hell of a lot about this, only what Cary told me."

"Must have been a stiff premium."

"Thirty million francs or so. Distributed among several companies."

"How much is thirty million francs?" Nikki wanted to know.

"How much is it?" Shep turned the question off on the Earl.

"About a million sterling, I sh'd think."

"How much is that?" Nikki inquired again.

"About five million dollars," Shep said.

"Well, go on," Nikki said. "Tell us about the ship and the beautiful blue brilliants of the first water and what happened."

"Well, leave me tell you. You keep interrupting."

Nikki said she never heard of such a thing.

The diamonds, Shep said were deposited in the purser's safe in the ship's strong room.

Single Lady

Off the coast of Portugal the ship was torpedoed.

"She was torpedoed and sunk," Shep said, "and there were no survivors. At least no survivors were picked up."

"I'm sure I didn't pick up any," Nikki said. "But what about the diamonds?"

"Somebody's got to pay more attention to the ordering around here," Shep complained. "It seems hours since I had a drink. Why I'm practically on the wagon. Think of that, Nikki," he declared, "I've been on the wagon for ten minutes!"

Stewart waved to the waiter.

"What about the diamonds?"

"Well, of course," Shep said, "the ship and the passengers and the rubber and the ivory and palm nuts and the whole thing went to the bottom of the sea."

Some more drinks came and they addressed themselves to their drinking for the moment.

"Well, now," said Shep, "all this didn't mean a thing to Wiffy except a piece for his paper, d'you see. But it was different with Cary. He decided to go after the diamonds."

"Cary did!" Nikki exclaimed.

"Oh, sure," Shep said, "Cary is a high-powered egg—with Thousand Island dressing. You don't know how high powered he is. He's a kind of Zaharoff or Lawrence or something."

"I think that's cute," Nikki agreed.

"But how could he ever expect—" began the Earl.

"Leave me tell you how he went about it," Shep said.

Cary had reasoned that there was perhaps one man who knew where the *Belleville* lay, and that was the man who had sunk her, the commander of the German submarine. So he had gone into Germany.

"What did he do? Just go around asking people, I s'pose," Nikki said.

"Oh, sure," Shep said. "he just traveled around Berlin and Strasbourg and Weisbaden and Leipzig and Dresden."

"Not to mention Munchen," Nikki said.

"No, no," Shep said, "I wouldn't mention Munchen. No," he protested, "he went to the German admiralty and got a line on him. The old duck was living in some little village in West Germany and had rheumatism."

"And turned out to be his father, *I* know," said Nikki.

Shep said he didn't know how Cary had ever managed to find the man or wangle the information from him.

"There was a revolution going on in Germany when the subs came home," he explained, "so the officers had nobody to report to. They just kept their records and things and settled down anywhere. Why, hell! Cary actually copied the page out of the log book that described the sinking of the ship. And besides that, the old man sat down and plotted out the position of the wreck on a chart. Cary looked up the soundings and found out that she lay in only about a hundred feet of water off Cape St. Vincent or somewhere."

"The man's a wizard," Nikki said. "And I don't believe a word of it."

"*Now,* leave me tell you what he did," Shep said. "He went to the insurance company that insured the diamonds and told them he knew where the wreck of the *Belleville* was and that she could be salvaged."

Nikki was visioning Cary during the account: at the little cottage in Germany; presenting himself, in his quiet assured manner before the directors of the insurance company.

"Why the insurance company?" Stewart asked.

Shep said he thought that Cary had figured that the insurance company, having paid the loss on the diamonds, would be the party most interested. They proved to be. Cary was the only person alive at this time in full possession of the facts concerning the *Belleville*. The submarine captain, sequestered in his little village did not know that he had sunk a ship full of diamonds. No one else knew where

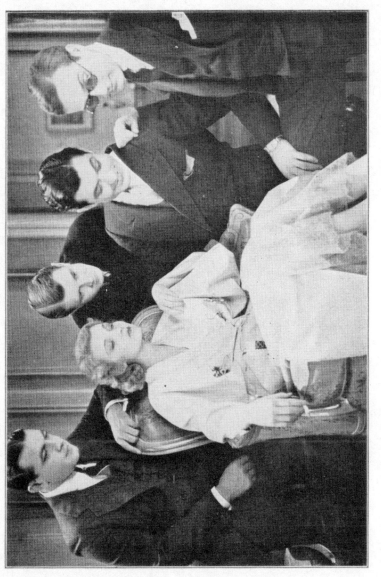

A *First National and Vitaphone Production.* *The Last Flight—Movie of Single Lady.*
NIKKI REVIVES AN OLD TURKISH CUSTOM BY HAVING HER TOENAILS PAINTED.

the wreck lay, except Cary. Cary refused to sell his information. He had prepared a plan for the recovery of the treasure. His plan was, in brief, to organize and equip a modern deep-sea diving expedition for the purpose.

He had proposed, first, to locate the wreck of the vessel by dragging the sea floor at the point indicated by the U-boat Commander. Once the hulk was located and marked with a buoy it was a simple matter to conduct diving operations from a salvage steamer anchored above.

"Anyways," Shep said, "they fell for it. They agreed to finance the expedition and Cary was to get a share of the treasure."

"Did they find the ship all right?" Nikki inquired.

As to the details of the diamond fishing excursion, Shep was a little dim. They hung a cable between the prows of two ocean-going tugs and scraped the sea floor and hooked the wreck all right. Then they sent some divers down to dynamite the strong room. They raised the safe to the deck of the ship with powerful electro-magnets.

"Is that where Cary's been all the time," Nikki demanded. "Was Cary there?"

"Oh, sure, Cary was right on deck."

Shep lighted a cigarette and then began to laugh. "I don't know why I think this is

funny," he said, "but I can't help it. They
made a big ceremony out of opening the ol'
safe after they got her up on deck. People
from the company and divers and sailors and
Cary and the whole outfit. They all stood
around while a machinist's mate cut 'er open
with a blow torch.

"The safe was empty," Shep said, and burst
into a wild and immoderate fit of laughter.

"The safe was *empty?*" Stewart asked.

"The safe was *empty?*" Nikki repeated.

"Sure, empty as a peanut shell," Shep
roared. "Empty as hell. A couple of Belgian
francs, maybe. Wasn't that a hell of a note?"
and Shep kept on laughing like a crazy idiot.

"Wasn't there anything in it at all?" Nikki
said.

Shep kept laughing and shaking his head.
"Not a damn thing. Not even a whisper of a
diamond."

Tears stood out in Nikki's eyes. "Poor
Cary," she said, "was he dreadfully disappointed?"

"Cary said there was only one answer.
Somebody took the diamonds out of the safe
before the ship sank. He says whoever took
the diamonds perished at sea in an open life-
boat or else escaped to the mainland."

"Poor Cary," Nikki said. "Where is he
now?"

"Here."

"Here in Paris?"

"Yep."

Nikki was incredulous. "Well," she said, "well,—well, how about . . . . ?"

"I don't think you can find him tonight," Shep said, "he went off some place."

"How about tomorrow?"

"It would have to be kind of early. He's leaving at ten."

"Why? Where for?"

"Sud Express. Lisbon."

"Lisbon? Spain?"

"No, my precious lamb. Portugal. Lisbon is in Portugal."

"Well, whoever went to Portugal?"

"Nobody that I ever heard of."

"Well, what does Cary want to go there for?"

"He's going to look up the diamonds."

"My lord," said Nikki, "he's going to a lot of trouble."

"Well," said Shep, "there's a lot in it."

"I suppose so. But why——"

"I think it's important to Cary."

"Why," said Nikki quickly, "does he need. . . ."

"It's stiff going up at Oxford," Shep said, "for a lad with a scholarship."

"Well, couldn't you ——"

185

"Me? Cary wouldn't take a sixpence from me. He's proud as Lucifer."

A profound depression settled upon Nikki. "How long will he be gone?" she asked Shep.

"God knows."

Nikki relapsed into thoughtfulness.

"Shep," she said.

"Yes, darlin'."

"Shep, have you ever been to Portugal?"

"No, darlin'."

"Have you, Stewart?"

The Earl said he'd never been.

"Well," said Nikki brightly, "how about going?"

Gloomily the Earl said he couldn't, and Shep, unaccountably, said he was against it himself.

"Let's go to Portugal," Nikki said again.

"No," said Shep firmly.

"Oh, Shep, come on and go to Portugal."

"No," said Shep, but he added thoughtfully, "but I'll put you up a nice lunch."

"Come to Portugal."

"I'll put in a hard-boiled egg and a bottle of olives," Shep said, "and some potato salad and a pimento cheese sandwich, and a napple and a banana—a nice big yellow banana—a little too ripe maybe."

Nikki turned to Stewart and asked him why he couldn't go.

"Got to go off," he announced.

"Where?"

"Ameddica."

"Whatever for?"

"Going to Bill Brown's."

"What's Bill Brown's?"

"A health camp sort of thing."

"Great lord, what do they do there?"

"They get you up at six and push you in steam cabinets and under cold showers and run you around the country and pummel you about."

"What's the point in that?"

"Make you fit."

Shep was looking at Stewart with flickering interest. The idea seemed to seize him for a moment. A health camp—stiff routine—daily workouts—cold baths—hikes in the hills.

Ah, but no, not for Shep. He had a wild fear of being trapped. Trapped where he couldn't take a drink at the very moment when he wanted one. With his morbid hatred of officials, of discipline, of order, he couldn't endure it. It would be like putting himself in a strait-jacket. Nevertheless, he eyed the Earl a little admiringly.

"You really going to Bill Brown's?"

Stewart nodded.

"Ever been before?"

"Once."

"How long?"

"Seven months."

Shep couldn't believe it. If it took seven months to bring Stewart around. . . . Shep measured himself against Stewart. Stewart wasn't a hell of a long ways from the supreme tremors, you could see that . . . those jerky gestures. It was kind of marvelous, though, how a chap like that could put himself in some one else's hands. Shep couldn't do that. The Earl must have only just decided about the Bill Brown thing after hearing about Cary. He would have gone on and married Nikki if she'd marry him.

"Come along," Stewart invited Shep, "we'll do it together."

"No, thanks," Shep said.

"Shep," Nikki said, "let's go to Portugal."

"Not your Uncle Shepard," Shep said.

"Why not?"

"How do I know how the drinking is down there?"

"Oh, the drinking is first rate," Stewart said.

"How so?"

"Great wine country. Porto flips sort of thing."

"That's where it comes from," Nikki said.

Shep was not convinced. He had a superstitious fear about leaving Paris. He was afraid to entrust himself to strange people, strange streets, strange forces. He couldn't let himself be caught too far away from a bottle.

The Ritz bar was nearly empty. They had talked a long time. Nikki was restless. Shep knew she was thinking about Cary going away in the morning.

When the check came the Earl took it and looked helplessly at the figure. Shep looked up and saw Nikki giving him some kind of office.

"Here give me the check, old chap," Shep said.

"What's the figger?"

Shep covered the check with a five hundred franc note and put it in the waiter's tray.

"Oh, look here . . . !" But Shep waved Stewart down. "I have to have some change anyway."

Stewart, it appeared, was stopping at the Ritz. Nikki insisted on leaving him there. They left him at the lift in the lobby to make his way to his room under his own power.

Shep and Nikki took a cab outside in the Rue Cambon.

"He's so sweet," Nikki said, "he's so sweet and he's going blind."

"Blind?"

189

"He couldn't read the check even. You have almost to lead him around."

"That's a shame," Shep said. "I noticed something about his eyes. What's the matter with them?"

"Poison liquor. In New York. It's a terribly sad story."

"Most of them are."

A year ago, when Stewart was in New York, Nikki said, he was going home from a party and he asked the cab driver to take him to a speakeasy. The driver took him to a dreadful hole on Lexington Avenue, near Grand Central.

Stewart drank a double Scotch and went to his apartment on Fifty-ninth Street. In the morning, he said he had double vision and was frightfully ill, up-chucking all over the place. His phone was out of order, so he put on a robe and crept out into the hallway. They found him unconscious by the lift.

He was taken to Roosevelt Hospital, where he nearly died. "They sent for the mater," Stewart explained. "I was solid blind."

He pulled through all right except for his eyes. He said he had to grope about now. Nikki said that Stewart really made a screaming tale out of his blindness and had people rolling on the floor, what with the stomach pump and all.

"But his eyes are bad again," Nikki said.

"Poor chap," Shep said, "he seems such a good sort."

"He's a peach," Nikki declared vehemently. "He's the sweetest soul that ever lived. I feel so sorry for him I could cry."

"Go ahead," said Shep. "Go on and cry."

So Nikki began to cry softly.

"That's a terrible way to treat anybody in New York," Nikki wept. "Make them blind. Make a fine boy like that blind."

"Terrible."

"He comes to America for the first time and we make him blind."

"Pretty bad all right."

"When an American boy goes to England, they don't make him blind."

"No, the English don't make people blind."

"It's terrible to think of what happened to Stewart in New York."

"Fantastic," Shep agreed and drummed on the cab floor with his crook stick.

"I wish I could do something for him," Nikki said.

"You can."

"What? What can I do for him?"

"Don't marry him."

"Why not?"

"You two would kill each other off."

"All right," Nikki said. "You come to Portugal and I won't marry Stewart."

"Anything to please a lady," Shep said.

BOOK II

BOOK II

CHAPTER VII

THE Sud Express (Train de Luxe) quotidian, leaves the Quai d'Orsay, Paris, for Lisbon, Portugal, at ten-forty in the morning.

On the fifth floor of the Carlton Hotel, an hour before train time, Shepard Lambert was organizing his quiristers for the Portuguese expedition. He was, after several brief excursions, downstairs to the bar, marvelously alert and efficient.

Since Nikki was going, it had taken no persuasion to induce Bill Talbot to come along. The Washout, who seemed to soak up vitality from Bill, couldn't be left behind. The presence of The Washout would make Bill uncomfortable, but Shep took a certain sly pleasure in Bill's discomfort.

The whole idea of the expedition, Shep explained, was a Big Joke on Cary. Here Ol' Cary was a slippin' off to Portugal to find a feller with a sockful of diamonds. So they would all go along, too. Ain't we got any rights?

But Nikki was going on account of Cary, and Bill was going on account of Nikki, and Francis was going on account of Bill, and the whole enterprise was the sum of their several motives.

To every question about how or why or what about passports and transportation and luggage and everything, Shep would reply stiffly: *"C'est commandé."* His fifteenth man, he said, was attending to all that. As a matter of fact, Shep had collected the passports the night before and placed them in the hands of an agent of a travel bureau (of which Shep was a valued client), who was at this moment collecting the proper visas. Shep's operative would no doubt be at the station with the papers and space.

In the meantime it was important to get Nikki organized. Shep went to her rooms and assured her that he would be a Big Help. Maria, in her dark, silent Austrian manner, was folding and packing Nikki's things with quick, expert hands. Nikki moved helplessly about. She was no good at packing, because she couldn't put her head down. The walls started wheeling about, she said.

Although she paid no attention to him whatsoever, Shep was at great pains to explain the whole idea to Maria.

They were taking Nikki down to the Portuguese Riviera, Shep said, on account of she looked so poorly. She'd been in the hospital, d'you see, and had gotten all wan and pale and she needed some fine Portuguese air and sunshine. Swim in the sea sort of thing.

Shep talked as though he felt he ought to explain things to Maria, although he knew as well as anyone that this Austrian maid was, by now, beyond surprise.

"We'll only be gone a minute or two," he assured Maria over and over, "and we'll bring her back the very pitcher of health." This was Shep's way of letting Maria know that she wasn't being taken along. Maria had no fears for Nikki; she knew well enough that Nikki was safe where numbers were concerned. Safe as a fish.

Nikki's bags were now ready and Maria rang for the porters.

"Keep a light burnin' in the window," Shep told Maria, "it might be dark and stormy when we get back."

Nikki, with the approach of train time, was getting apprehensive. "Shall we go?" she appealed to Shep.

Shep started for the door and then stopped and turned around for a last look at the apartment.

"Play me out with music," he said suddenly, "play me out with music."

Single Lady

Nikki said please could they go before they missed the train. But Shep was unaccountably obstinate. He insisted on being played out with music.

Nikki went to the victrola, wound up the spring, tripped the release and set the needle down on a record.

> *"Co-me un so-gno d'or scol-pi-toe nel co-re*
> *Il ri cor-do an cor di quel—la—mor*
> *che non e-siste piu . . ."*

It was Toselli's "Serenade," that strange, sad composition that haunted Europe at the close of the war.

> *"Ma fu mol-to bre-ve,*
> *La dol—cez-sa di quel ben——"*

Shep stood listening to the music, while the porters cleared Nikki's bags out of the room. "My, my," he said to Nikki, "but you play me out with sad music."

> *". . . cu-poe l'av-ve-nir—sem-pre piu tri-sti-i di*
> *La qui-ven-tu pas-sa-ta sa-ra . . ."*

Nikki took Shep's arm, turned him around and walked out of the doorway with him. Bill and Francis were coming down the hall. They all moved along the corridor to the lift. Bill rang the bell and the cage came up for them. The boy opened the grilled cage door.

For a single instant, before she stepped into the cage, Nikki was seized with a queer panic. Where was she going? What was she doing? The vague dread of leaving Paris, which Shepard Lambert felt, was fleetingly communicated to her. She suddenly felt terribly guilty and responsible for Shep. She wanted to take him by the hand and turn him around and lead him back to her rooms.

From far down the empty passageway came the last strains of the Serenade:

> *"Oh rag-gis di so-le*
> *Sul mio cam-mi-no ahime non bril-li piu*
> *Mai piu! Mai piu . . ."*

Nikki stepped into the cage. The others followed her and the door clicked behind them. They were descending.

Shep's low-swung cab, the old Santa Maria, was standing outside the hotel. They climbed in, Nikki, Shep, Bill Talbot and Francis. Another taxi followed with the luggage. Nikki had so many bags. She had insisted on taking her turtles along in a basket.

Serge drove dispiritedly, looking back reproachfully at Shep at intervals. He was reluctant to get them to the station on time.

The signs of Paris stared down upon them as they passed across town. Cinzano. Société Lattiere de Blanc. Grand Marnier. L'Echo de Paris. Cyber. La Grande Maison de Blanc. Comptoir Nationale. Ripolin. Chocolate Suchard Cacao. Dubonnet. Citroen— Aida AIDA Aida——

"This is your idea of a joke on Cary, is it?" Bill inquired.

"Yep," said Shep, looking sidewise at Nikki, "this is my idea, all right."

"Do you s'pose he'll be mad?" Nikki queried innocently.

"Sure he'll be mad," Shep said.

"I still don't believe all that about the diamonds," Nikki said. "I think it's a forgery."

"If Cary's at the station, will you believe it?"

"Maybe."

The cab pulled up at the curb in front of the Gare d'Orsay. Behind them came the second with the bags. They all unloaded on the sidewalk. Shep took command and engaged the porters. Shep gave Serge a folded bank note from his wallet. The big Russian seized Shep's hands and began to kiss them wildly. Shep, embarrassed at the demonstration on the sidewalk, withdrew his hand and patted Serge on the shoulder, whereupon Serge burst into tears.

"So long, old boy," Shep said and followed the porters in the station.

"Can you imagine the big loon?" he demanded of Nikki. But Nikki knew that behind his dark glasses Shep was strangely moved.

Bill Talbot bought a Saturday Evening Post at the newsstand. (Eight francs in France.)

Shep's agent, a multiloquous little chap in a black suit and bowler hat, was standing at the gates with a long, pale manila envelope. The two conferred importantly and the whole party passed through the gates and onto the station platform.

"Now, if Cary isn't here . . . " Nikki began apprehensively.

Halfway down the platform, standing beside a coach was Cary Lockwood. He was dressed in gray flannel trousers and blue single-breasted coat with white mother-of-pearl buttons. He was wearing a gray felt hat and his ashwood crook stick hung from the curve of his arm. He was cutting the leaves in a paper-back book.

Nikki went straight up to him. He looked quite thin and brown and a little tired.

"Hello, Cary."

Cary looked up in astonishment.

"Well—hello," he said. Then he saw the others coming up.

"Well," said Nikki, "you still have your white teeth."

"Thanks. You're looking very lovely."

Nikki curtsied. She was very trim in a black canton travelling suit, with a severe little coat with wonderful big dull silver buttons. She had on a close-fitting black hat and her feet were encased in small round-toed gun-metal pumps.

Shep went down to the end of the coach with the porters, and unbeknownst to Cary, directed the distribution of the bags inside.

Cary appeared puzzled and uncertain. "I say, what are all you chaps doing down here?"

"You're going to Portugal, aren't you?" Bill said.

"That's right."

"Well, we just wanted to put you on the train."

"Very thoughtful of you," Cary said.

"Have you got a nice seat on the train?" Bill inquired solicitously.

"Right by a window," Cary said.

"Let's go in and see Cary's space," Bill suggested. "Cary, come on and show us your space."

Bill took Cary by the arm and led him to the end door of the coach. They all followed him inside.

"Well, well," said Bill, "what a swell train."

"My boy," said Shep, "this is the Sud Express, Train de Luxe."

"Train de Luxe," Bill repeated, "that sounds like Gala de Nuit."

"Same idea," Shep assured him. "Slight extra charge."

Nikki sat down at a table for four across the aisle from the table for two occupied by Cary.

"This is a fine train," she said, looking around.

She picked up a folder from the table, examining it casually. "What time does it—let's see—Arr. and Dep. Dep. ten-forty."

Cary was looking at his wrist watch. "I think you all better get off," he said.

"Get off!" Bill said. "Hell, no. We like this train. This is a Train de Luxe. We like trains de luxe, don't we, Nik?"

"That's right," she agreed.

Cary was getting anxious. By now the coach was filled up with the exception of the table where the four sat.

Cary got up. "Well," he said, "the train's going to start."

"Let 'er start," Bill said. "Who cares? Let 'er go Gallagher."

"Who cares?" echoed the others, "who cares?"

"Look," said Cary, "you better get off."

201

"Can you imagine that," Bill said, "trying to put us off the train. We ain't going to get off no train. Not for you nor anybody like you."

"Suit yourself," said Cary, "only there goes the whistle."

The train had begun to move. Cary looked at them in dismay.

"Isn't this fine," Bill told Shep. "We're all going to Portugal with Cary."

The perfect composure with which they all took the departure of the train told Cary that it was a conspiracy.

"Honestly," he said, "you all ought to be ashamed. What's the idea?"

"We thought we'd just come along is all."

"I see."

"None of us has ever been to Portugal and Nikki here needs the sea air—she's been ill —and besides we want to help you find the man with the diamonds."

Cary winced a little at that last.

"Nikki ill?" he said.

"Nikki's been very ill," Nikki said. "Nikki was in the hospital."

"I'm so sorry."

"She's all right now," Shep said. "She's fine."

Cary saw the deep purple crescents under Nikki's eyes.

"She's fine now," Shep said, "only her legs are thinner."

Nikki extended her legs out into the aisle and surveyed them. "They *are* thinner," she agreed after a careful scrutiny.

"Well," said Shep, "thin or fat, hot or cold, wet or dry, they're still the best legs in the world—in *my* estimation."

Nikki thanked him warmly.

"Are you really all going to Lisbon?" Cary asked as the train left the station.

"That's right," Shep said.

"You have to have tickets and passports and things," Cary reminded. "Have you got passports?"

"Sure," said Shep reaching in his coat pocket, "what kind of passports do you like?"

Nikki and Bill sat on one side of the table and Shep and Francis on the other. Cary sat across the aisle. At his table sat a young chap in a gray tweed cap, reading a French journal. They all arranged themselves comfortably and looked out of the window. It began to be hot.

It was hot. They found that out as soon as the train pulled out of the shadow of the Gare d'Orsay.

Cary opened a brief-case, got out some maps and folders, spread them on the table in front of him and began to study them.

"How long does it take to get to Lisbon?" Nikki asked.

"Thirty hours," Cary said without looking up.

Bill took off his coat and his tie and displayed some wide, high-powered figured braces that brought the waist line of his gray trousers nearly up under his arms.

"Those certainly are sporting braces," Shep said admiringly.

"Very fruity," Bill agreed.

The Washout sat with half closed eyes, looking out of the window. No one ever knew what he was thinking about. Shep was thinking about his next drink. Like a diabetic who must weigh his ounces of food in order to keep an exact balance, so Shep had to measure his drinks to maintain the proper degree of intoxication.

Once out in the bright noon sunlight, the interior of the coach became smotheringly hot. The fat man in the black suit behind them took off his collar and began fanning himself with his hat.

Shep looked at Bill, miserably hot and perspiring.

"You know what I could go for?" he demanded.

"What could you go for?"

"A bottle of beer. A nice cold bottle of beer."

"So could I," cried Bill.

Shep pushed the little mother-of-pearl button under the window. After a while a waiter came down the aisle.

Nikki said she wouldn't have any beer, just some mineral water. Shep ordered four bottles of beer. He asked the chap across from Cary if he wouldn't have a bottle of beer, too. The chap said yes, rather.

"Have a gasper?" he invited, holding out his cigarette case.

He introduced himself as Lennox and presented his card. It always embarrassed them to have people present their cards. They looked at you as if waiting for yours. None of the troupe ever had cards. They all looked at it politely and Shep thanked him and put it in his pocket.

Lennox was the European Representative of the Chase Thrashing Machine Company of Racine, Wisconsin. He said he was on his way to Morocco to sell tractors. He had the blue and white of the D. S. C. in the buttonhole of his coat lapel.

When the beer came it was ice cold and beaded with perspiration.

"Oh baby!" Shep said and took a bottle in his two hands. It was Bière de La Meuse, a pale cold beer, refreshing beyond all description. It had a nice oval brown label with a lovely young girl seated beside a gushing fountain. The waiter ripped the caps off the bottles and set them down. Bill poured out a glassful.

"Well, men," he said, holding up his glass, "fire and fall back."

Shep told Lennox confidentially, that Bill was an old Civil War drinker and pay no attention to him.

Bill rang for some more beer. "This is a fine day for beer," he said. "How come you to think of it, Shep?"

"I can't explain it," Shep said. "It was really just like I seen a message in the sky. Letters of fire in the sky. Couldn't you go for some nice cold beer, Nikki?"

Nikki said she couldn't go for beer.

Nikki is a fancy drinker, Shep pointed out. "She only goes for fancy drinks. We like our beer, don't we Bill?"

"Don't we just," Bill agreed.

"We can do fancy drinking, too," Shep said, "only we can do plain drinking, also. Plain *and* fancy drinking is what we can do."

"That's right," Bill said and burped a little.

"Now, Bill," Shep said, "no plain and fancy burping. You can have all the beer you like so long as you don't burp."

" 'Scuse me," Bill said. "I didn't mean to. Did you ever hear about the man who burped during the Two Minute Silence?"

"No, what about it?"

"Well, that's all there is to it."

Nobody appeared impressed, so Bill, crestfallen, subsided in his seat.

"I guess a boy's best friend is his mother," he concluded.

Cary and his English friend drank their beer moderately, but Shep and Bill addressed themselves earnestly to the business.

"You have to drink it kind of fast," Bill pointed out, "on account of it gets warm so quick. Just as soon as you sit it down, it gets warm. You can't drink warm beer."

"That's right," Shep agreed, "and besides cinders fall into it. It gets full of cinders."

"Cinders're good for you," Bill said. "Make you lay hard-shelled eggs."

Cary kept studying folders and Lennox read and The Washout slept gently, and Bill and Shep drank beer and every little while Nikki leaned over and sprinkled her turtles with mineral water. She had them in a shallow little square basket with straw on the bottom and a criss-cross net work of twine over the top. Abélard kept sticking out his neck and trying to shoulder his way through the lacings. He escaped every once in a while, but somebody always brought him back. People would retrieve anything for Nikki.

In an hour and a half they were in the huge station at Orléans.

Shep and Bill got out and went to a bar along the station platform. "All that beer left a sweet taste in my mouth," Bill said.

They had a couple of Amer Picons to fix the taste before they got back on the train.

"This is a hell of a big place," Bill said. "I thought all the Frenchmen were supposed to be in Paris."

Cary managed to get tickets for all of them for the premiere service, so they trooped back to the wagon restaurant together. The four of them—Shep, Bill, Nikki and Cary, sat together. They put Francis with the Englishman.

A woman in a uniform came down the aisle, "Coktail! Coktail!"

Shep hailed her immediately. He found he could get Martinis, so he ordered six.

"This is a fine train," he said. "Isn't this a fine train though?" he asked Nikki.

"Practically perfect."

He ordered three more Martinis before the hors d'œuvres came. As soon as he'd eaten a sardine, Shep called for the wine card.

"What are you trying to do, get us all tight?" Nikki said. "In the middle of the day?"

"That's what I'm trying to do," Shep

agreed, "get you all tight in the middle of the day. On a train."

"Beautiful thought," Bill said. He was beginning to look a little sleepy.

"Will you all leave me order the wine?" Shep asked.

Nobody objected, so Shep ordered two bottles of Turpin Monopole. "It's a fine Sauterne," he said, "not too sweet and not too dry. Make you bark like a fox."

When the omelette came, everybody was hungry and they enjoyed it.

"Well," said Bill, when the omelette was taken away and they brought in the Escallope Viennoise, "they give you enough to eat."

"You have to have something to go with the wine," Shep pointed out. "It's always nice to have food with your lunch."

After the cut meats and peas and sauté potatoes had been cleared away, the entremets appeared, then dessert.

Shep cared little for sweets when he was drinking. Nikki was usually smoking at this point and didn't eat dessert. But Cary and Bill went for theirs.

They all thought the lunch was over when the cheese appeared, and then came the fruit and then the small blacks. Nikki cut some slices of apple for her turtles.

The wine women went by with a large

basket of corks under her arm. "Liqueurs!"

Shep asked Nikki if she would have a cordial.

"Could you go for a benedictine?"

"Oh, sure."

Bill said he could go for a kümmel, so they all had liqueurs. The bill for the drinks wasn't so stiff, considering, and Shep insisted on paying. "You'll all get a chance later," he said.

The coach seemed hotter than ever when they got back to it. The fat man in the black suit unlaced his shoes and took them off. Shep gave him a disgusted look and got up and went off.

At Angoulême, where they stopped four minutes, he found the Chef de Train on the station platform and went into a huddle with him. A hundred franc note passed between them. Back in the train, Shep led the troupe back into an empty compartment. He invited Lennox along, too.

It was much nicer in the compartment. They all took off their coats and neckties and opened their shirts at the throat. Nikki took off her hat and jacket and revealed a flame-colored blouse.

"You're so cute," she told Shep. "You think of everything."

"Aren't I just."

They had the compartment to themselves

all the way to Hendaye. Lennox turned out
to be a hell of a fine chap. They called him
Captain right away, but he said he wasn't a
captain. He'd been a sergeant-major was all.
He said he'd been offered a commission many
a time toward the end of the war, but he
didn't want to leave his pals. He started out
with some chaps d'you see and they'd been
together a long time and he wanted to stay
with them.

They all agreed that he'd done right. What
the hell was a commission if you had to leave
your pals. They called him Captain anyway.

Nikki was sleepy after lunch, so without the
slightest trace of self-consciousness, she curled
up on the seat with her face to the wall, and
went to sleep.

The sight of Nikki lying asleep on the seat
gave the boys a strange sense of pride and
responsibility. She seemed so utterly helpless lying there, fast asleep on an express train
headed for Portugal. Her pleated skirt had
fallen away from her legs; you could see the
back of her knees smoothly encased in filmy
silk stockings. Her legs looked long and pa-
trician from the tip of her gun-metal pumps
to where they disappeared under her dress.
There was a nice curving line from her hip
to her shoulder. She slept with one hand under
her cheek and her head resting on a tiny lace

and satin baby pillow she had taken out of her travelling case.

The presence of the sleeping girl in the compartment was exciting. *Elle dort comme un enfant,* peacefully, gently; you couldn't tell that she breathed. From her hair and from her person there rose a faint aromatic fragrance, like fresh gardenias, that refreshed the dust and smoke-filled interior of the compartment. In sleep, with her black, near-sighted eyes closed and her hand under her cheek, she seemed so pathetically alone and unprotected, dependent upon the presence of all of them. She belonged to all of them and she belonged to none of them. "She's not very good looking," Shep said to the Englishman, "but her mother always said she had the nicest hair-ribbon."

Lennox said, on the contrary, he thought she was stunning.

Shep said, "well, she has got eyes like an Assyrian Queen. She's got eyes like an Assyrian Queen has got eyes," Shep said.

"Assyrian Queen," Bill scoffed, "you don't know no Assyrian Queen. You never even saw no Assyrian Queen," Bill challenged him. "You don't know what you're talking about. You're just a-makin' that up."

"I did so see an Assyrian Queen," Shep retorted, stoutly.

"In whose gray fedora?"

"In the Metropolitan Museum's gray fedora, that's whose gray fedora."

"What was her name?"

Shep said he didn't remember. "It was only a head," he said, "carved in ivory and painted."

"Semiramis," Cary Lockwood said, looking up from his book, "and she was noted for beauty, wisdom and voluptuousness."

"There you are!" Shep cried triumphantly.

"All right," Bill said, miffed, "I can't stand off the two of you."

Lennox accepted Nikki's presence among them in the same spirit that he accepted the whole thing. He was an Englishman and not inquisitive. They were jolly good company and he was glad of it.

Shep found that he had caught a fine drinking companion in Lennox and he was delighted. Following a suitable respite after lunch, Shep had proposed a nice cold bottle of beer as a refreshment. But Lennox, had somewhat apologetically expressed his preference for Scotch and soda. He found beer came up in his throat a little.

So they got in a bottle of White Horse Cellar and some Schweppes and went to work on it. Bill stuck to beer.

"He's the type," Shep explained.

Single Lady

Cary sat quietly in a corner going over papers in his brief-case, and Francis slept quietly in another corner.

Suddenly the chiming watch in his waistcoat pocket went off. Francis sat up, leaped to his feet, reached for his hat and started off.

"Hey," Shep said, "where you going?"

Francis blinked uncertainly.

"You aren't going anywheres," Shep said. "Sit down."

Francis, suddenly conscious of his surroundings, blushed and sat down.

"You're on a train," Shep said.

"Tsorry," said Francis and went back to sleep.

It developed that Lennox knew Portugal and spoke French, Spanish and Portuguese.

"What the hell kind of a language is Portuguese?" Shep wanted to know.

Lennox said it was a hell of a language right enough. He said it had everything in it but the kitchen stove: Spanish, French, Latin, Finnish, and even a couple of Chinese diphthongs.

"A couple of Chinese diphthongs, hey? They must feel lonesome. They're a hell of a long ways from home. Is it a hard language to learn?"

Lennox said he wouldn't like to hang by his thumbs while Shep learned it.

Shep wanted to know what the Portuguese were like.

"Banties," Lennox said.

"Banties?"

"Remember the bantam regiments England had in the war? The little Yorkshiremen? Coal-miners?"

"Oh, sure."

Lennox began to laugh at the recollection.

"I remember one time we went in to replace a banty outfit. Poor devils were so short, they couldn't see over the top of the trench from the firestep. A squad of Prussian guards about eight feet tall came over one night and bagged the lot of them."

"Little fellers, eh?" Shep said, thinking about the Portuguese.

"Undersized. They're a mongrel lot, you know. Cross-bred and all that. Down around Lisbon you'll find 'em strongly crossed with negro."

"I remember something about them in the war," Shep said. "What the hell was it? 'Take back your monkeys.' Something like that."

"Something like that," Lennox said. "You know down at the southernmost tip, they're just like that—monkeys. They chatter like monkeys. Down in the Province of Algarve. Excitable little monkeys."

"How about the women?" Shep wanted to know.

"In what way? Looks or what?"

"Well . . . you know."

"Couldn't say. Not much for looks, although you'll see a regular rip snorter now and again in one of the fishing villages."

"How is Lisbon?"

"You'll find it dull. Not many Americans there. Not more than four, I sh'd think."

Shep said it would be funny if they found any place dull.

"It's a poor country, you know," Lenrox said. "Poor as poor. What made you chaps ever start for Portugal?"

"I don't know," said Shep. "It seemed like a good idea at the time."

Lennox laughed.

"As a matter of fact," Shep said mysteriously, "we're on a big treasure hunt."

Cary looked up sharply.

"We're looking for some diamonds," Shep went on regardless.

"Diamonds in Portugal?"

"Certainly, why not? Portugal is practically full of diamonds."

"How so?"

"Big shipwreck off Portugal during the war," Shep said. "Boat-load of diamonds.

Feller landed in Portugal with diamonds. We're lookin' him up."

To Shep's surprise Lennox didn't laugh. Instead he said thoughtfully, "I heard somethin' about that. Torpedoed, wasn't she?"

"That's right," Shep said.

"French or Belgian——?"

"Belgian."

"What was her name?"

Shep looked at Cary.

"The *Belleville.*"

Lennox looked at Cary with new interest. "You figure the diamonds are in Portugal?"

Cary shrugged his shoulders. He was annoyed with Shep.

"They have to be," Shep said. "They're not in the ship. He found the ship and raised the safe and cracked her open. Empty."

"I read somethin' about that, too," Lennox said. "So you're the chap, eh?"

Cary made a wry grimace.

"For God's sake, Shep, what's the idea?"

"He'll find the feller all right," Shep went on unperturbed, "unless he's at the bottom of the ocean." Shep was very proud of Cary's pertinacity. Incapable of any sort of sustained effort himself, he admired Cary no end.

Lennox could see that Cary was studying road maps of the coast of Portugal.

"Goin' to do it by motor, eh? You'll find it rough enough."

"I expect so."

Lennox went over the thing in his mind. It wasn't such a needle-in-the-haystack quest as it sounded. The length of the coast line of the narrow little country was but three hundred and fifty miles. It was only a hundred and thirty miles wide, less than half that distance. He might pick up a trace of a castaway somewhere along the coast.

At Bordeaux they all got out and had a couple of quick ones at the station bar. They had a couple of quick ones, too, at Dax and at Bayonne and La Negresse. They had to be quick ones because the train only stopped four minutes.

Lennox said they ought to go in to dinner right after they left La Negresse because they got you out for baggage and passport examinations. So they went back to the wagon restaurant and started in and began ordering dry Martinis. As a special favor, Shep treated Nikki to demi-bouteille of Mumms' Cordon Rouge. "Not too sweet, not too dry," he said. "Make you leap like a tuna."

Nikki said she really didn't want to leap like a tuna.

Shep said he knew how to make a Big Joke about tuna. "When the waiter comes you say,

218

'Waiter, have you got any tuna?' and the waiter says, 'No, sir, I'm all out of tuna,' and you say, 'That's what I thought,' and you see," Shep said, "that's how you make a Big Joke." He looked very pleased with himself.

Nikki looked at him very sadly and asked him if he really had to go to all that trouble.

More food was offered at dinner than at lunch. "Boy," said Shep, "don't the French eat on trains, though."

They all had to get off at the Spanish border to show their passports to a little Frenchman seated at a deal table in an office at the station. This baggage and passport examination was an ordeal for Shep. He had a morbid hatred for all officials. He didn't like being questioned or having anyone go poking about in his things. The double ordeal—the French at Hendaye and the Spanish at Irun—put him in a state. Nikki didn't seem to mind. She had six cases altogether, besides the turtle basket, and although she just drifted dreamily along paying no particular attention, still she never seemed to lose anything.

At Irun they passed through the station, showed their tickets at the gate and boarded the Wagon Lit for Lisbon.

Nikki had a compartment by herself, Shep and Bill were together and Cary and the

Single Lady

Washout were alone. There were few passengers on the train.

It was still oppressively hot. Shep and Bill went into Nikki's compartment to see that she was all right. Shep lifted up Nikki's overnight case and opened it for her on account of Nikki couldn't put her head down. She couldn't pack or unpack. She wouldn't have anything more to drink so Shep got a bottle of mineral water and a glass full of ice for her.

"If you need help, darlin', just pull the emergency cord," Shep advised her, "and stop the train."

Nikki gave him a tired smile. It had been a long, hot, jolting day, full of dust and cinders, and she was exhausted.

Shep showed her how to open the wash basin and then they said good night to her.

When they had gone, Nikki could not help but marvel at Shep. He was so tight and so alert and so thoughtful of her. Who else but Shep would remember that she couldn't put her head down after she had been drinking, or that she'd never figure out that Spanish collapsible wash basin that you pulled out and down.

Nikki locked the door of her compartment. She took her mules out of the suitcase on the bed and laid out her kimono. She began to undress, taking off her blouse first, undoing

the snaps along the left side, beginning at the
bottom. She unhooked her skirt at the waist,
dropped it over her hips and stepped out of it.
She hung her blouse and skirt under a sheet
to protect them from the dust that filtered into
the compartment from the dry roadbed.

She sat down on the side of the bed and took
off her pumps and undid her garter clasps.
She peeled off her stockings and slid her bare
feet into her mules. She unbuttoned the single
button that held her brassiere together at the
center of her back and slipped it off. She got
out of her step-ins, and taking a small silk bag
from her traveling case, she stuffed the lacy,
discarded lingerie into it and put it back into
the case.

Turning on the high pointed heels of her
mules, she caught the reflection of her white
naked figure in the glossy black glass of the
train window. Unconsciously she arched her
back and lifted her chest and surveyed herself.
She had fine lines in the dark window glass.
The contours of her body appeared much
rounder and softer than in a mirror. It did
not occur to her to draw down the curtain.
The train was rushing through the darkness.

The words of Toselli's Serenade, heard in
the morning, kept recurring in her head, like
a solemn litany. She wished she had played
something else, when they left.

Single Lady

". . . all be-yond is dark
And sad-der ev-'ry day
For youth it-self will soon pass a-way . . ."

Nikki slipped on her kimono and took a small red leather case from her bag filled with toilet articles. She sat down by the washstand and took them out, distributing them haphazardly about: creams, soap, mouth wash, tooth brush, tooth paste, eye wash, witch hazel, talcum and eau de Cologne. The train lurched about so it was hard to keep them in their places. She tore the paper wrapper off the soap and washed her hands in the bright metal wash basin. She combed her hair straight back from her forehead so that she might cream her face easily. She let her kimono slip off her shoulders. As she removed the cream from her face with a soft cloth, she kept turning to look at her reflection in the window glass. I like myself best in a train window at night, she thought. And then she wondered if other people liked themselves in train windows, too.

". . . la-ment-ing re-mains a-lone,
my tears and bit-ter grief of heart . . ."

Suddenly the blackness outside was streaked with a long, blue-green lash of lightning. A clap of thunder shook the train and the window glass was spattered with rain drops. Startled and frightened, Nikki instinctively drew her garment about her shoulders. She thought, of course, the train would stop, but it kept right on plunging through the rain and the winds and the darkness. Over the rumble of the trucks beneath her feet, she could hear the roar of the thunder. The window was washed with rain. Nikki, who could scarcely endure being alone, found herself alone at night in a strange compartment on a strange train, ripping through an electric storm on the way to a strange destination. She was filled with wild panic. She wanted to rush out and summon the others, but in some mysterious way her panic graduated into a queer ecstasy. She felt that she was being carried along to swift, splintering destruction. The roaring rhythm of the car wheels, the rush of the wind, the battering of the rain drops against the glass, acted upon her like the crescendo of a powerful symphony. And together with the stunning, bewildering cacophony of sound was the thrilling knowledge of Cary's presence near her. They were plunging to destruction together and there was something terrible and exciting about that. Intoxicated, she wanted the train to speed faster, the lightning to flash, and the thunder to burst again and again. She wanted to sing, to cry out, to dance. She understood what Shep Lambert

had meant when he told her he liked to yell
and scream and whistle and sing and curse
when he was flying an airplane at night. The
sense of loneliness and speed and power was
almost unbearable.

Nikki's hysteria diminished as the fierce-
ness of the storm died away. She scrubbed
her teeth and poured a few drops of the red
dentifrice (*du Docteur Pierre de la Faculté
de Médecine de Paris*) in a water glass. It
clouded the water white and tasted a little
like licorice, but it was very refreshing and
took away the dull taste of cigarettes. She
washed her eyes in the eye-cup and patted
away the lotion that ran down over her cheeks
and dripped on her throat. She stood up and
slipped off her kimono and bathed her throat
and arms with witch hazel from the bottle.

"*. . . O rays of the sun-shine
Upon my way, a-las, ye shine no more . . .*"

Nikki put talcum on her skin with a huge
puff and sat down on the bed to comb
her hair. She took off her kimono and slipped
a chiffon nightgown over her head, tying a
coral ribbon around her waist in a bow at the
left side. She put the fan at second speed,
fixed the pillows, slid her feet out of her mules,
swung her legs under the sheet and switched
off the light.

CHAPTER VIII

A T nine-thirty in the morning Bill and Shep were awakened by a persistent knocking on the door.

Bill reached out of his berth and opened the door. It was Lennox, in a gray tweed suit and cap.

"Hello, you chaps," he said, "you'd better get up."

"What the hell for?" Bill said.

"They'll be after your passports in half an hour. We're getting close to the frontier."

"Thanks," said Bill.

The train came to a stop and Shep looked out of the window.

"We're in Spain all right," he said. He pointed out two little yellow painted structures standing primly side by side. One bore the legend, Retrete de SENORAS; the other Retrete de CABALLEROS.

"Bill," he said, "I never seen such an idea expressed so pretty."

"We're a couple of Caballeros," Bill said, "and make no mistake."

Shep and Bill had a terrible time shaving in the rushing, jolting, little compartment.

Single Lady

"These little ol' Spanish trains go like hell," Shep said. "Just arootin' and atootin' along."

Lennox was standing in the aisle, looking out of the window when Shep and Bill came out. He said that Mr. Lockwood and the other chap had been up for some time, but not the young lady.

Shep went and knocked softly on Nikki's compartment door. "Rise and shine, Senorita," he said, "rise and shine."

There was a faint stirring within.

"You're practically in Portugal," Shep said, "and you've got to show yourself."

Shep heard a sleepy murmur inside, whereupon he delivered a matutinal oration at the locked compartment door; about the glories of the Spanish morning and what was the idea of lying in bed like that. He concluded with a plaintive petition to be allowed to come inside and render the necessary morning services. Couldn't he raise the blinds or find her tooth brush for her or lay out her shaving water or something? Help her with her hair? Untree her shoes? Anything? Sprinkle her turtles.

Since there was no reply to these entreaties, he abandoned his post at the door and went off, muttering philosophies about the general incomprehensibility of women. Lennox led him back to the wagon restaurant.

"You'll not find it like the other," he warned.

It was too late for breakfast. There were no aperitifs, so Shep and Bill had to choose between Johnny Walker whiskey and Lisbonne beer. Shep and Lennox went for whiskey, but Bill went for the beer.

Nikki did not appear until the train reached Vilar Formoso, the Portuguese frontier town. The others saw her first on the station platform. She was bareheaded and she had on a simple, sleeveless slip-on of French blue silk. She looked cool and fresh and young in the drab little station. She was almost immediately surrounded by scrubby little urchins who gazed up at her out of inflamed eyes. Flies swarmed in clouds about their close-cropped bullet-shaped heads. Nikki looked like some kind of a precious wild flower swaying in a patch of rag-weed.

"Will you look at that creature!" cried Shep to whom Nikki was always, on first appearance, an astonishing revelation. He went up immediately to kiss her cool hand and present his morning respects.

They all had to go back to their compartments and open their bags for the inspection of the custom officials. Then they had to get down from the train again and present their passports for scrutiny at a tiny office in the station. These formalities were very trying to Shep.

"I don't think you will like Portugal," Lennox told Shep. "It's hell's own shakes of a place for officials. Swarmin' all over the shop. Everybody has got some civil job or is maneuverin' to get one, so he can bear down on the others."

"Sounds like the U.S.A.," Shep said.

"Your Portygee only talks about business and politics. You never saw such indolence."

"Such what?" Shep asked.

"Indolence."

"Well," said Shep, "they's a certain virtue in good, well-placed indolence."

"Time or distance don't mean a thing to your Portygee."

"I like that," Shep said. "I think that's fine."

"Wait 'til you have a business appointment."

"A business appointment," Shep said, "is something that is not likely to enter our lives. In fact," Shep said, "if our business appointments were laid end to end they wouldn't re, quire more'n a split second to pass a given point. Isn't that right, Bill?"

"Right you are, Caballero," said Bill.

When finally they got their passports back from the quick-eyed little man in the black fedora hat, they reboarded the train.

"One thing I know about your Portygee,"

228

Shep said (he got that 'your Portygee' from Lennox), "is he wears a black fedora."

"That's right," Lennox agreed.

"He wears a black fedora and he snaps his brim. You see how acute my powers of observation are," Shep said. "Your Portygee wears a black fedora and he snaps his brim and if he wore a black cape, he'd look like any bandit."

"Or any musician," Bill said.

"That's right," Lennox said, "and if we go right into the restaurant car, we'll be first in and we can get lunch."

They collected Nikki and went in the wagon restaurant.

"Well, here we go again," Shep said, as the sliced cucumbers and sardines and potato salad appeared.

Nobody could find a wine they liked, so they all drank Lisbonne beer, except Nikki.

Through the wide, long window the country outside looked mountainous and picturesque.

"So this is Portugal, hey?" Shep said. "Looks like a fine place for highwaymen."

"Oh yes," Lennox said, "you daren't go about the mountain roads alone. You'll meet the banditry right enough."

For the rest of lunch they had an omelette

and then some cold sliced lamb and a salad and cheese and fruit.

"This is our last meal aboard the train, isn't it?" Shep asked. "What the hell time do we get to Lisbon?"

"Ha' pas' six," Lennox said.

"Hurray," Shep said, "this is a fine train, but it's too dusty."

They all went back to Cary's compartment. It was Shep's humor always to make Cary's space his headquarters, so Cary had to be polite and couldn't escape.

"We'd better get some beer in here," Shep said, "it's going to be hot." He rang the bell and ordered some Lisbonne beer.

Nikki sat by the window and looked out at the scenery.

"It's not so much from this side," Lennox told her, "but along the coast it's beautiful."

Nikki wasn't very much impressed with Portugal from the car window. It looked rugged and mountainous and barren. There seemed something sinister and fatal about Portugal. She had never known such heat on a train or such dust and cinders. She raised her glasses now and then to look out, but quickly put them down. It was better if the country went by in a blur.

"How did you sleep last night, Nikki?" Shep inquired.

Nikki said she didn't know what time it was when she got to sleep. It was awfully hard getting to sleep.

Since the Sud Express had left the Gare d'Orsay in Paris, Nikki had seemed to become very quiet and thoughtful.

"You ain't blue, is you darlin'?" Shep ventured.

Nikki said that she didn't know it was going to be so hot in Portugal.

"It will be cooler in Lisbon," Cary told her. "You get a nice breeze from the sea."

"Nikki's letting up on her drinking," Shep complained. "You ought not to do that, Nikki. It ain't right. A girl of your reputation and standing."

Nikki finally agreed to drink some vermouth if Shep sent for it. She brightened up a little after that.

Shep was expressive about the train. "This here is the gosh dangdest train I ever did see," he would say whenever they came into a station. "It takes three blows on a whistle, two toots on a horn and seventeen bells to get this here little old train out of a station. We're just arootin' and atootin' and aringin' and adingin' and a peep-peepin' our way along to Lisbon. Now you listen."

Sure enough, every time the train was ready to leave a station, there would come a long

231

blast from a horn, then a couple of shrill whistles and a lot of ringing and tooting from the cab of the locomotive.

At Santa Combo, where they got off for a stretch, Lennox showed them the little charcoal boxes underneath the coaches which heated the train in winter-time.

"Antique, isn't it?" he said. "If you want to do anyone a dirty trick, just open the slide and dump the coals on the road bed, and the poor beggars inside will freeze all right. It gets cold up here in the wintertime, I can tell you."

A shy little creature in a white pinafore with half-socks and Mary Janes came along with an orange water jug and glass. Shep was enchanted with her and took the first drink of water he'd had in a year.

"Fantastic!" he said.

Lennox gave her a coin and she ran off.

Then a little boy in a white smock came along with a tray of sticky nougats and a shallow basket of grapes. Lennox gave him a coin, too, but nobody went for his sweets.

When they got back in Cary's compartment Shep picked up a little red handbook lying on the seat.

"Manual of Conversation," he read aloud. "Boy, don't this come in handy. Here's where I learn Portuguese."

He turned to the first page: "the stars," he announced, "*'estrellas'*—Say, that's pretty —*'estrellas'*. . . ."

Lennox said you pronounced it *eestraillas*.

"That's even better," Shep said, "let's see the sun, *O Sol*. Hell, this language is a cinch Let's see what's the milky way—the *via lactea*. Why land sakes, I could learn this lingo with one hand tied behind my back . . . let's see what Nikki is . . . a young girl . . . *uma menina* . . ."

"Yes," said Lennox, "but you pronounce it *ooma meeneena*."

"Say," said Shep, "whilst I'm a learnin' this here language, I better learn some important words. What the hell is wine in Portygee? Let's see wine, wine, wine . . . wine . . . w-i-n-e . . . here we are—no—here's garters, Nikki; it's *ligas* and its feminine plural, *leegaas,* how's 'at, Cap? Now, here's a whisker comber and a second breakfast and a sick-nurse and a cupping glass and orange-flower water and a drunken man and confinement and a sweetmeat box and a hip-bath. . . ."

"What's a hip-bath?"

"A hip-bath? A hip-bath is *um semi-cupio.* Now, let's see where's that there wine . . . ah boys, here she is . . . *vinho.* . . ."

"*Veeneo,*" said Lennox.

"Red wine is *vinho tinto*."

"Look," said Lennox, "all those H's are Y's."

A slight diversion occurred at this point. Bill (Bronko) Talbot had set his glass of beer on the window sill. Dust and cinders immediately began to accumulate on the surface of the beer and when Bill picked up his glass again, an expression of deep disappointment over-spread his features. He looked around for some place to empty the glass. The windows in the compartment were screened, but the window in the corridor just outside the open compartment door was open. Bill stepped through the open compartment door and tossed his beer out the window with one mighty heave. Almost immediately some kind of uproar broke out further down the corridor and Bill hastily ducked back into the compartment.

A moment later three gentlemen appeared at the compartment door. They were foreign gentlemen and their faces, hair and coats were splashed with beer. It seemed that these three unfortunates had been standing at an open window but five or six removed from the one out of which Bill had hurled his tall glass of Lisbonne beer. The rush of wind outside the car had caught the beer neatly and hurled it back into the open window at which stood the three gentlemen admiring the scenery. The result was a fine baptism of beer.

Thus it was that the three, with streaming faces, appeared simultaneously at the door of Cary's compartment looking for the miscreant who had thrown the beer. They were, for a brief moment, nonplused at the quiet literary hour they found in progress there, but the guilty expression on Bill's face and the empty glass in his hand told them the story. It was exactly like an old cinema two-reel comedy. The three insulted ones, fixed upon Bill the most withering looks of scorn and rage, and burst forth into excited Portuguese.

Bill shrugged his shoulders and shook his head and said he no spik English. But he was red and ashamed and anybody could see he was as guilty as Dr. Crippen. When the temper of the three Portuguese increased, Bill got up and took out his pocket handkerchief and clumsily attempted to police up their clothes. These offices the three gentlemen haughtily disdained. Eventually they withdrew along the corridor with great dignity.

Shep was weak with laughter. "Can you imagine that big chump!" he cried, "dousing people with beer!"

But Bill's embarrassment as usual had changed to anger. "Those monkeys," he growled, "if they'd've said anything more, I'd've knocked their heads together."

Shep told Lennox about the time Nikki got

pinched in Paris and Bill gallantly smacked
the wrong man for the offense. Bill wasn't so
ashamed of that now, either. He said he was
glad he hit *some* Frenchman, anyhow.

Shep told Bill not to interrupt any more
and went on with his reading.

"I never saw so many words in my life,"
Shep said, "so many beautiful words . . . why,
look at all the beautiful words, porosity, loz-
enge, yesterday, celibacy, usufruct, benefice,
cicatrice, whitlow, humpback, mint water
. . . whoever heard so many lovely words
. . . extract of Saturn . . . Peruvian bark,
antiscorbutic wine. Why, Cary, this is the
swellest collection of assorted words I ever
did see. Pelerine, rice powder, a dozen oysters
. . . for God's sake . . . lark pie, oasis, kirsch,
woner shrim . . . what in God's name's a
shrim. . . .?"

"Didn't you never go for a shrim?" Bill
inquired.

". . . warming pan, pepper, caster, spring,
mattress, wash-hand stand, water, pot, night-
light, pot-hanger, door-porter, Schaffhauser,
flower-bed, tubular-bridge, cornrick, vegetable
mould, coffee-house keeper, pork butcher,
pastry cook, spizzerinktum (the others knew
he threw that one in) splurk (that too), cap-
stan or capstern, generalissimo, culverine, se-
quin, licentiate. That's ol' Johnny Swann.

Pounce-box loto, to play at puss-in-a-corner, touch-hole, tench, what an awful tench, bear's ear, boodlestorff, bindlesnitch, ogglesburg, splaff, splunk, zooch and spleewitchet!"

"Spimf," said Bill.

"My, my," Nikki said, "you tired you'self all out."

"I never *seen* so many words," Shep said, "I never *seen* so many words all in one book. Can you imagine so many words? So many words you can use in Portugal. Well," he said with a deep sigh, "we certainly learned a lot of nice words."

"Are you all through?" Bill wanted to know.

Shep turned another page. "Hell no!" he exclaimed, "we've just come to the practical exercises. Now that you've learned all the words, children, we shall take up a few simple exercises. Let's see, *I have a book* . . . well, that's not so good. *She has the scratchers* . . . that's better . . . *she has the scratchers.* Boy that there is important news. Now let's see here, *thou hast bought a nosegay* . . . can't use that. *Gustavus Adolphus was killed at the battle of Lutzen* . . . dear ol' Gus. *You are invited to the ball* . . . that's ever so nice, isn't it? Now here is something choice in the reflective verbs. *Having joined in the conversation he revived it by felicitous sallies* . . . how's 'at for a practical exercise. Here's something swell in a umpersonal verb. *Must mortals be happy only in dreams* . . . I don't believe a word of it."

"Can't anything be done about this?" Nikki demanded.

"Take the book away from him," Cary told Bill.

"Oh, que felicidada!" Shep proceeded in Portuguese, *"you see me deeply afflicted.* Now here we come to the conversations. *Show him into the little drawing-room* . . . hey, hey there. Now here we have something select!

"B. Allow me to retire, Madam.

"A. You want to leave me already?

"B. Deign to believe that I am very sorry that I cannot stay any longer with you.

"A. I equally regret that your visit has to be so short.

Polite chap, your Portygee," Shep observed.

"Now we've got to find something we can use. *Look and see if my ear-rings are properly fastened* . . . no, that won't do. *Put on my shawl, but don't let it drag on the ground* . . . that's hardly what we're after. *Are not my moustaches too long* . . . what do you think about that as a piece of polite conversation? *Do you wish me to give you a friction*

and a touch of the curling irons, sir? . . . a
great lad for barbers, your Portygee. . . ."

"It is unnecessary. My hair curls naturally."

"And boot blacks," Lennox noted.

"Now we are at the perfumes," Shep went
on. "A gentleman enters and says, *'Give me
some cold cream.' 'We have white and pink,
sir. Which do you prefer?' 'White. Put
up two pots. I also want almond paste for the
hands, toilet vinegar and rice powder.'* Your
Portygee is a kind of dandy," Shep said.

"Well," said Shep, "I'm torn between two
common phrases here: *'I can refuse you nothing,'* and *'It is a very sad affair.'* Now, which
do you think is the more useful?"

They all seemed to favor "It is a very sad
affair," so Shep began to repeat *Isso e' muito
triste.*

"Still," he said, "here is a good one. *'Give
me my stockings, my garters and my wrapper.'* "

"You better get set on one," Bill advised
him.

"I have a hollow tooth," Shep said. *"I have
a hollow tooth, and your little daughter, Clau-
dine, how is she? Fair Marchioness, your
beautiful eyes make me die of love. Waiter,
can we have a private room? The wind sits on
this side. Thank God we have got out of that*

dismal hole. Do you like emotional excursions? At last we are on board. Drink a drop of gin. Now there is a sensible piece of advice. *I want a bolster and two pillows. Have you any vapour baths and douches? Give me a night light. . . ."*

Lennox was looking out of the window. Suddenly he exclaimed and pointed.

"That's the Tagus."

They all looked out to see flat green countryside with a great green bosom of water in it like a mirage.

"Just five hundred years behind the times," said Lennox. "Look at those oxen pulling that Arab plow—that's wood—that plow."

"What they should have," said Shep, "is something in unbreakable glass with an outboard motor."

"—and plays twelve records without stopping."

"—and has a cigar lighter."

"—and tzippers front and back."

"—and you can entertain your Aunt with."

"—or rub it in your hair."

"You see those fishing boats coming up the river? Those are the real Portuguese. You'll not see anything like the cut of those boats anywhere else. Best sailors in the world, the Portuguese."

Shep said, "Well, we must be getting into the hoopskirts of the city."

"You mean the inshoots?" said Bill.

"I mean the upshots."

"Oh, I see, the excerpts—"

"Well, anyway we're in the rhubarbs—"

"What you must see first-off," said Lennox, "is the Portuguese fleet."

"Is it any relation to the Swiss army?" Shep inquired.

"It would be about a Mexican stand-off," said Lennox. "The Portuguese fleet is lying in the harbor of Lisbon and certainly looks a fleet. The on'y trouble is the ships can't run. Old English cruisers built in eighty-seven—haven't fired a boiler in years."

"Why not?"

"The Portuguese haven't money enough to support 'em."

"Now that's my idea of a career," said Shep, "enlisting in the Portuguese navy. Have they got admirals and things?"

"Wait till you see one," said Lennox. "He's the most beautiful thing going—well, here we go into the tunnel."

"Everybody'd better drink their beer," Shep advised, "because you know how it is when it comes out of tunnels."

"How far is it to Lisbon?" Nikki wanted to know.

"The other end of the tunnel," Lennox told her.

"You mean we're coming right into it."

"That's right," Lennox said.

They were actually coming into Lisbon! Nikki could scarcely believe it. Lisbon! Lisbon, Portugal! Of all places!

"You mean we're right there!"

"That's right," Lennox repeated, laconically.

They were in the great, gloomy, glassed-in station at Lisbon. They all left the compartment and the porters came in and put their bags out of the window onto the station platform.

"What about taxis or something," Shep said.

"It's only just upstairs," Lennox said, "the porter'll carry 'em right up for you."

They all walked to the gates where men in uniforms and rifles demanded their tickets. Nikki couldn't find hers, of course, but it developed that Shep had it. Shep said it was a forgery, but finally produced it.

They were all surprised when two men came up and spoke to Cary. Mr. Lockwood? Yes. The three of them fell behind the others—talking earnestly.

"Can you beat that?" Shep said to Nikki, "he's got secret agents all over the world."

It was true what Lennox had said, you just

walked upstairs and there you were in the lobby of the Aveniaa Palace Hotel. And very nice, too. The clerk spoke French, assured them of their reservations, and directed them to the lift. They found they had a cluster of rooms on the fifth floor overlooking the Avenida da Liberdade.

Shep and Bill had a room together. The Washout was alone, so was Cary and so was Nikki. Cary disappeared into his room still talking earnestly to the two men. Shep begged Nikki to go down and find the bar with him.

"No, Shep," she said firmly. "I'm going to take a bath and change first."

"Well, but one drink—"

"You run along and take a bath, too, and *then* we'll find the bar."

She shut the door softly against his plaints.

"Don't be too long, Nikki," he pleaded.

Bill was already in the tub when Shep came in. "By gosh, Shep," he said, "the Portuguese hot water is the hottest hot water I ever fell into."

"Let's see how the Portuguese bathrooms are for singing," said Shep as he took off his clothes and got ready to shave.

"Here we go," said Bill, and began:

> *"The bells of hell go ting-a-ling-a-ling*
> *For you, but not for me . . ."*

Single Lady

"Pretty damn good," said Shep as they sang along together. "I wish to hell we had Cary in here to sing baritone. Boy, the harmony sure drips from his mouth like honey from the comb . . . and get the hell out of that tub—and rinse it out—you hopeless Hungarian—and let a gentleman get ready for a large evening. Hell, we're losing out on a lot of drinking, everybody relaxing like this." Shep's tic was working again.

When Shep was dressed, he went and pounded on Nikki's door. She wasn't ready yet—but she was dressed, so she let him in. Bill came in, too, while she brushed her hair and made up her mouth.

"You certainly are a swell-looking gal," Shep said admiringly, as he sat on the bed watching her.

"You used to not think that," Nikki reminded him.

"That was before I appreciated all your sterling qualities."

"So now you think I'm nice."

"Yes, sweet lamb, I think you're everything nice. You're the nicest thing going."

"That's very, very sweet of you, Shepard." she said bowing to him in the mirror.

"But if you don't hurry up, I might change my mind on account of the bar might close or something."

"It couldn't close before seven," Nikki said.

"Well, you can ever tell about these furrin countries. Anything is liable to happen."

When Nikki's mouth was all ready they left her room together.

The Washout was waiting for them in the hall. They banged on Cary's door and he said that he would be down in a minute.

Shep's eye caught the sign the moment the lift stopped at the lobby. "American Bar."

He opened the door and they went down two steps in the barroom. It was clean and shining and empty.

A tall, dark, almost handsome bartender in a crisp white coat was polishing a glass behind the bar. The four of them climbed onto stools.

"Do you speak English?" Shep demanded.

"Yes," he said, "a few."

"What's your name?" Shep said. "It's very important to know your name and then we'll get on like anything."

"I give you my card."

The card read:

BENJAMIN LOPEZ

BARMAN

They all studied the card with great interest. Shep said he couldn't make up his mind to call him Bennie or Benjy.

"But I like Ben-ja-min!" Nikki said. "That's a powerful name—if you kind of hold onto the Ben."

"Allow me to introduce Benjamin Lopez," Shep said to Nikki. "Senhor Lopez, I want you to know Senhorita Nikki—the Queen of the Rum Runners, otherwise known as Little Goody Two Shoes. She desires a half bottle of Cordon Rouge or Dry Monopole! Veuve Cliquot yellow label? Whatever you have on the ice. And three dry Martinis for the men."

As Benjamin said he was enchanted and set to work behind the bar, Shep proceeded to introduce the others.

"This, Benjamin," said Shep pointing to Bill, "is Bronko Bill Talbot from Big Forks, Montana, variously known as Bill the Bombardier, or Bill the Busman. Sometimes referred to as the Diving Horse, The People's Choice, The Barefoot Burglar, Eric, or Little by Little, and," he said, leaning over confidentially, "sometimes suspected of being the Left-Handed Lover of Mrs. Gertrude Green. Sexually precocious at the age of twenty-seven. Known to have relations with petty thieves, counterfeiters, narcotic addicts, swindlers, confidence men, gunmen's molls, boll weevils and plumber's helpers. In short, a fellow to be reckoned with. Accord him some of your best service, Benjamin."

Benjamin acknowledged the introduction with a deep bow and placed the drinks on the bar. Shep tried the cocktail while Benjamin looked anxiously on.

"Dry enough for you?"

"Fine," Shep said, "you make a fine Martini, Benjamin. Oh, I forgot to introduce our young friend," he said, turning to the Washout. "This, Benjamin, is Fwancis, once described as Fer de Lance, The Deadly Nightshade, The Scarf Dance or Mendelssohn's Spring Song. . . ."

Francis whirled on his stool, wild with anger, "Tsay," he said in a toneless chilling voice, "go easy."

Shep turned and looked into a pair of yellow eyes, snapping and flickering with pale cold light.

"Well for gosh sakes," Shep said. "This is Shep speaking, old boy. This is your Uncle Shepard."

"I know. Go easy."

Shep got off his stool, took Francis by the shoulders and shook him gently. "Listen, old son," he said reproachfully, "this is old Shep."

The malignant glint died out in Francis' eyes.

"Tsorry," he said softly and turned away.

Shep resumed his place at the bar. "Dangerous if disturbed," he explained to Benja-

247

min. Benjamin pulled down the corners of his mouth as if he understood. For the first time Shep saw how far Francis had gone. Why, Francis was as brittle as Shep himself. It wouldn't do to cross him again.

"How is the life down here anyway?" Shep inquired.

"Pass along those potato chips," Bill commanded Shep sternly.

Benjamin turned and began to strop his left arm with his right hand as if he were sharpening a razor.

"Clean shave, eh?" Shep said.

"Nothing in it," said the barman, pulling down the corners of his mouth again. "Poor country. No money. Can't do no business."

"No business, eh?" Shep encouraged him.

"Two and half hours work a day," Benjamin said, pouring the drinks. "Nine-thirty to ten-thirty in the morning—a few early customers—one, two maybe—and eight-thirty to nine-thirty at night—maybe t'ree, four customers—otherwise dead."

"I guess we're a big help to Portugal," Shep said. "Are you Portuguese, Benjamin?"

"Spanish," he said, looking around.

"So it's kind of quiet down here," Shep resumed.

"They woke up at twelve o'clock," Benjamin said. "They go to cafe an' talkin' an'

talkin' an' talkin". H'in the afternoon they
went to a football game an' talkin' an' talkin'
an' shoutin'."

"Football?" said Bill.

"Sure, you know English football—kick—
kick the football."

"Oh, soccer," said Bill, disappointed.

"Sure, they gone crazy on football."

"I thought they had bull-fights or something," Shep said.

"Bull-fights!" snorted Benjamin. "What
does it take to makin' a bull-fight? Heat, sun
and flies! An' w'en you t'ink they havin' their
bull-fights in Lisbon? At night!"

"I never heard of a bull-fight at night," Shep
said.

"On account football in the h'afternoon,"
said Benjamin.

"What time at night?"

"Ten to twelve."

"What do they do after?"

"H'after! Hangin' about! Talkin'!"

"Where do they go?"

"The streets. Maxime's maybe. The Bris-
tol. But," said Benjamin, "nothing in it!"
The room, apart from the four Americans at
the bar, was empty, and Benjamin was warming to his subject.

"You gone to Maxime's. You see one, two,
t'ree maybe seven peoples at a table. What

do you see? Here one glass water, next one glass beer, here one glass water, there one cup coffee for the rest—nothing in it!"

"Doesn't sound like high-powered drinking to me," Shep observed. "How long do they stay?"

"Four, five, six h'o'clock in the morning."

"Just talkin'?"

"Talkin' an' talkin'."

"On one glass of beer and a cup of coffee?"

"For seven peoples. But if you go to Maxime's you think something doing. They talkin' like this." Benjamin began to gesticulate wildly, waving his arms, shaking his fist under somebody's nose, glaring ferociously, shaking his head.

They all began to laugh. Nikki clapped her hands. "Benjamin, you're lovely. You should give up your career and go on the stage."

"Nothing in it," Benjamin pursued, "nothing in it. You think they goin' be a fight. Nothing in it."

"Don't they ever fight?"

"Never!" said Benjamin emphatically. "W'en you see them shoutin' at each other on the street—don' stand aroun' an' wait for a fight. You won't see one. They just talkin' an' talkin'."

"Didn't you ever see a fight in Lisbon?" Shep asked.

"Not one. At firs' I think *everybody* goin' fight. Now I am sure *nobody* goin' fight."

"How long've you been here?"

"Nine months."

"Why are you here, Benjamin?"

"By mistake. So soon I finish my engagement—I go."

"Well, don't go before we do," Shep said.

By now they had drunk six Martinis apiece and Nikki was starting her second pint of champagne.

"What are we going to use for money down here?" Bill asked Shep.

"Well, we can charge the drinks to our rooms and go to the bank in the morning."

"Ho, ho, ho!" Benjamin said. "You go to the bank! Ho, ho, ho!"

"Yes?"

"You gone to the bank," Benjamin repeated, "you gone to the bank and you givin' you check to the window. Pretty soon he comin' back an' he says Meestaire so-and-so is not here. Back in two t'ree minoots.

"You standin' with you elbow like this an' you smokin' one, two, t'ree, four, fi', seex, seven, eight, nine, ten cigarette. Pretty soon you handin' in you check once more. Meestaire

251

this-and-so here but Meestaire somebody else
not 'ere now.

"You smokin' ten, twenty cigarettes and
pretty soon you handin' in you check and the
window is close. Is lunch time—twelve o'clock.
So you goin' to lunch and you comin' back to
the bank and you waitin' like this an' nobody
come. You smokin' ten, twenty, t'irty, forty
cigarette. Is t'ree o'clock. Is four o'clock.
Meestaire so-and-so is 'ere. You handin' in
you check. You gettin' you change. Is finish.
The day is finish too. I don' think you goin'
to the bank."

"No," said Shep. "I think I'll cash a check
with the porter."

"You won't gettin' so much," Benjamin
warned him.

"What's a couple of escudos either way."

Shep went off and came back with two thousand escudos. "It's only money," he said,
apologizing for the roll of chiffon in his hand.

"Now," he said, "you'll have to let me do all
the spending on account of you don't know
how much an escudo is and besides you can't
speak the language."

"Neither can you," Nikki said.

"That's right," said Shep, "but my mother
always said I had the nicest hair-line. We'll
all have another drink, Benjamin."

"Do you know," Shep continued, "I like

Benjamin's Portuguese dinner-party better than his visit to the bank. Which do you like the best?"

"I like the dinner party better," Nikki agreed, "on account of it has more action."

"I wonder if he would do it again for us?" Shep inquired.

"I tell you what," Nikki said, "you give your celebrated imitation of the man from Marseilles boarding a street-car and maybe he will do it again."

"Have you ever been in Marseilles, Benjamin?" Shep asked.

"Shoo!" said Benjamin.

"Well, you know what they are like—those provencals? What importance they give to everything?"

"Shoo!"

"Well," said Nikki, "Mr. Lambert is going to give an imitation of a man in Marseilles boarding a street car if you will do the Portuguese dinner-party for us again."

Benjamin agreed readily.

Shep got down off his stool and told them which way the car was coming and then went to an imaginary curb and played out the scene. Shep was tight by now and he gave a fine show. Benjamin laughed so hard during the performance that he couldn't shake the cocktail shaker. When Shep finally boarded the street car and came to his place at the bar, Benjamin said he should be an actor, too.

"Now give us the seven Portuguese with three drinks between them," Nikki commanded.

Benjamin had just begun when Lennox came in through the street door and Cary entered from the hotel side. The four were screaming with laughter, but at the sight of the newcomers Benjamin halted instantly.

"You just missed a fine show," Shep told them. "What did you do with your secret agents? Come and have a drink," Shep presented them to Benjamin with some formality.

"This here," said Shep, indicating Lennox, "is the sole surviving member of the Royal Welch Fusiliers, and this," nodding at Cary, "is the Seattle Kid, of Fire Station No. 5."

Benjamin thanked Shep for making their acquaintance known to him.

"He's been telling us all about the Portuguese," Shep said.

"He must be a Spaniard," Lennox said promptly.

"He says the Portuguese make a lot of hostile passes but they never go into action."

"He's right."

"He says they've gone crazy on football and have bull-fights at night. I wonder if there's

a bull-fight tonight. Is there a bull-fight tonight, Benjamin?"

"Not tonight. Tomorrow night. But," he
added, "nothing in it."

"How so?"

"They don't kill the bull down here. It's
forbidden by law," Lennox explained. "And
they wrap his horns and nobody gets hurt."

"An' the bull fighter's one 'undred years old
an' bald headed and run for the trenches w'en
the bull come," Benjamin said.

"The only thing about a Portuguese bull
fight," Lennox said, "is the parade at the beginning. You'll see some good riding."

"Well, what in the hell is a fellow to do in
Lisbon?"

Lennox shrugged his shoulders. "Go to
a cinema."

"Ten years old," Benjamin said.

"We don't go to cinemas," Shep and Nikki explained.

"Well, there's an amusement park up the
street. Port Mayer."

Nobody said anything.

"You'd like to see what a bunch of Porty-
gees look like, wouldn't you?"

"That wouldn't be for our own improvement, would it?" Shep inquired. "We've tried
improving ourselves and it doesn't work."

"No. It won't improve you any. I'll guarantee that."

They had some more drinks and then went upstairs for dinner in the huge, ornate dining room of the Avenida Palace.

During dinner Nikki discovered how exhausted she was. Shep was all for going out and finding out how drinking conditions were in Lisbon. But Nikki knew they would never get home and so she begged off. If Nikki wasn't going out, Bill said, he wasn't going either. Tomorrow night they would all go.

Shep would have been annoyed if he hadn't discovered through Francis that Cary was setting out early in the morning by motor car on some kind of exploratory expedition along the coast. He thought it would be a good joke on Cary for everybody to get up early and go along with him.

They took Nikki to her room.

"Kin I come in and help you undress," Shep pleaded at the door.

"No thank you, Shepard."

"Aw, please."

"No," said Nikki firmly.

"Not if Bill comes along, too?"

"No."

"Not even scrub your back?"

"No, Shep. But thanks for thinking about

me.   Good night." She closed the door gently
against them.

"Can you imagine that ungrateful old trol-
lope?" Shep demanded of Bill as they went
down the hall.

CHAPTER IX

AT six-thirty Cary was in the little breakfast room off the main dining room and overlooking the Avenida da Liberdade, having rolls and coffee, when Shep led in the others.

Cary looked up in a kind of dismay. "Hello," he said.

"Hello yourself. Do you mind if we sit down?"

"Help yourself."

"What time do we take off?" Shep wanted to know.

"You coming with me?"

"Ra-ther-r," Shep said. "The whole smear of us. What did you think we was agoing to do?"

"It will be a pretty long day," Cary said, looking at them doubtfully.

"The longer they are the harder they fall," Shep said.

"And I'd like some coffee," said Nikki, "if anybody should ride up on a pair of spanking chestnuts and ask you."

"Or pop up out of a bed of daisies," Shep

258

said, "or peek out of a gopher hole or anything, and say you're looking dandy this morning. How do you feel?"

"Just dandy," Nikki said.

"That's a very fruity outfit you have there," he observed.

Nikki was looking exquisitely fresh in a smart sports suit of white linen, white and gleaming as beach sand, patterned in a Fruit d'Afrique design, with pineapples and citrons and ships and tropical trees in orange and brown. She had on an extraordinarily large straw hat with a floppy brim and she was wearing white high-heeled sandals.

They all ordered coffee and rolls and wigged Cary, who was getting impatient.

"Where are we going today, Captain?" Shep said.

"Nowhere," Cary said, "unless we get started."

"Don't get your drawers in an uproar," Shep advised him. "They's plenty of time down here. Why, they tell me they've got more time down here in Portugal than anywheres else in the world, practically."

"Well, if you're all going, I've got to go down and arrange about it."

"Go ahead," Shep said, "go ahead and conclude all the arrangements necessary for the transportation of the Delegation."

Single Lady

Cary left them and Shep said, "You have to fix that fellow every once in a while. He gets too precious."

When they went downstairs Cary was waiting for them out on the sidewalk. A black seven-passenger touring car was standing at the curb in the little square driveway at the entrance to the hotel. It was a Steyr, an Austrian car, with a battleship prow.

Cary presented a thin, dark, tall man to Nikki first. "Joseph Travassos," he said.

Travassos had square wide shoulders and was remarkably flat for a man of fifty or so. He carried himself like a soldier only he had a peculiar shuffling, sliding way of moving, not bobbing up and down, but keeping his head on the same level, like a professional tango dancer. He had thick dark eyebrows and a very dark skin. His eyes were quick, black and direct. Shep liked him.

Travassos introduced his friend, Senhor Calderon, a short and polite little Portuguese, as the second largest exporter of sardines in Lisbon. He begged the privilege to be allowed to have Sr. Calderon accompany them as Sr. Calderon had packing plants along the coast which he wanted to visit and he would be glad to show them whatever they wanted to see. Sr. Calderon, a particular friend, did not speak English, but he understands, Travassos said.

"'E h'understand h'everything," Travassos said, "sympathetique."

Cary had no objection to the presence of Sr. Calderon. Shep was delighted to find that it embarrassed Cary a little to have to present the Delegation to the two Portuguese.

The Washout, because he had a very thin backside, sat up in front with Sr. Calderon and the driver. It wasn't likely that any earnest conversation would spring up in the front seat, as the driver spoke no English. Sr. Calderon only 'understood' and The Washout was pleasantly dizzy with whatever it was he was addicted to.

Travassos and Cary and Nikki sat together in the back seat and Bill and Shep adorned the jump seats.

Shep, with his usual precaution, had brought along a bottle of brandy. Travassos told him it wasn't necessary. You could stop anywhere for a drink. Shep put the bottle on the floor of the car where it rolled and bumped around during the whole day.

"This is a powerful car," Shep said as they drew out into the early morning traffic along the Avenue of Liberty.

Travassos said the Steyr people used to make fine firearms during the war, but on account of the peace treaty had to stop, so now they were making fine motor cars.

Cary had evidently worked out his route with Travassos the night before. The driver had his instructions and drove as if he knew exactly where he was headed.

They passed a tall statue in the middle of a circle.

"The poet Camoëns," said Travassos, "the most scientific man we ever had in Portugal. 'E contribute the greatest service to his country."

"What did he do?" Shep inquired politely.

"'E modificate h'our langidge," said Travassos.

There was little traffic on the cobbled streets at this hour. A few fish girls with bare feet and shallow baskets of fish on their heads passed by, calling their wares.

The car made its way rapidly through the city and pulled up at the ferry slip at the water front.

Travassos waved pleasantly at the old English cruisers lying low in the water. "Part of h'our tin can fleet," he said.

Shep said he'd like to be an admiral of that fleet.

"Fifty-two years old," Travassos said. "They couldn't fight nor they couldn't run away."

Shep noticed a string of pennants run up from the flagship.

"What's the idea?" he wanted to know. "Acute distress or something?"

"Holiday," said Travassos. "As we can't get nothink else down here we shall have holidays enough so we giving ourselves holidays."

Shep said that he'd never heard of a more sensible notion. Give yourself a holiday. Give yourself a flock of holidays. No harm in a holiday.

They found they had to wait at the ferry slip. There were a lot of leather-faced women and little boys sleeping around on sacks in the morning sunshine waiting for the boat. Shep and Bill and Cary got out of the car, followed by the others.

"This is a hell of a place for old women," Shep announced. "I never seen so many, so many old women."

"Don't talk like that," Bill reproved him gently, "they might be somebody's mother."

"That's right, they might be somebody's mother."

With his customary cunning Shep located a wine shop just back of a warehouse and dragged Bill in. They came out beaming when they heard the boat whistle; beaming all over the place.

From the ferry, drawing away from the ship, they could see the great gray city of Lisbon, lying serene and beautiful in the morn-

ing sun. It was magnificent. They had all
got out of the car and were standing on the
deck of the ferry, looking back at the receding
city. Lisbon . . . Lisboa . . .Lisbonne old
as hell, tragic as hell; poor, proud, sunken
Lisbon.

Shep was strangely moved. "Isn't that a
swell city. Look at that thing. Isn't it fantastic? Isn't that the most fantastic thing you
ever saw?"

The city of Lisbon from the harbor looked
like a buff and gray mirage of roofs; terribly
beautiful, terribly unreal.

Nikki peered at it through her glasses and
shivered.

"They had a terrible earthquake here once,"
Cary said. "Shook the whole city down. Sixty
thousand people killed in six minutes."

"Fantastic," Shep said.

"Most of them were in church."

"That's what you get for going to church,"
Shep said. "That ought to teach people to
stay out of churches. Saloons is the place for
people."

"There was a long marble quay running out
here into the harbor," Cary went on, "and
thousands of people ran out on the quay.
They couldn't go to the hills because the hills
had split open and fire was pouring out of the
cracks; fire, and sulphur smoke."

They all looked at the hills back of the city.

"So they all crowded down onto the quay. Then the water ran out of the harbor and came rushing back in a tidal wave sixty feet high. Swept the quay clean."

"The poor Portugeezers," said Shep.

"Then the bottom of the bay cracked open and the quay fell in and all the ships in the harbor. And none of them ever came up, not a mast or stick or a spar or anything."

"Who ever heard of such a thing," Shep said. "When did all this happen?"

"About a 'undred fifty years ago," Travassos said.

"The Portuguese have a theory that nature requires a hundred years to produce an earthquake on a grand scale," Cary said. "Isn't that right?"

Travassos said yes, the people lived in a dread of the *terremoto*.

"This is the most sensitive earthquake sector in the world," Cary said.

"Tell us more about the tidal wave, Mister Lockwood," Shep said. "Tell us some of your speriences."

"Well, the tidal wave swept clear past the city and then poured back into the harbor," Cary said obligingly, "the backwash carried all sorts of things on its surface."

"What kind of things?" Shep demanded.

"Oh things from the yards and houses and streets and shops of the city; chairs and cradles and bedsteads and broken doors and fences and mattresses. . . ."

". . . and cushions and tables and brooms and ironing boards and tea cozies. . . ." Shep chimed in.

". . . and flocks of geese and pigs and cows and sheep . . ." Bill said brightly. The assortment of debris on the backwash of the tidal wave fired their imaginations happily.

". . . and bed-springs and clothes pins and spare tires and toupees and false teeth and hot water bottles. . . ." Shep suggested, "and hunting seats . . . and that old cherry highboy your Aunt Lucy never liked. . . ."

"Do tell us more about the earthquake, Mister Lockwood," Bill said. "This is fine hearing about the earthquake." Bill and Shep were starting to get ribald. "You're so informative."

Cary eyed them suspiciously.

"Are you two tight already?" Cary demanded.

"Tight!" Shep demanded with astonished innocence. And then drawing himself up with great dignity, he said, "You better look out who you're calling tight."

"That's right," Bill said, "you'd better look out. Who are you anyway? You and your

earthquakes. Who cares about your old
earthquakes. You think just because you can
tell about earthquakes you're all shakes of a
fellow. You probably read it out of a book.
I bet lots of other people can tell about earthquakes, too. Better earthquakes than yours.
Better earthquakes than you ever thought of
or your father either. Shep," said Bill, "this
one and his earthquake, what's he trying to do
anyway? Did we ask to hear about any earthquakes? Did we? Did we, or did we?"

"I believe they're both tight," Cary said.

With supreme dignity Shep linked his arm
in Bill's, drew himself up to his full stature,
turned about and stalked off to the far end
of the vessel. The two thus drawn apart from
the others conversed earnestly in hushed tones.
The two Portuguese viewed the proceedings
with some alarm.

Presently Bill alone approached the rail
where Cary stood with the others. He bowed
stiffly and cleared his throat.

"My friend has been affronted," he announced. "My friend has been affronted and
demands satisfaction."

Cary eyed him sternly.

"Ask your friend what kind of satisfaction
he wants."

Bill bowed stiffly. "I will go and tell my
friend," he saluted and turned on his heel.

Single Lady

He came back after an earnest consultation with Shep.

"I have spoken with my friend," he said. "I have spoken with my friend and my friend desires more information. What kind of satisfaction you got?"

"Three kinds of satisfaction," Cary said, "strawberry, chocolate and vanilla. What kind you like?"

Bill bowed. "I will tell my friend," he said and returned to the afterpart of the ship where his insulted friend stood in wounded solitary pride.

When Bill returned again after the third conference he uttered only one word, and that in a kind of treble peep-peep voice. All he said was "Pineapple," and a delicate affair of honor was settled.

The Portuguese looked gravely perplexed at these strange formalities, but Nikki gave them a bright smile and being of a sensitive and sympathetic people, they took it that everything was all right.

The ferry pulled in, touched at the other side of the harbor and they all piled in the big Steyr. The driver slipped through the streets of Almada and in a minute they were out on a wide white road racing through the country. The sunshine was clear and golden and the air was scented and spicy. Shep suddenly became aware of the clear beauty of his surroundings.

"My, my," he said, "but isn't this fine. Did you ever smell such air, Nikki?"

"Not at these prices," Nikki said.

"How about you, Bill, ol' boy, ol' boy?"

"Not in these pants," Bill said.

They were passing through the loveliest countryside Shep had ever seen.

It came to Shep, flying along in the car, that he was in an enchanted land; a land of green meadows, wooded hillsides, winding streams, sweet smelling heaths and soft sea breezes.

"My goodness me!" he exclaimed joyfully, "but isn't this fine. Who ever heard of such a place? Why didn't someone ever think of this before?"

Shep was a thousand miles away from the close atmosphere of the Paris bars. He was out in the open air, filled with sweet wine and speeding through gorgeous country. He exclaimed constantly at everything he saw, like a child on a holiday.

At this time of the year the embankments were spangled in honeysuckle and wild roses and starred with azaleas, camelias and rhododendrons. The moors were carpeted with brilliant yellow cistus and the orchards were heavy with ripening fruit. Along the roadside you could identify box hedges, lady slippers, wandering jews, and Monte Cristoes.

"I never seen so many posies," Shep said.

Shep's wild enthusiasm for every new thing communicated itself quickly to the two Portuguese. They had deep feeling for their native land and they were happy to explain things to him. Travassos, from the back seat, told Shep about the yellow moss on the great rock they passed. And old lady, believing that it contained hidden treasure had pelted it with eggs in order to break it open. She did not succeed, but the yolks left a golden imprint.

The legend appealed enormously to Shep.

"So the old hussy tried to break the rock open with eggs, did she?" he exclaimed. "What an idea! What an idea!"

Shep was enchanted with Travassos. He engaged him in a spirited conversation and discovered to his astonishment that the slender, dark Portuguese had once been a lightweight prize fighter and that he had fought Joe Gans at Coney Island. The man, black-haired and black-eyed, and dark-skinned, was not young, but he might be thirty-eight or fifty-four. It was from the battered lips of the ex-lightweight that the quaint little legends of old Portugal fell along the way. He explained that to the Portuguese fisher girls the fuchias were "tears," the anemones were "little kisses" and the down-hanging creepers were "weepers." The creepers were sentenced always to climb downwards because one of them had once grown so fast that God thought it wanted to reach Heaven.

Shep applauded everything Travassos had to say. Calderon encouraged by his enthusiasm interjected little cues from time to time.

The car was bowling down the long white road to Cezimbra, a Portuguese fishing village on the coast.

"You won't seeing no fishing," Travassos had warned them, "unless you getting up at four-thirty in the morning. Besides you must come back in August for the fishing. Is better in the fall."

"But we'll see the fishing girls," Shep said.

"Sure you see the fish girls."

"I'd druther see fish girls than fish," Shep said.

They passed small farmhouses of gray granite standing by cattle-yards and sheds and orange and lemon trees and patches of garden. Mighty sand dunes rose up around a lagoon where the bold headlands ran out into the sea. On their left the hills were covered with pines and cypresses.

"We got more variety of trees in Portugal than any country in the world," Travassos told them.

"What kind of trees you got?" Shep immediately inquired.

"We got cork trees, we got more cork trees than anybody; we got limes and magnolias, junipers, maples and monkey puzzles. . . ."

"Monkey puzzles!" Shep exclaimed. "I wonder if my little Josie would like one."

Nikki wanted to know the name of the tree with the great flowering of pink blossoms.

"Judas Tree," Travassos said, "the very special glory of Portugal h'in the springtime."

"The Judas Tree," Nikki repeated. "The Judas Tree. Do you mean the tree that Mr. Iscariot hanged himself on?"

"So it is said."

"It's a very beautiful tree to hang yourself on."

"That's the kind of a tree for me," Shep said enthusiastically, "only I should like it to be in blossom, like now."

The big Steyr pulled around a huge wooden-wheeled cork laden bullock cart and entered a steep little thoroughfare winding down through the village of Cezimbra to the seashore. The name of the street was the Rue Alecrim. Shep asked Travassos what it meant, if any, and Travassos said "Rosemary Street."

Shep was enchanted with Travassos. "He whips out so many nice words," Shep said, "just ask him anything."

And now Shep said that his idea of a place

to live would be a net-mender's cottage on Rosemary Street in the village of Cezimbra on the coast of Portugal. "Jesus," he said, "what a euphonious layout. How's the climate," Shep asked Travassos, "the year around?"

"Fine," said the Portuguese, "no extremes. Not too hot, not too cold."

"For God's sake," said Shep, "make you laugh and play."

The car pulled up on the cobbled street just at the edge of the beach. A great assortment of Portuguese were collected along the sand. They all got out and mingled in the crowd.

Shep came to a full stop before a fisher girl standing just by the edge of the water, washing a fish. Her tucked-up skirt gave him a glimpse of her bare legs, strong and brown and gracefully flexed. Her full rich bosom was lashed tight and high in thin cambric. Her throat was bare; her hair bound in an orange-colored handkerchief. She was tall and dark and lithe and alive with the full-blooded vitality of the Portuguese peasantry.

"Bill," said Shep reverently, "do you see what I see?"

"I hope to kiss a pig," Bill said, "or smoke a rubber herring."

"That there is practically a museum piece in my estimation."

The two stood in silent admiration of the creature. "She can come Tooseday," Bill said.

Travassos came up behind them.

"You could trying all your life and you couldn't do nothing with her."

"Ask her how old she is."

Travassos spoke to her politely in Portuguese. She replied over her shoulder without looking.

"Fifteen," he said.

"Is she married?"

"She says she is unpromised."

"What's her name?"

Travassos persuaded her fluently to tell her name, but she refused. A little group gathered about them. A small boy volunteered the information. "Nina Candida."

"Nina Candida, fifteen and unpromised," Shep said. "How's 'at for a portrait in a line? Where's Nikki?"

Nikki had found it hard going in the sand in her high heels, so she went back to the car and took off her shoes and skinned off her stockings. She came back and wandered barefoot in the sand. The five of them, Bill, Shep, Nikki, Francis and Joseph, wandered aimlessly about in the sunshine among the fisher-folk, looking at the fish spread out on the plain wooden boards before the fishermen. Cary was

274

back in the village somewhere with Calderon.

Shep noticed that all of the little green and gold painted fishing boats had little designs and names on the prows. He got Travassos to read them for him.

"*Flor do Cezimbra,*" he read promptly, "The Flower of Cezimbra."

"Isn't that nice, Nikki?" Shep said. "Damn romantic these Portuguese. How'd you like to go fishing in the Flower of Cezimbra?"

Nikki thought it would be cute.

"Most of the fishermens naming their boats after their sweethearts," Travassos said. They read the names *Mariana* and *Aurora* and *Lucinda.*

"That one saying 'We leave it to the Gods.' "

"Bright idea," Shep said. "And what's that saying?"

Travassos was puzzled. "That sa-ays, 'She come, but she didn't come.' "

"How pale the princess looks tonight," Shep said understandingly. "I wish I could buy a dead fish, but I don't know what I'd do with it."

"You could feed it to a seal," Bill offered, "if you could find a seal, or you could th'ow it."

"Tain't polite," Shep said, "to be th'owin' dead fish about."

Cary and Calderon were in the car when they went back.

"Find the diamonds?" Shep inquired casually.

"No," said Cary shortly.

"Too bad. We saw a girl with legs like Nikki's, only brown. Her name was Nina Candida. She's fifteen and unpromised."

The driver turned the car around and they drove up through Rosemary Street and out of the village, the little village with the green window boxes of red geraniums. Nikki borrowed a handkerchief from Shep to whip the sand off her toes. She returned it to his breast-pocket and struggled into her stockings and shoes.

"You know," said Shep, "I've only just got this diamond thing all figgered out."

"That's interesting," Cary said.

"Now, here is the way Lambert, the old Sardou, has it. This fellow . . ."

"What fellow?"

"This chap that escaped from the ship with the diamonds got washed up on the beach here at Cezimbra."

"That's right," Cary agreed.

"Now, he is in a pretty bad repair on account of he has been knocked about a lot by dat ol' debbil ocean. In fac' he's just a piece

A First National and Vitaphone Production.   *The Last Flight—Movie of Single Lady.*

A CLIMAX TO THE MAD ESCAPADE OCCURS IN THE AMUSEMENT PARK.

of spindrift or something th'owed up by the sea."

Just a piece of driftwood, they all agreed.

"Now, who should come along but Nina Candida," Shep proceeded. "Who should come along but Nina Candida, the Flor do Cezimbra. Who should discover the poor diamond bestudded castaway but the flower of Cezimbra, the Posy of Portugal. She takes the poor man to her cottage . . . her mother is a net mender and she has no father to speak of . . . and there nurses him back to health and strength."

Shep asked Travassos if that part of it wasn't all right.

"Oh sure, they would taking care of 'im," said Travassos firmly, "if he was left astray on the beach. Sure they are very kind, the Portuguese people. They would taking care of 'im."

"You see," Shep returned to Cary, "you see."

Shep wanted to know what kind of a life Left Astray would have in a village of this kind. He said he wanted to kind of get the general background and atmosphere. What would he eat, for instance.

Well, Travassos said, for breakfast he would having a couple of sardines broiled, say, and a glass of red wine and a piece of bread.

How about lunch?

For dinner, Travassos said, he would having fish with onions, and bread . . . soaked with olive oil. For supper, the same as breakfast. "They eat anything comes out of the sea," he explained.

Of course, it wouldn't be like stopping at the Avenida Palace Hotel ("a very expensible place," Joseph observed). He would have to get used to a hard bed and getting up at four-thirty in the morning to go out for the fish. "Nine o'clock at night everything closed."

There was a little shop he could buy anything he needed: hats, shoes, brooms, cheese, candles, grapes, wine, bread.

Shep wanted to know if there was any excitement in a fishing village. Oh, sure, Joseph agreed affably. Fights. Peoples get dronk and fight. "You want to be very careful when you mixing it up here," Joseph said. "The knife," he added significantly. As for the social administrative structure of the village, well, "the beach is the school and the judge is everybody."

With these facts satisfactorily arranged in his mind, Shep proceeded with his fiction.

"Now," said Shep, "Left Astray has the diamonds and he thinks he ought to return them. His first intentions are honorable, mind you. He's a fine young chap of a purser or first officer or something. But the longer he hangs about Cezimbra, the more he begins to think about it. Powerful temptation to keep the diamonds, you know, powerful temptation. Sole survivor of ship and all that. Nobody knows he's alive. Been accounted missing. Practically a dead man. Hell, he *is* a dead man. A dead man with a million of diamonds. Why should he come back to life? Why give back the diamonds? Why, hell, this is a marvelous story," Shep exclaimed. "Are you all paying attention? Why this here is a masterpiece that's being unravelled in front of your big blue eyes."

Very deftly Shep began to dispose of the difficulties in connection with the plot and to paint in the details. Left Astray couldn't get out of Portugal anyhow, could he? He had no papers or anything. You couldn't get anywhere without papers. Not when there was a war on. Portugal was a belligerent, wasn't she? Sure she was. Everybody remembered the Portuguese troops in action.

Travassos and Calderon nodded and beamed.

Why, hell, the man with the diamonds was practically sealed away whether he liked it or not. He couldn't pass any frontier without papers, could he? He'd probably be searched and the stones confiscated. If he'd try to slip through the mountain passes into Spain with thirteen thousand carats of diamonds on him, the bandits would nab him; those assassins in the black fedoras.

Shep didn't need any help from anyone now. He was in full grip of the plot.

"So you see," he explained, "this fellow just decided to stick around Cezimbra until the war was over. And very nice, too. Grew a beard and fell in love with Nina, the Flor do Cezimbra, and cultivated a taste for fish. Became a fisherman himself. Hid the diamonds under a floor board in his cottage. Very mysterious character in village. Years pass.

"Now," said Shep, "now the war is over. Left Astray is free to go at last. Free to return the diamonds. But what the hell! He wants to keep the diamonds. Feels he's earned 'em by now. Besides he wants Nina. Powerful, powerful mental conflict. Pow'ful struggle. Decides to keep diamonds. Whew," said Shep. "I'm all tired out.

"But look," he went on, "look. He wants Nina to go away with him. Tells her about diamonds, shows her diamonds. Nina is very conscientious. Very conscientious and respectable fishing girl, Nina. Simple flannels of the poor and all that. Simple morals. Religious." Shep asked Travassos if Nina wouldn't be a religious girl.

Travassos stoutly affirmed that such would be the case. You couldn't making love to Nina if you trying one hundred years. The girl is in the window, the boy is in the street. If you sitting in the parlor with the girl, her mother sitting here, too, Nina must respect herself. A decent girl won't leave the house alone.

"You see," Shep said, "the only way Left Astray could have her would be to marry her." He asked Travassos if that wasn't right, and Travassos said, yes that was right.

"But Nina wouldn't have him if he kept property that didn't belong to him. So Left Astray had to choose between Nina and the diamonds. Powerful conflict, you see. Powerful conflict.

"Well, sir," Shep said, "you'd be surprised, but he takes the diamonds and clears off. Goes to Paris. Tries to forget Nina. Tries to forget Portugal and Cezimbra."

"I saw him myself," Nikki broke in.

"Who?"

"Left Astray."

"Where?"

"At the Claridge Bar, talking to himself."

Shep investigated the idea in his mind. "That's your man," he told Cary.

"And then what?" Bill wanted to know. "And then what?"

"Oh well," Shep said, "then comes the happy ending. Just before Cary catches him, he returns the jew-els, goes back to Nina, who has been waiting for him all this time. Light in the window and all that. And they get married and live happily ever after. On codfish."

"Now," said Shep, "if that isn't a high-powered plot, I never heard one." He bet if he'd sit down and write that up, putting in all the touches, he could practically sell it anywheres. As it was, since he had so much drinking to do, he was going to turn it over to Cary. Cary would get rolling rich with that plot. Torpedoed ship, missing diamonds, mysterious castaway, Portuguese fishing village, beautiful fisher girl, romance, separation, pursuit, return; it was practically the best story he'd ever heard. And all made up right out of his own head, too, by—What was a good resounding Portuguese oath? he inquired of Travassos. But in the presence of a lady, Travassos and Calderon, being polite gentlemen, only smiled and shrugged their shoulders.

Anyway, Shep said, there was a fine high-powered plot, and he hereby gave it to Cary. Hell, it was practically an epic.

Cary thanked him kindly and asked what was the title of it—Love Expectant or something?

Bill suggested "The Fisherman's Daughter," or "Duck Foot Sue."

"You're all trying to spoil something very beautiful," Shep complained. "How about stopping somewheres for a drink?"

CHAPTER X

TRAVASSOS said they were going to another village, a larger one up the coast, Setubal. Only he pronounced it Shtubal.

"How far is it?"

Joseph said it was half, three-quarters of an hour, and the others had their first example of the Portuguese sense of time and distance. It took three hours. Nobody minded much because the car went racing along the white ribbon of a road, tooting oxcarts and donkeys out of the way. Nikki held down the wind-blown brim of her floppy straw hat with both hands on either side of her face.

"The King of Spain has a siren on his car and goes like hell," Shep said. "Everybody gives him the right of way. We ought to put a siren on this bus and pretend Nikki is the queen of Spain. She has the figure for it. And a very fine dame was she." Shep immediately started off on a lot of ribald verses about the queen of Spain and had to be shushed down.

Setubal was different. It was large and

had sardine-packing factories and a quay and docks and a fleet of big fishing boats.

Calderon insisted upon taking them into one of his packing plants. So they drove down along a cobbled street toward the sea and stopped by a sliding steel door at the side of a great corrugated iron structure. Inside they were overpowered by the odor of olive oil; heavy, thick and warm.

"Waco," Shep murmured.

Nikki pressed a tiny handkerchief to her nose and looked helplessly about. It was gloomy inside the building. At the far end they could see rows of girls sitting on wooden benches working rapidly with their hands. When they approached, they saw that the girls had little nickel-plated scissors with which they dextrously snipped off the tails and fins of the sardines before they placed them in the cans. The cans, neatly cradled in wire trays, were submerged in tanks of olive oil.

Shep asked Nikki if this wasn't all too divine. But Nikki wouldn't reply.

The girls, for the most part, were an ill-assorted lot, drably dressed in black or brown. Their hands were brown and deft and they all had black hair and dark eyes. Shep said you'd bust your braces trying to find a blonde in here. He said that, judging by the standards of this place, Nikki was an albino.

Single Lady

None of the girls looked up nor gave the slightest sign that they were aware of the presence of the visitors. But just as they were leaving, one of them gave quite a good imitation with her scissors of Nikki and her lorgnette. Nikki couldn't see across the room, so she was spared the mimicry. It would have amused her anyway. She knew she looked helpless with a lorgnette.

Calderon insisted upon giving them all mementos of the visit to the packing plant. He loaded them down with fine skinless, boneless sardines in bright new cans with green and red labels. On the labels it said:

NICE SARDINES

contents
6¼ ounces
Boneless Portuguese
in Pure Olive Oil

They all received them solemnly and marched back to the car, bearing their gifts.

Outside the packing plant, they deposited the sardines in the car and walked down toward the sea. Girls stared surreptitiously at them from upstairs windows behind window boxes.

The section below the packing plant was a bit on the disreputable side. A young Portuguese in a black hat and a brown suit lay on the sidewalk snoring peacefully in the bright Portuguese sunshine, with his head pillowed on a stone doorstep. Only the flies paid him any attention. Shep regarded him wistfully. He said he wished he could get as tight as that. For anyone who could sleep, Shep had the most envious regard. To sleep in the daytime was for him out of the question. The most he could expect was a few frantic, phantom-ridden hours at night.

Scores of battered little shacks with crazy stances and burlap curtains were huddled along the fringe of the town.

Scrofulous, swollen-bellied children played about in the sand under shifting clouds of flies. A hulking idiot boy stood by a boat eating live snails, which he picked out of their shells with a wooden splinter.

Nikki was unhappy, so they took her back to the car.

"Did we see a condition?" Shep inquired of Cary.

"Sure you saw a condition," Cary assented, "a condition with flies on it."

Shep discovered a low, villainous *taverna* on the opposite side of the street from the parked car, and insisted on dragging the others in for a quick one before lunch. Nikki leveled her glasses at the place and resolutely refused to leave the car.

Single Lady

"Bring me back an ice cream cone," she said.

Inside the tavern it was dark and low-ceilinged. There was a bar across one end, as in an English public-house, presided over by a swarthy slattern with stringy black hair and a wart on her chin. Three fishermen sat at a table in the open space before the bar, playing cards, and a fourth sat with his chair tilted back against the wall, plucking a guitar and singing a very melancholy ballad indeed.

Shep and the others stood up to the zinc-lined bar. Through Travassos they ordered beer; Shep called for a pony glass of brandy.

Joseph explained deprecatingly that this was by no means a first-class place; just a low drinking resort for fishermens. Shep said he found it charming. Cary studied the place with quiet, alert interest. His eyes settled upon a shelf behind the bar filled with a miscellany of bottles and odd bric-a-brackery. Behind some tall green narrow-shouldered vermouth bottles he saw a clock. It was not a large clock; it was possibly a foot tall and he could see that it was covered with dust and had been in long disuse. While the others were conversing, Cary spoke to Joseph and asked him if he thought the old lady would let him look at the clock.

Joseph spoke to her, pointing to the clock. She looked at it indifferently and shrugged her shoulders. Joseph turned to Cary. "She says it doesn't march."

"Ask her to let me see it anyway."

Again the old lady shrugged her shoulders, but under Joseph's persuasion she dragged a stool along behind the bar, stepped up on a rung, and pushing aside the bottles, lifted down the clock. She blew the dust off the top and set it on the bar in front of Cary, as if it had been a lot of trouble.

Cary took out his pocket handkerchief and whipped off more dust, rubbing the exterior surfaces. It was an eight-day, satinwood bracket clock with a square dial and brass basket-top. The inlay finish was blistered, scratched and stained. It had long, graceful, elaborately pierced steel hands. Studying it more closely, Cary saw that here was a stray specimen of early eighteenth century clock making. The metal spandrels at each of the four corners of the dial were ornamented with gold cherubs' heads with wings. Then Cary discovered something which made him catch his breath. In the brass fretted mesh below the Roman numerals on the face of the clock he made out the legend: *"Tho. Tompion, Londini, Fecit."* He turned the clock around. It had a pull repeater at the back and there again on the brass plate was written in scroll: Thomas Tompion.

"Ask her how much she wants for it," he told Joseph.

"You want to buy it?"

"Yes."

"But it's broke."

"Tell her I want the broken down old clock for a souvenir."

Joseph entered into a spirited conversation with the old creature. From her attitude it was obvious that she was not comfortable about it. She made as if to put the clock back on the shelf, but Cary kept it in his hands.

"She says she not wanting to sell the clock," Joseph said.

"Tell her the American will pay two hundred escudos."

Joseph gave Cary an astonished look. "For the clock! For the clock!"

"For the old clock."

"Not worth a pants button! Not worth a pants button!"

However, Joseph went into conversation with the woman behind the bar. She shook her head.

"She saying it has been here a long time. She saying she must asking her husband."

"Where is her husband?"

"Where is your husband?" Joseph turned back to Cary. "Her husband is drunk. She will have to wait."

"How long will he be drunk?"

"How long will your husband be drunk, Madame? She does not know. T'ree days. Two weeks."

Finally Cary bought the clock for two hundred and fifty escudos, against the misgivings of the old woman. She replaced the vermouth bottles carefully on the shelf to conceal the space left by the missing clock. Cary wrapped his purchase tenderly in an old Lisbon newspaper and tied it with a piece of cord.

"Cary bought a tclock! Cary bought a dead tclock," Francis informed Nikki excitedly when they got back to the car.

"Not dead," Cary said, "just a little tired."

Nikki was mildly surprised. Cary held the clock in his lap, refusing to put it down on the floor of the car.

"Must be a genawine antique," Shep remarked. "What are you going to do with it? Sell it to the British Museum?"

Cary said he might have it stuffed.

Travassos had an idea it would be a fine thing if they went to the Esperanza Hotel in Setubal for luncheon. It was a charming place, facing the main street and overlooking the square. Cary refused to leave his clock with the driver in the car. He carried it along with him. Inside it was cool. The dining room was on the second floor. Nikki dis-

appeared for a time and the boys found a
retreat de Caballeros where they treated themselves to a washup.

Shep was first out and immediately found
a big round table in the circular alcove overlooking the public square and the harbor. He
ordered Martini cocktails. Cary came and set
his clock down on an empty chair at a nearby
table.

When everybody was collected around the
table, it was decided to let the Portuguese select the luncheon.

Travassos asked them if they had ever
tasted red mullet. Nobody had and they were
all terribly happy that they hadn't, because it
delighted Travassos so much to have a surprise
for them.

Calderon nodded happily. He agreed with
his friend. He was in sympathy with every
one. Travassos was quite right about his
friend Calderon. He not speaking English,
but he understanding everything.

They began with cucumbers and sardines
and a light clear soup. The Portuguese conferred industriously over the wine for the mullet. Here it was that Shep discovered the wine
of Collares, a pale yellow wine with a sweet
singing flavor in a tall slim necked bottle; "a
sun within the mist and darkness of the
world."

When the red mullet came, grilled like mountain trout, it was tender and had a delicious flavor. Shep, to the infinite gratification of his hosts, continued to exclaim over the mullet and the wine.

"You will not eating that fish outside Portugal," Travassos told him. "That fish won't stand no transportation." The flesh of the red mullet, he explained, was too tender for packing or shipping. It bruised easily.

Shep could not help but say that Nikki was like that, too. She bruised easily and wouldn't stand much transportation. Just a Red Mullet.

Shep was exalted by the red mullet and the wine. He devoured two red mullets and drained off a bottle of Collares and called for another. He noticed with vast gratification that Calderon was staying with him, glass for glass. The others were too wise.

Travassos said he was glad Meestaire Lambert enjoyed the wine so. He would like to drink more himself, but he had enough already. Ordinarily he didn't drink that much. Feel his pulse, he said.

Shep felt the flickering pulse in the flat brown wrist of the ex-prize fighter.

"Not so young as you used to be," Shep said.

"Not like when I fight Joe Gans at Coney Island."

"When was that?"

"December six, eighteen ninety-six."

It was too amazing. They all stared at him. Why, that was before any of them were born.

"Did you lick him?" Bill asked.

Travassos smiled and shook his head. "Not Joe Gans," he said. "He was the old master. He knocking me out in the twenty-sixth round."

"Good Lord," Bill said, "you stayed twenty-six rounds?"

The Portuguese nodded. "I fought them all," he said, "Terry McGovern . . . George Dixon . . . George Elbows McFadden." They used to call him the Portygee, Joseph said. He wore green and red trunks, the Portuguese colors, and he fought under the name of Young Travis.

Bill asked him about Joe Gans.

"He was the best," Travis said. "He was knock-kneed, spindle-legged. Like Fitzsimmons. He hitting me awful hard. He hitting me hard.

"My right weight was a hundred forty-four," Joseph said. "I had to reduce to a hundred thirty-six to fight Gans. I was living on the juice of a steak. Run four miles and jump into ice-water tub. No man in the worl' could beat Joe Gans."

Bill wanted to know how he had wound up his pugilistic career.

"My last fight in eighteen ninety-eight," Joseph said, "in 'Azeltown, Pennsylvania. I was supposed to fight Jack Leon—for eighty-five dollars and train fare. He didn't show up. They want me to fight Terry Magerry, the nègre. Out of my class. I refusing to fight, but they holding back my railroad ticket. I was broke. Boxers are always broke. I can't get back to New York unless I fight the nègre. They tolding me he go easy."

Joseph sipped his wine sadly.

"H'in the firs' round he try to knocking my head off. He had what you would calling a dangerous right hand. At close range he drive against my ribs and tear me apart." Joseph said he stayed fifteen rounds with this colored boy, but he took a bad beating and afterwards he not liking to fight any more. He became a steward on the White Star Line and eventually came home to Lisbon, where he was born. "I 'ave a lot of contrary things in my life," he said with a sigh.

Calderon had ordered a bottle of Three Star Collares brandy. He raised his glass to Shep and Shep responded happily. This was a fine idea, to Shep's way of thinking. Many times during Travis' account of his career in the States, Shep raised his glass to Calderon. The little Portuguese always brightened up and returned the courtesy.

"You better leaving the cork out of the bottle," Joseph said. He had been observing the performance out of the corner of his eye.

He was a little worried about Shep. "You frien' like to drink," he told Nikki.

"He does it to make the rest of us interesting," Nikki replied.

Travassos said that Calderon on account of being accustomed to the wines of the country would not be so much affected. But Meestaire Lamber' . . .

Bill told him not to worry.

"Your frien' there," said Joseph indicating Cary, "looks a good boy."

"He's all right."

"A quiet fellow," Joseph observed, "a nice fellow."

"Our moral tutor," Bill explained.

When the brandy bottle was empty, Calderon looked inquiringly at Shep. Shep nodded agreeably, so Calderon ordered another. Travassos looked worried, but he was a little tranquilized by the equanimity with which the others regarded the affair. It was obvious that the exchange of courtesies between Shep and Sr. Calderon was rounding into a contest.

With the arrival of a new bottle of brandy, Shep settled down to his drinking with cheerful anticipation.

Travassos' concern changed shortly to puzzlement and thereafter to astonishment. He was treated with the awesome spectacle of a man drinking himself sober. The more brandy Shep consumed the more serene he became. His manner was natural and composed. There was no outward indication that he had polished off some twenty brandy *fines* in the last three-quarters of an hour.

Sr. Calderon returned smiling graciousness although a slight fixity might have been detected in his expression and a new glassiness in his eyes.

At intervals he leaped to his feet, threw out his chest like a pouter pigeon and drew in his stomach till his abdomen rubbed against his spine. You could have stuffed a football into the gap between his stomach and his silver belt buckle. Being a small man and incapable of entering the table conversation, this was his method of establishing the fact that he was physically in his prime and a fine figure of a man. Everyone nodded sympathetically at this recurrent display of prowess.

He said something in Portuguese to Travassos.

"He wants me to say to you," Joseph said, "that there are no frontiers between us."

Everyone smiled gratefully at Calderon. He was very happy.

The others had long ago given up the contest and were sitting back as mildly interested spectators.

Calderon could not easily suggest leaving off while his guest was still enjoying the brandy.

The result was, therefore, that poor Sr. Calderon's features became set in a kind of frozen smile and the movements with which he raised his glass became stiff and labored.

It must be said for Sr. Calderon, however, that his deportment on this occasion was admirable. He would have gone on certainly until unconsciousness overtook one or the other of them.

However, Travassos' concern, once so great for the young American, had been displaced by anxiety for his compatriot. At the conclusion of the second bottle, he suggested that on account of the necessity of catching the ferry at Almada, it would be better if they arranged to depart sometime soon now, if they expected to be back in Lisbon for dinner.

Shep arose and helped Nikki on with her jacket. The others rose, too, but Sr. Calderon, although his mind seemed to be functioning normally, could not apparently operate under his own power. He got to his feet, but his knees declined to lend him the proper support and he would have sat down abruptly again had not Bill lent a supporting arm. Shep perceived the state of affairs, so he took his place at Sr. Calderon's left and the two of them, Bill and Shep, helped him navigate without appearing to offer the slightest aid. They each had an elbow and bore Sr. Calderon's weight between them. Sr. Calderon's feet trod as if on air. It was all very tactful and diplomatic. Once downstairs, and in the motor car, Sr. Calderon stiffened himself into a fine, upright sitting position. Cary followed with his precious clock under his arm.

The ride back to the ferry landing was accomplished in the slanting rays of the declining afternoon sun. Portugal was lovely in the morning. It was beautiful in the late afternoon.

Back at the Avenida Palace, they stopped off at the bar to have a couple of cocktails before going upstairs. Benjamin was there, but froze up at the sight of the Portuguese. He was practically no good at all as a matter of fact—not being half himself in the presence of the Portuguese.

Lennox came in and sat down with them and said he'd been doing a job of work. Said he'd planned to get away in a couple of days, but it looked more like a fortnight. Could do absolutely nothing with the beggars. Took their own sweet time. It was always tomorrow. Tomorrow. Tomorrow. "How about the bull-fight? Are all you chaps going to the bull-fight tonight?"

"Certainly," Shep said, "where is it?"

"Campo Pequeno," Lennox said. "On'y it's at ten o'clock."

How about Nikki? Did Nikki want to go? Would it be safe to take Nikki? You know the blood and all that. The horses and everything.

Lennox roared with laughter. She won't see much blood, you bet your hat on that. Not at a Portuguese bull-fight. Not likely. The horses are armored.

Shep wanted to know how you got the bull out of the ring, since you don't kill him.

"Just send in a flock of steers," Lennox said. "He'll foller 'em out."

Benjamin enjoyed the way the Englishman talked about the bull-fight. It was different in his own country.

"In Spain," Lennox said, "you've got to kill your bull. You're for it. They throw bottles at you else. If they can tear up the balustrade, in it goes. But for good work," he said, "cigar cases, cigarette cases, hats . . ."

"Peanut brittle," Shep suggested brightly.

He was afraid the Portuguese would take offense. But, on the contrary, they smiled apologetically. The Englishman was right. The bull-fights in Lisbon weren't so good any more.

Calderon shook his head and shrugged his shoulders. He was sorry that the Americans were going to attend a bull-fight in Lisbon. They saw that he was a little ashamed.

Still, Joseph said, he wasn't crazy about the bull-fights in Spain either. "I don't like to see anybody abuse a horse," he said. "It's cruelty. Blind his left eye besides. I don't like to see that."

Lennox asked him if he had ever seen a bull-fight in Spain. Joseph said he had seen one. "I seen the bull charge the 'orse," he said, "and then the next I know someone is fanning me outside with a fan."

Lennox had got a little red and blue handbill somewhere, which he was examining with interest.

"Inauguracao Das Corridas Nocturnos," he read, "10 de Junho as 22 h. (10 horas de noite).

"There are going to be eight bravissimos touros," he said.

"Hurray," said Shep.

"The names of the cavaleiros are Ricardo and Marcelino."

"I think Francis would go for Marcelino," Shep said.

"The espada is Juan Ramillito."

Benjamin let flee a little snort of laughter. When they looked up at him he said, "One 'undred forty-two years old an' bald-headed, an' if the bull run his way he jump over the fence. He staying right by the trenches so he can jump quick."

"Got a lot of bandarilheiros here," Lennox continued.

Shep said to read just their first names so Lennox said Felipe, Antonio, Julio, Jose, Carlos, Eduardo, Joaquim; Francisco and Fernando.

"Isn't that a beautiful bouquet of names though!" Shep said. He was pleased and delighted with the names of the Portuguese bandarilheiros. "I never heard so many beautiful names."

"Atencao! Atencao! Atencao!" Lennox cried. "As an added attraction, they have the famous faquir Travisco in an assombroso exercicio de catalepsia."

"I'll take vadilla."

"Travisco will be enterrado vivo under the sand in the middle of the bull ring during the fights and he'll be dug up after."

Travassos took the handbill and studied it. He began to laugh, too. He said the famous faquir was a shoemaker's assistant and lived next door to him. He thought that was pretty shameful, but Shep thought it was fine. Must be a very imaginative cobbler who could pass himself off as an East Indian Fakir.

Lennox said to expect nothing of the bull fight, but that the parade was worth looking at. Good horses, fine ridin'. See some first-rate horsemanship.

A dark, thick, ragged, bristle-headed little young-old monster came in the bar with a shoe-blacking box swung over his shoulder and stood expectantly in front of them.

"Great Lord," said Shep, "what's that?"

"That is a cross-breed between a monkey and a man," Joseph said, "with a little dash of billy goat. He wants to shine your shoes."

"Tell him to help himself," Shep said.

Travassos said he would arrange everything about the tickets and everything for the bull-fight, and meet them at the bar at nine-thirty. He told them not to dress. Lennox said not to dress either. Nobody dressed for the nocturnals. They would be conspicuous if they dressed. They said they wouldn't, but they knew they would dress anyhow. They had a few more cocktails and then went upstairs to bathe and dress for dinner and the bull-fights. Cary carried the clock to his room.

The Portuguese bull-fight was as bad as advertised. But everybody seemed to enjoy it because it was so terribly bad. Only the parade was fine. The Delegation had beautiful seats in the first and second rows back of the trenches. They had to sit close down so that Nikki could see things.

The sound of the bugles was fine and brave, and the costumes were gorgeous. The bandarilheiros, matadors and picadors made a powerful entrance through flung-open gates at the far side of the bull-ring and marched directly across to where Nikki sat. The riders did not turn their horses when they retired from the ring, but simply backed them out through the gates, keeping perfect alignment.

Lennox said that now the show was practically over, unless they enjoyed laughing.

It was true about the famous Portuguese bull-fighters. The ace was fifty anyway and bald-headed and nervous. The bandarilheiros were pretty bad. One of them missed so badly as to stick a banderilla in the bull's rump. How the audience whistled at that.

Before the first bull was let in, the East Indian Fakir, in silver tights, flanked by two buxom wenches in pink fleshings and ballet

skirts like circus bareback riders, came march-
ing in with a tremendous fanfare. He minced
all around the bull-ring whilst a half dozen
bull-ring servants dug a grave in the sand in
the middle of the arena. Travisco was lowered
into the pit. A wooden lid was placed above
him and the sand shoveled in upon him. The
bull-fight went on over his interred body.
Travassos thought it would be fine, if after
the bull-fights, everybody went off and forgot
about him.

Old Ramillito refused to venture far from
the trenches. At the first sign of a charge
from the bull, he would scamper back over the
barrera to the hoots, howls and cat calls of the
audience.

The picadors were pretty sad, too. They
fell off their horses. The bandarilheiros
couldn't seem to make their flags stick.

"You can't stick a banderilla in those ani-
mals," Lennox explained. "They've been
stuck a hundred times. Their necks are all
scar tissue. They use the same bulls for all the
bull-fights down here."

"So the picadors can't pic and the bandarilheiros can't banderil and the old bull-
fighter runs for his life," Shep said. It was
all a great joke. Once the bull was fixed for
the sword, all the bull-fighter did was to pro-

file, sight his blade over the bull's horns and then retire.

It was all Cary and Shep could do to keep Bill Talbot in his seat. If he could borrow a cape from one of the bull-fighters he said he bet he could run one of those bulls ragged. It was all dodging about, wasn't it? Just pull the bull one way with the red cape while you pivoted. Anyway he couldn't be worse than anybody else.

They thought Bill was kidding at first. But Bill was pretty tight and his instinct for combat had been aroused. He was crazy to get into the ring and play the bulls. He was looking around for the nearest way into the trenches.

"Don't be a damn fool, Bill," Shep said.

"Hell," said Bill, "I'll run those bulls bow-legged."

"You stay right where you are."

Bill got sore and began to sulk. Francis hardly took his dreamy eyes off the bull-fighters. He had never seen such tight trousers. He didn't see how they could bend without splitting them.

Bill was sore as anything because they wouldn't let him go into the ring with the bull.

"You get sore because we won't let you get yourself killed. You're a funny guy, Bill."

"It's not so easy as it looks," Lennox said.

"It takes a long time to make a bull-fighter."

Bill refused to believe it. A broken field runner, he had a natural instinct for feinting and dodging and he knew he wouldn't get hurt. He'd have a fine time with that bull.

One bull was lame and the crowd jeered so they sent in the steers. He followed them out. One bull refused to charge at anything, horses, capes or men. He just stood and looked around and pawed the sand with his hoof. The bull-fighter approached him and made a couple of passes at him with his cape. The bull did not respond. The bull-fighter, insulted, turned and walked away, shrugging his shoulders. He refused to fight that bull, so that bull was let out, too.

Lennox said he thought the bull was color blind or had only one eye or something.

The whole business seemed kind of silly anyway. Like sending two fighters into the ring to shadow-box. When the last of the bravissimos touros loped out of the arena with the tame steers, the attendants ran into the center of the arena with their shovels and began to disinter Sabio Fakir Travisco. The two bareback riders, with arms folded, took up stately stations on either side of the diggers. The lid was lifted off and out popped the pink tighted figure. He rushed frantically toward the higher-priced seats, leaping, bounding, and throwing kisses in the manner of a delivered martyr. Accompanied by his two juicy consorts, he made a complete tour of the arena, sharing the joy of his deliverance with everyone. Only one little circumstance marred the glory of his exit. A hundred feet from the gates, a seat cushion came sailing through the air to land in the sand at his feet. Instantly a medley of whistles, groans, cushions, programmes and paper fans filled the air. Oblivious to the shower of foreign objects, Travisco continued his impetuous bounding and kiss throwing and swept out in a burst of glory.

Afterwards the Delegation went to investigate conditions at Maxime's. They found conditions pretty strange at Maxime's. It was a gorgeous place with terrific high ceilings and a powerful winding marble staircase and balustrade and great gleaming glass chandeliers. The ballroom proper was large and red and ornate, with the orchestra on a dais at the far end. The orchestra played nothing but tango music. But it was beautiful Portuguese tango music.

The Americans were the only ones in evening dress. There seemed to be a lot of Portuguese admirals about, gloriously festooned with medals. Shep said he guessed they saw a lot of service at Maxime's. There was a Portuguese army Captain, too, likewise ornamented. Cary wanted to know about the medals. Lennox said he only recognized one —the Victory medal . . . on the left side. The others were civil decorations no doubt . . . perhaps an African campaign. Been through three revolutions. On the right side, you see. God help the sailors on a night like this and all that. A party of Swedes occupied a long table next them. The girls wore formal dresses and the men were in blue naval uniforms. You could tell the girls were Swedish because they had so many elbows and they danced as if they had on big shoes. They wore no make-up and their cheeks were red as red, red apples and they had ever so many white teeth and they looked so serious. The color flared through the white skin over their cheek bones. They wore white dresses and Shep said he bet there was fire under the snow. He said he was so affected by the sight of Swedes dancing the tango in Lisbon that he would break down and buy champagne.

The Portuguese weren't terribly comfortable at Maxime's. Calderon looked around and said something to Travassos. Travassos told Shep that Calderon said it was all a pile of cod-fish.

Bill left the table and when he didn't come back, Shep went to look for him. He was sitting on a sofa in the hall talking to a big blonde with a lot of ear-rings.

She was holding his hands and speaking persuasively in his ear.

"Hey, Bill," Shep said, "for gosh sakes."

Bill stood up.

Shep led him back to the table. "I just rescued him from a blonde," Shep told everybody.

"English Annie," Travassos said. "In the hall?"

"The one with the fallen arm-pits?" Shep inquired.

"That was English Annie," Travassos said. English Annie, he explained, had been left astray in Lisbon.

Shep began to marvel at how many people were left astray in Portugal. Practically everybody was left astray.

At four in the morning they were still at Maxime's. An American boy named Johnny, who worked in a bank in Lisbon, came over to their table. He was surprised to see them. There were only three other Americans resident in Lisbon beside himself, he said. Nobody came to Lisbon. Nothing happened in Lisbon. You could walk up the street and see seven-year-old motion pictures just arrived at the Tivoli. What were they doing here?

Shep said they came down to investigate conditions in Lisbon.

"Conditions!"

Drinking conditions, mostly. They would like to see a Portuguese earthquake, too, if anyone would be so polite as to break one out for them while they were here. They had all brought along their earthquake clothes just in case.

Johnny looked at them all quickly. He said he would see what he could do about the earthquake. They talked desultorily about the bullfight.

Shep had been drinking since early morning and his face, for once, seemed congested. His forehead was colored with a deeper red flush than the half-lights of Maxime's showed.

He excused himself and was gone for quite a while. When he came back he was white and shaking.

Cary shot an inquiring glance at him. The cuff of his dress shirt was stained a light pink and there were light pink stains on the white starched bosom. Oh Lord, Cary thought, he's had another hemorrhage.

The others were drinking wine, but Shep ordered brandy.

It was after five when they left Maxime's.

Cary had planned to visit the Lisbon waterfront in the early morning. Travassos had ad-

vised him that the fish market was in full blast
around five-thirty. "You seeing them h'auc-
tion off the fish."

Since Cary was determined to carry out
his plans, the Portuguese insisted that they accompany him. Shep was determined to come
along, too. Nikki was tired, so Bill and The
Washout were delegated to take her home.

The other four, Cary and Shep still in their
smokings, took a cab for the fish market. It
was only a short ride. The market was all that
Travassos had said, loud, fish-smelly, rough
and alive with bare-legged girls. They bought
the fresh-caught fish at small shrill auctions,
piled them on flat baskets and hoisted them
atop their heads, setting out through the
streets.

Travassos pointed out the toughest girl on
the Lisbon waterfront, a great strapping creature, with a fine straight back, a brown column
of a neck and arms like a beer swamper's.

"I seen her fighting once," Travassos said.
"She lick t'ree womens. The police couldn't
holding her. Stronger than two men, she is."

"She play too rough," Shep murmured.

"Ooh," said Joseph, "she turns mad, that
one. She screws up her face like a bool dog.
She left a girl bare naked."

The girls with quick, observant eyes, had
noticed the two young Americans in their eve-

ning clothes and tossed remarks back and
forth.

"What are they saying?" Shep wanted to
know.

"Oh, they are naughty, those girls," Travassos said. He and Calderon were laughing
constantly. "I can't telling you what those
girls saying. The worst things," Travassos
translated a couple of remarks that the fish
girls tossed to each other. "That one say, how
would you liking to . . ."

"Nice girls," Shep said.

Travassos said it was a funny thing, but
those girls looked rough and talked rough, but
you wouldn't finding no more decent girls nowhere.

"You should see the underneath of those
girls," he said. "You would be surprise. Lace
h'underwear! Clean! They washing all the
time."

Shep said he would like to see their underneath.

"Those girls not touchable," Travassos said
with some pride. "Not touchable."

"You should be here," he said, "when the
fishermens sail away for the Grand Banks for
five months, maybe a year. Then you will
hearing some screeching and howling," he said.
"The wives all come down to watching the
boats sail away. An' no matter how long her

'usban' staying away, you can depen' on those womens. Once they do something no one shall look on their face again."

A slight early morning drizzle began to fall on the fish market. Shep and Cary had no coats. They all started back for a cab.

"Not possible to rain this time of year," Joseph said, looking perplexedly upward.

Calderon looked up happily when Shep suggested finding the nearest bar. He said something to Travassos, who explained that Calderon's stomach was leaping and grabbing.

They found a place called The American Bar. Shep wanted brandy, but Calderon sheepishly ordered Martini cocktails. They sat at the bar and got good and tight and then went back to the Avenida Palace. Shep and Cary said goodbye to the Portuguese at the bar there. Shep had a couple of drinks with Benjamin and then went into his room. The housekeeper passing along the hall, noticed a torn cuff pinned to the door. On it was written:

Do Not Disturb

CHAPTER XI

LIFE had become an inexplicable chaos to Shepard Lambert. He could not sleep. He could not remember when he had last dropped off into a simple, refreshing slumber. Sometime before the war, sometime before he began to fly. Sleep, the precious release of sleep, was denied him. He wondered sometimes, when he was very tight, why it was that he couldn't fall asleep naturally. Why didn't Nature step in and put him to sleep, just once? One good night's sleep would make all the difference. It would be like being born again. With a good night's sleep behind him, he would have enough resistence to carry him through the day without a drink—maybe till evening. Then maybe he might catch another night's sleep, and so on. Soon he would be saturated in beautiful, restful slumber. He was so tired. So tired of those terrible mornings when he was exploded into dry, searing, blinding consciousness. The prospect of facing another morning filled him with shivering dread. The thought of it drove him to drinking more fiercely, to postpone the inevitable moment of waking. His drinking, begun so light-heartedly after the war, had become a roaring furnace in which he was being consumed. Boy, this was the real hell-fire.

It had come to seem to Shep that life was just one long terrible morning-after. Each morning he would tell himself this was the last, that he had had enough. A human being could endure no more. He could never, never face another morning like this one. Why should he go punishing himself like this? This morning was positively the last. This was really the last. Of all the other resolutions he had ever made, this was the one that would stick. The realization that he had at last come to the end of his drinking would break over him with a beautiful, shining light. This was the last.

But first he had to silence his tic and gather some kind of strength to hold firm to that resolution. The muscle under his eye, quieted the night before by thousands of drinks, was leaping and clamoring. What a hell of a visitation that was. That terrible little tic was a leaping, bounding, clamoring, insane, shrill little alarm clock that summoned him out of his unconsciousness. Shep got up and found a half bottle of Martel Three Star Brandy on the dresser. The muscles around his mouth were twitching, too. He was stiff and brittle as a bread-stick.

The first hooker of brandy didn't mean anything so far as his determination not to drink was concerned. It was purely medicinal. Any doctor would prescribe a couple of ounces of brandy for one in his condition, rattling like a paper in the wind. Any doctor.

That first drink was just to take the stiffness out of his tongue, to warm his vitals, to start the circulation in his wooden limbs and put the quietus on that tic. Lifegiving, it was. Then he could sit up and see where he was and what time it was. The thing about the Claridge Bar was they had a clock there and a calendar. You could kind of keep track of things. Shep's eye fell upon a sheet of hotel note-paper:

THE AVENIDA PALACE
LISBON, PORTUGAL

Well, for gosh sakes! Look where I am. He studied his wrist watch. It was two o'clock. The old brain was stiff, too. He couldn't even think without a drink. He'd have to have a couple of more ounces of brandy to start his brain working. A nurse would have fed him the brandy out of a spoon, no doubt,—one in his condition. But he'd drink it right out of the bottle. Medicinal. Purely medicinal. Brandy was considered medicinal, wasn't it?

317

Single Lady

Well, now, this is better. There. Wash his teeth now and bathe and shower and dress. One of these days you'll miss your baby. One of these days you'll feel so lonely. . . .

Ol' Bill was lying asleep in the next bed.

In the bathroom Shep took one look at himself in the glass. Oh, my Lord. Look at those eyes, would you. Where the hell was the eye-cup. Where the . . . hell was the eye-cup, the old Collyrium Wyeth. He found the tall blue bottle of eyewash with the cup on the top and took out the stopper. It chattered against the bottle in his hand. I've got the shakes all right. He poured the lotion into the cup, splashing it all over the place, and held it to his right eye, tilting back his head. He nearly fell over backwards, and finally sat down on the edge of the tub. He rolled his eyeball around in the lotion. It felt marvellously cool and wet to his stinging lids. You could see a nice blue light through the eyecup. In some curious way you could see your own lashes in the eye-cup, sweeping up and down in the cold, wet lotion. Good old eyewash. God bless you, eyewash.

One of these days you'll miss your baby . . .

Shep bathed his right eye and let the lotion stream down his face. It ran across his mouth and he tasted it experimentally with his tongue. Not bad, not bad. When he looked in the glass, it looked as if he had been weeping. It was interesting to see himself like that because he had never cried since he could remember and he liked to see how he would look if he cried.

Well, that was better, but the glass stopper rattled in the bottle when he put it back. He took his auto strop razor out of the cabinet and began to strop it on the strop hanging on the hook. He stropped it jerkily because his muscles inside his elbows worked spasmodically. He stopped. Hell, this is no good. He tried again. It went a little better. But when he raised his arms to shave they came up in staggered steps and he dared not put the razor to his face.

A couple of more hookers of brandy would fix that. You had to shave. So he brought the brandy bottle into the bathroom and took a pull out of the bottle and put it on the side of the washbowl. His arms jerked a little as he shaved, but he shaved in easy spells and then rinsed his face and head with cold water. Drying his face with a towel, he wondered what in God's name he'd of done without that brandy. Lifegiving. He held the bottle up to the light. At first he wondered who had been drinking out of that bottle. It was getting empty. He couldn't remember quite how it was when he took his first drink. He thought about it as he tilted the bottle again. Wham!

He turned the water on in the great porcelain bathtub and listened to the rush of water. He had another swallow as he watched the tub fill up. When it was half full, he unloosened the cord of his pajamas and let them fall to the floor, and stepped into the tub. It was pleasant lying in the hot water. The brandy bottle was out of reach. He kept turning his head to see if it was still there on the wash bowl. The tide line went down so fast in that bottle, it seemed like three or four fellows must be working on it. He soaped himself and rinsed and then pulled the stopper out of the bottom of the tub by hooking his big toe around the chain. The water ran out fast. Then he stood up and turned on a rush of cold water. He took a wash cloth and sluiced himself all over with cold water. You got fine reaction. You'll miss my hugging. You'll miss my kissing. You'll miss me, honey, when you're away.

He stepped out of the tub and surveyed himself in the glass. He was certainly thin. Thin as a spinster. Thin as Miss Beasely who used to sing soprano in the choir. Drunks were supposed to be paunchy, weren't they? Shakespeare's drunks were fat old tosspots.

But Shep was thin and straight. His stomach was flat as a gramophone record. He was certainly thin around the waist on account of he never ate anything hardly. He supposed his insides were all tangled up anyhow. All this drinking. How about a milk diet? He understood a milk diet would straighten out your insides. Certainly couldn't cap that medicinal brandy with milk now, though. Go on a milk diet tomorrow. Wouldn't everybody be surprised, though. Well, Shepard, ol' boy, ol' boy, here's to you in Portugal. He tilted the bottle again.

He combed and brushed his hair and bathed his hands in Yardley's lavender water. The alcohol made them feel thin and cool and clean. Before he left the bathroom, he polished off the brandy and dropped the bottle in the towel hamper.

Now he had a fine edge on. And when I leave you, you know it will grieve you. You'll miss your little dad-dad-dad-dy one of these days.

He went back to the bedroom. The only problem now was to hold that edge. The moment it faded ten thousand demons assailed him. All the troops closed in.

Bill was still sleeping in the other bed. Shep put on a robe, lighted a cigarette and sat down against the pillows at the top of the bed to wait for Bill to wake up.

Consciousness returned to Bill Talbot with a hot blast. His ears began to roar as if two conch shells were clapped tightly to his head. His head was big as a cannon ball and swelling with blinding waves of pain. His eyeballs felt seared at the back. His eyelids were red and swollen. His tongue was dry and sour as a tanner's thumb, and his lips felt like a couple of slices of assorted cold meats; mutton, for example. His body was stiff with poison. His stomach felt cold and old like a dead oyster. His breath came up painfully out of lungs scorched and seared from the smoke of countless cigarettes. An idiotic musical phrase kept buzzing about in the roaring cave of winds that was his head.

For the first time Bill was scared. He tried to move his brandy-stiffened body. He tried to lick his swollen lips with his dry tongue. There was no rallying power to his system. He had gone too far. Nature, called on one more swear-last time, failed to respond. I'm dying, he thought.

His teeth were covered with an unholy film; vegetable growths, fungus, foreign bodies, sword ferns, potted palms; Spanish moss, Shep had once described it. His mouth was as dry as the inside of a gourd.

The events of yesterday came back to Bill in slow procession. All those drinks. My God, all those drinks!

If I'm dying, Bill thought, Shep must be dead. Surely Shep, with half his strength, half his vitality, would be pickled in that ocean of brandy. He must be extinct.

I'll never drink again, he swore to himself. I'll never smoke another cigarette. All this terrible punishment. This time I mean it.

He raised himself on his elbow and opened his eyes to look across at Shep. Shep, bathed, shaved and looking bright as a robin was sitting up in his bed, grinning at him.

"Tonight," said Shep, "we're going on a real party."

"Oh, my Lord," Bill croaked and fell back in bed.

For Shepard Lambert the days and nights in Portugal melted mysteriously into each other like chemical dissolves on a cinema screen. He lost all track of time. At the bar he scolded Benjamin daily for not having a calendar where you could see it. Each day Benjamin promised to have one, but it never appeared. As for the hour of the day, Shep would sometimes stop short and holding out his arm, study the hands of his wrist-watch with the utmost gravity. Shep's two eyes would no longer focus distinctly. He always closed one eye, cocked his head a little to one side and looked at the time. By some incomprehensible twist, it always turned out to be two o'clock. Shep had often observed that since he had taken up drinking time had stopped. He would sadly scrutinize the hands of his wrist-watch and say, *"Marche pas."* The hands never advanced. Time was dead. It must be the same with people in hospitals or prisons, he conjectured. It was wrong to say that time flew. Time, since the war, was dead.

Yet none of the others knew what Shep suffered for his drinking. Alcoholic depression sat upon him in the early hours of the morning when the others were asleep and he faced it out by himself. For the rest, he remained blissfully tight and stoutly defended drinking. Alcohol attacked the higher cerebral centers first, he declared, and broke down your self-control. It swept away all your protective barriers and released you from your inhibitions and made you honest. You couldn't prevent yourself saying and doing the things you really wanted to say and do. You revealed and exposed your charming self—or otherwise—and that was beneficial for all concerned. Yes, it was a splendid idea and he wondered who invented it.

Shep had forgotten his early premonition

about Portugal. In Lisbon, blissfully and magnificently drunk on the tawny wine of Collares, he felt a strange kinship with the Portuguese. He found a fatal attraction in the sinister sunken old city of Lisbon, with its slanting terra cotta roofs, its harbors filled with the red lateen sails of the fishing boats. He found himself in a world of gliding barefooted fish girls, of golden sunshine, of old-world indolence. For the Portuguese women, with their fine straight backs, their splendid vitality and unremitting industry he came to have the greatest admiration. By the old gray fort which they frequently passed on their way to the beach (Shep's Portuguese Riviera) he saw groups of barefoot girls, with tucked-up skirts, at work repairing the road. They earned about five escudos (twenty-five cents) a day. Others he saw piling seaweed into their oxcarts to be used as fertilizer. He tried to keep a list of the articles he had seen Portuguese women carrying on the little circular pads on their heads; baskets piled high with purple and red chunks of codfish, loads of slate slabs, jugs of water and wine, a baby asleep in a cradle, but Shep's imagination got too much for him and he invented such bizarre things that finally none of the others would believe him. He learned to buy freshly boiled shell-fish from the women on the street corners, to crack and eat in the car on the way to the sea.

He was in great sympathy, too, with the youth of Portugal. He found them very original. Their favorite pastime, he discovered, was posing for roadside photographers. On any Sunday afternoon, you could find your young Portygee, in a new suit, with a red flower in his buttonhole and with freshly oiled hair, bravely facing a camera. He carried a pocket-mirror and a comb with which he frequently whipped back his long black hair. For their minor vanities, such as their love of lottery, use of perfume, and having their shoes shined, Shep readily forgave them. Splendid chaps, all of them. You could count on his hearty cooperation.

Shep gave up trying to follow Cary's movements. Cary left the hotel early each morning and did not appear till late at night. Shep discovered a fine bathing-beach not far up the coast and carried the others off to it every afternoon. "Nikki in a bathing suit," he said, "is one of the sights I want these old eyes to dwell upon before I leave this here vale of tears."

Nor did Nikki disappoint him. Superbly hipped and breasted, Nikki, in a one-piece bathing suit was enough to take away the breath.

"Look at that girl," Shep told Bill, the first time Nikki came out of her bathing-wagon and took off her cape. "Just look at that tender grape. Don't tell me that's standard equipment."

"De luxe," said Bill.

"How would you like to enjoy the intimate favors of that creature?" Shep queried of Bill.

Nikki, who usually paid no attention to Shep's observations, in so far as they concerned her, warned him that he was getting fresh again.

"Pay no attention to me," Shep said, "I'm just a cab-talker. I'm like those Portuguese fish wives. I say things but you can depend on me. Once I do something you shall never look on my face again. You should see my underneath. Besides," he said, suddenly bridling up, "what are you getting exercised about. Who invited you into this conversation? You don't belong in this conversation. We'll leave you to your wine and cigars. Bill and I are going into the conservatory. Come along, Bill."

Bill, however, refused to move from Nikki's side. He stretched his magnificent torso out in the sand and gazed at Nikki like an awed, wondering little boy.

"You know," Shep said, "I can't get this whole thing straight in my mind. This here wench is too good to be true. I think all the time some dark stranger is going to turn up and claim her. You don't find gals like this running around loose like this, not with legs like that, and all those charms. No mother to guide her or make her come in when the street lights go on or anything. No sense to it. No sense to it."

Nikki always became very remote when Shep talked like this.

"Say listen," Shep demanded of her. "What's your idea anyway? What's your angle? Everybody's got an angle. You have to have an angle."

"What's yours?" she countered.

"Who me?"

Nikki looked out across the blue-green sea.

"What would you druther do than anything?" Shep inquired. "What are you after? What do you want most in the world?"

"You know what I want most in the world?" Nikki said. "An African address."

"A *what?*"

"An African postal address."

"No sense to it," Shep said.

"Don't you understand," said Nikki. "If I lived in Africa I could write letters to all my friends, and don't you see how excited they'd be about getting a letter from Africa? Did you ever get a letter from Africa?"

"No."

"Did you, Bill?"

"Nope."

"Did you, Francis?"

"No."

"Well, then," said Nikki, "there you are. Wouldn't you be thrilled? You'd show it around and somebody would ask you for the stamp and you'd cut it out and give it to him and have a fine time. Now, wouldn't you? Wouldn't you?"

Shep studied the matter in his mind. "I wonder if I'm getting all there is out of life," he pondered.

"What would you do in Africa?" Bill wanted to know.

"Learn stomach dances," Nikki replied promptly.

"You've got the stomach for it," Shep observed. "Well, Bill, I don't see how we're going to provide this girl with an African address. That's about the one thing we'll have to deny her. Until her eighteenth birthday, anyway."

Bill admitted that it was quite a problem; you couldn't go around establishing people in Africa so they could write letters around.

"What else about you, Nikki?" Shep pursued. "Tell us more. Do you believe in God or anything?"

"You don't have to tell him," Bill said. "He's just an old atheist himself. He doesn't believe in anything."

"I do so believe in things," Shep retorted fiercely. "Certainly I believe in things."

"What do you believe in?"

"Well," said Shep, "I b'lieve in a lot of things. I b'lieve that a snappin' turtle never lets go till it thunders. . . . I b'lieve that a dead snake's tail never stops a-waggin' till the sun goes down . . . an' I b'lieve that if you step on a spider it'll rain . . . and I b'lieve that if you handle a hoptoad you'll get warts on your fingers . . . an' I, why land sakes, boy, I'm religious and I b'lieve that anybody coming to Europe ought to bring their own soap."

Minor manifestations of Shep Lambert's disintegration began to appear during these long sunny days in Portugal. He would look up suddenly and demand of the others what day is this? Wednesday? Wednesday what? The twentieth. But what month I mean? June. That's right, it's June. To be sure it was June. Even to himself it seemed incredible that he shouldn't know the month of the year. Then strangely, later on, he would hear himself asking again, what month is this?

An hour after breakfast one morning, in his room, he turned to Bill and said, "Well,

how about breakfast? You order breakfast.
Let's have breakfast."

"We've already had breakfast," Bill said.

"Did we?"

"Sure."

"How can you tell?"

Bill pointed to the breakfast-tray. Shep
stared at it with puzzled eyes. "I guess I belong in a benevolent institution," he said finally, "the Bide-a-wee Home, or somewheres."

"Pull yourself together," Bill advised him.
"You're all bathed and shaved and dressed
and had your breakfast and everything."

"I thought that was yesterday," Shep said.

But there were other things more serious
than this temporary amnesia; the night-sweats,
for example, and those hemorrhages of the
stomach. They were no fun. The first one
had shaken him up a bit; that sudden gush of
blood from his throat. He thought it was his
lungs and he had dismal thoughts of Switzerland and six months on his back and all that.
But one of his drinking companions had soon
set him right. Just a little rupture of a vein
in the lining of his stomach, nothing to worry
about. He'd soon get used to it. All the same
they were no picnics, nor were the sinking
spells afterward.

Shep maintained toward Nikki the most
considerate and worshipful attitude. In the

mornings he always greeted her with formal continental politeness. He would bow ceremoniously and kiss her hand. For some unexplained reason she was always Madame to Shep, in the mornings. Kees the hand, Madame? And how is Madame this morning? Did Madame rest well, he trusted. Madame was looking well. Indeed, Madame looked in very good repair. And such a smart frock and what a becoming hat.

It always set Nikki up to be taken such notice of in the mornings. She had brought along a lot of smart white sports clothes.

Following the payment of these morning respects. Shep would inquire of Madame what he could order for her to drink. Nikki usually begged off on account of it was so early in the day. She'd grown to understand that it was folly to start drinking with Shep right at the start. You couldn't keep up with him.

Whereupon Shep would act very hurt and shake his head sadly at Nikki's decline, and begin to abuse her. She was just a sissy drinker and for the life of him he couldn't understand why he permitted her the pleasure of his society. As a matter of fact, when you got right down to it, she was nothing but an old hussy. A wizened ol' witch doctor was what she was.

"And you're an old fuddy-duddy," Nikki would retort.

She had so many things the matter with her. Always losing her key, never having any matches, leaves the taps running, spills her drinks, blind as a bat, queer as a witch, no better than she should be.

"I would take advantage of the girl myself," Shep said, "only she's so vulnerable. It wouldn't be right."

Nikki said he'd better look out or she'd steal his passport.

"I'm in favor of euthanasia," Shep would state emphatically.

For the most, Shep would heap gentle reproaches upon Nikki, for he was terribly devoted to her. But it was Nikki who gave Shep his zest for living. In the blackest depths of his depressions, it was the thought of the whiteness of Nikki's skin, the curving line of her back, the touch of her well-kept hands, the warm tones of her voice, the fragrance of her hair, that recalled him to life. Like a discharged battery, he was re-energized by daily contact with this pure vessel.

Shep took Nikki and Bill and Francis all over the place. They motored to the Royal Palace of Ajuda and Necessidales and the Basilica of Estrella. He insisted that they go to the Se' Cathedral where lay the Braganzas;

the assassinated Monarch, King D. Carlos, and his unfortunate son, Prince D. Philippe. Shep had taken a melancholy turn. He became steeped in the countless little songs of the land; everywhere in the taverns he heard a penitent, sad singing. He found a vein of melancholy in the Portuguese, as deep as any in Ireland.

Mostly they went to the seaside resorts at Cascaes and Mont 'Estoril, scarcely an hour's motoring from the Avenida Palace, where they swam in a sea tempered by the Gulf Stream. They saw little of Cary during these days. He was preoccupied and enigmatic when they did see him.

Shep saw Travassos in the bar late one afternoon and asked him about Cary.

"Your friend gone crazy on clocks," Joseph said. "He buying all kind of clocks."

From Joseph they learned that Cary was rooting around in waterfront warehouses, pawnshops, stores, and taverns, for old clocks.

"What *is* all this about clocks?" Nikki demanded of Cary when she saw him. "I hear you have a roomful of clocks. What are you going to do with all those Portuguese clocks?"

"Not Portuguese. English."

"English clocks? *English.*"

"English."

"What are English clocks doing down here?"

Cary shrugged his shoulders. "Haven't the faintest idea. Only know they're here."

"How did they get here?"

Cary said he wished he knew. He said he'd heard something very vague about a boatload of clocks that left Liverpool for South Africa and was blown ashore in Portugal. Lisbon and its environs, a hundred years or so ago, had been flooded with English clocks.

"But are they so valuable now?"

"Not to the Portuguese."

"Why not to the Portuguese?"

"They don't march."

"But otherwise, I mean."

"How otherwise?"

"As antiques or something."

Cary said he was by no means an expert on old English clocks.

"You're very exasperating," Nikki said. "Please tell me. I'm terribly interested, really."

"Well, I won't know until they're properly restored."

"What are you going to do with them?"

"Ship them up to London."

But Nikki wasn't satisfied. She wanted some idea of the actual value of the clocks.

"Tell me, Cary, what is one of those clocks

worth—really? You must have some idea. Is it anything sensational?"

"No. Nothing sensational. The unsigned ones might fetch fifty pounds apiece. For the signed ones I might get, say, three hundred. Maybe less. Maybe more."

Besides his Tompion, Cary had come onto a Beverly and a Charles Gretton.

"Well," said Nikki, "I hope they're all perfectly priceless."

"That would be nice," Cary agreed.

"Tell me, Cary, did you really expect to find diamonds down here?"

"Well," said Cary, "sometimes the hundred-to-one shot comes home."

It was ten days before the Good Will Delegation was reconstituted in its original pattern and setting; Cary, Bill, Shep, Nikki and The Washout in the Avenida Palace bar. It was eight-thirty and they were all dressed for the evening. Nikki was wearing the black-and-gold dress with the golden sash (draped in the oriental manner) and the gold metal-cloth turban which she wore on the first evening in Paris. Lennox in gray tweeds and a cloth cap came in and joined them at the bar. They took him along with them upstairs for dinner. It was Lennox who suggested that, since there was no bull-fight to see and no cinema under the age of consent, they should go to the amusement park at Port Mayer. They did not leave the hotel till after ten. Outside the Avenida Palace, they turned left to walk along the Avenue of Liberty.

They had to filter through a chattering crowd of Portuguese in brown, wrinkled, unpressed suits, standing in front of an entrance beplastered with yellow bulletins.

"Football results," Lennox said. "That's a newspaper office."

They got into a cab and Lennox told the driver where to go and pretty soon the cab pulled up at the entrance to the park. Carnival noises issued from within. You could hear the music from a carousel.

"You can get a drink in here, can't you?" Shep said, hesitating at the entrance.

"Rather," Lennox told him.

The streets on either side of the park were lined with attractions; The Blue Pavilion, Little Egypt, Temple de Mystère. Concessionaires were barking through megaphones.

Nikki said that she would like to look in one of those places.

"You go ahead," Shep said, looking at a little open-air café. I see a place where a fellow can do a lot of good for himself. You can tell me about it after."

"We'll be right out," Nikki said, and led the

others into the Temple of Mystery. Shep found a table and sat down. He ordered a brandy *fine*.

After awhile the others came out and sat down with Shep.

"How was it?"

"Well," Nikki said, "you had to stand up and there was a gauze curtain over a little stage and there was a blonde sitting in a chair on the stage and she looked like Alice Terry."

"Amazing," Shep said.

"Then a man came out and delivered a disquisition."

"—in front of all those people?"

"—right out in front of everybody—and then he left off and they turned out the lights and pretty soon Alice Terry turned into a Greek goddess."

"Sensational," Shep agreed.

"Now leave me tell you. First she turned into a Greek goddess and then into a bunch of roses and then into a bowl of goldfish, and then she turned into a lighthouse in a storm, and then she took up a collection."

"—and right there is where you left—I understand," Shep said. "What will you have to drink?"

Across the street was a little shooting gallery. There were three girls behind the green baize counter yelling "Hi! Hi!" all the time.

A couple of flaring blue gas lamps lighted up the interior of the booth. Little white ducks on an endless chain kept swimming across the base of the range and disappearing with a happy clink-clink. A couple of orange-colored balls bobbled up and down on the tops of two slender columns of water.

"Let's shoot for the drinks," Bill suggested.

"Righto," Shep said. "How about it, Nikki? Want to shoot off a gun at something?"

Nikki had no objection, so they all crossed the street to the shooting gallery. They lined up at the counter. The Washout against the wall on the far right. Next him stood Lennox, then Cary and Bill and Nikki and Shep.

"What the hell," said Shep, picking up a rifle. "Haven't they got any automatics?"

They only had two automatics. Lennox had one and The Washout had the other.

"Well, then," Shep said, "one shot at a time and the first one to miss pays for the drinks. How's 'at?"

"—and for the shooting."

"What'll we shoot at?"

"Let's shoot at the clay pipes," Shep said. He took the bowl off a clay pipe with his first shot.

Bill knocked over a duck but claimed that was what he aimed at. One of the orange balls disappeared from the top of the water column when Cary fired, and Lennox accounted for an owl. Then, unexpectedly, The Washout cut loose with his automatic, shattering a whole row of pipes with his split-second firing.

"Hey," Shep yelled. "Gimme that there automatic. I'll show you some plain and fancy shooting."

But Francis refused to give it up.

"Let him keep it," Bill growled out of the side of his mouth.

Nikki raised her little target rifle to her shoulder. The end of the barrel described uncertain circles in the air. "How do you keep it still," she wanted to know.

They were all watching Nikki when they heard Shep say sharply, "Hey there! Watch yourself!" A little Portuguese in a colored shirt and wearing a cloth cap and wrinkled brown clothes and with a flat white face, had turned toward them and the muzzle of his gun was pointing directly into Nikki's side.

With the back of his arm Shep swept the barrel of the gun away from Nikki.

"You little monkey," Shep said. "Don't you know any better than to point a gun at anybody!"

"What's up?" Lennox asked.

"He was pointing his gun at Nikki. Tell

340

him for Christ's sake to keep his gun pointed the other way."

Lennox let go with a flood of Portuguese. The little mongrel stood looking at Shep, his eyes narrowing.

Shep turned away. "Go ahead and shoot, Nikki."

The little Portuguese, turning around to see if he had an audience, suddenly pointed his rifle directly at Nikki's head. "Bangbang! Bangbang!" he cried, at the same time screaming with shrill laughter and looking around at the crowd at the rail for approval.

Nikki turned her head and looked squarely into the muzzle of the gun, to the wild amusement of the little Portuguese. Shep seized the barrel of the gun and tore it out of his hands.

"Why, you crazy squirt!" he cried. "What in God's name are you trying to do! Did you see that?" he demanded of Bill.

"Smack him!" Bill said, "or I'll do it for you!"

Lennox, who had seen the whole thing, was raving at him in Portuguese. The uproar brought a cluster of curious people to the shallow entrance of the shooting gallery, railed off from the street.

"Should I slap him?" Shep asked Lennox. "He's so small——"

"Sure, give him a biff," Lennox said. "It'll teach him a lesson!"

But the gun-girl had caught hold of Shep's left arm and was pulling him around, turning him away from the Portuguese.

"Let go of my arm!" Shep cried. But she held on like a mad witch, and Shep, looking over his shoulder and down into the malevolent little face of the Portuguese, said, "When she turns loose of my arm, I'm going to slap you bow-legged."

The Portuguese was spitting curses at him. Then, without warning, he leaped upon Shep and locking his legs about Shep's middle, buried his teeth in his throat just under the ear and held on like an evil bat.

"Jesus Christ!" Shep tore himself loose from the gun-girl, got his hands on his assailant's throat and forced his mouth open and his head back. The two of them whirled about for several moments before Shep could free himself. He hurled the Portuguese against the side wall of the gallery with a crash.

Shep took out his handkerchief and pressed it to his throat. "Of . . . all . . . the . . . tricks . . ." he was saying. The little Portuguese was gathering himself in a crouching position against the wall.

"Atenceo!" someone shouted.

No one saw where the knife came from;

somewhere in the Portuguese's clothes, but there it was in his hands, a clasp knife. They all heard a metallic click as he pressed a release in the handle and the steel blade flew out —long and slender and sinister. Bill said afterward it was a regular toad-stabber.

"Uh, oh," said Shep in that mild, surprised tone he used when something unexpected turned up.

He halted for a moment, uncertain. Speaking over his shoulder and not taking his eyes off the face of the little Portuguese, he said: "Thought you said these little monkeys wouldn't fight, Captain."

"Steady on—" Lennox warned him in a low voice.

The appearance of the knife had stopped the breath of every person in the place. They stood, frozen in attitudes of arrested motion, staring hypnotically at the naked blade. Here, before their eyes, was murder.

The little Portuguese, his glittering eyes on Shep's face, was rising to a half crouch. His body was bent forward at the waist and he held the knife close in—like the knife-users around Montparnasse. He advanced on Shep, standing uncertainly. No one moved, no one spoke, no one breathed. He was closing in.

Shep did not back away. Instead he took a half-step forward.

Single Lady

"Drop that."

Someone screamed. Shep was standing directly in front of the Portuguese and his shoulders blocked out the action, so that those behind did not see exactly what happened. They were too close together, now, anyway, for anyone to see exactly what happened. But it seemed that Shep made as if to seize the hand that held the knife.

Tat-tat-tat-tat-tat-tat-tat—tat—tat——tat!

At the first report of the target rifle the knife fell clattering to the floor. As the lead poured into him the little Portuguese began to claw at his belly and doubled over. A torrent of blood burst from his mouth and nostrils and he fell face forward on the floor writhing and twisting.

Shep stood looking down at him. Not till the Portuguese was down on the floor did heads turn in the direction of the source of the firing. There was The Washout, back against the wall, the smoke curling from his automatic. His blazing yellow eyes were snapping like the rifle he held in his hand. He fired again across Bill's shoulder. Crack! The last shot took effect in the head. The jerking figure on the floor lay still.

Still no one moved. The Washout put his gun on the counter, slipped past Bill and the rest, put his arms around Shep's shoulder for a moment.

"Good-bye, Shep." From the pressure of his hands Shep knew it was for the last time.

He was gone. Swift as a cat he disappeared in the crowd. The Washout was gone.

A whistle sounded shrilly. There was a pounding of feet, coming nearer.

"Clear out!" Lennox said to Shep and Bill, "I'll stand by for the police."

"Come on, Shep," Bill said, taking him by the arm. "Let's screw out of this place." Followed by Cary and Nikki they slipped through the thick fringe of excited people fast gathering in front of the shooting gallery and made their way down the street toward the entrance. Nobody stopped them.

"Great glittering Jeeroosalem," Bill burst out, "did you see the way Francis poured lead into that baby?"

"Fast work," Shep agreed.

"Fast! *Fast!* Why Christ amighty that boy's chain lightning with a gun. He was the only one who did any thinking. The rest of us just stood petrified."

"Pretty good, all right."

"And did you see his face—his *eyes?* Did you see the whole thing?" he demanded of Shep. "It was the prettiest piece of work I ever saw. I didn't even know who was shooting until it was all over. Those bullets went whizzing right past my ear. If I'd a moved an inch I'd of got one in the jaw. They went right through *here*." He pointed to the angle between his shoulder and his head. "I didn't dare move. I was paralyzed anyhow."

Bill was terribly excited by the whole thing. "That lad's sudden death. Shep, it's a good job I didn't crowd him—the way I wanted to."

"I told you to look out for him," Shep reminded him.

"Boy, oh, Boy! You know where he shot that Portuguese first? Right in the belly. Then he just cut a line right up to his chin. It was the lung shots that brought out that blood. And then he put that last one in the head—just for luck."

"Nice shooting," Shep agreed again.

"Well, that's the last of ol' Francis," Bill kept on. "I'll bet we never see him again."

"What will happen if they get him?" Nikki asked.

"Don't worry, sister. They'll never get *that* one. He can take care of *himself*. I'd be sorry for them if they ever did corner him. That's the first time I ever saw him look happy," Bill said reminiscently, "when he shot that drunken little monkey."

They were outside Port Mayer. There were no taxis in sight.

"Let's walk a while," Bill said, "I'm so excited I want to walk."

"The hell with it," Shep said.

"Come on, let's walk."

But Shep was obdurate. He sat down on the curbstone. Pretty soon a cab came along and Bill hailed it.

Shep made no effort to stand up. Bill took him under the shoulders and lifted him to his feet like a child.

Nikki got in first, then Shep, then Bill. Cary sat on the jump seat facing them.

"Well, sir," said Bill to Shep, "the old boy came through—at last."

They were all silent.

"What's the matter with *you*, Shep." Bill wanted to know. "I've never seen *you* so quiet."

"That's right," Shep agreed. "I'm kind of quiet."

They rode along for a few blocks, the cab jolting over the cobblestones. Nikki took out her cigarette case and selected a cigarette. She offered one to Shep, but he shook his head.

"Your lighter working?" she inquired of Shep.

"Sweet Nikki," Shep said, "she never has any matches."

Shep reached into his waistcoat pocket,

347

searching for the lighter. He brought it out slowly, Nikki put her cigarette between her lips and bent her head. Shep struck the flint. The light flared brightly in the dark interior of the cab.

Nikki cried out. The cigarette fell to the floor of the cab.

Bill and Cary stared. The hand that held the lighter was wet with blood.

"Shep! Shep!" Nikki cried, "you're hurt!"

" 's a forgery," Shep said. But his body had already begun to sag against Nikki's.

"Bill! Cary!" Nikki cried. "Do something! Stop the cab! Something! Oh, Shepard!" She put her arm about him. His head was already heavy against her shoulder.

"Shep! Shep!" Bill cried in a frightened voice. "Are you hurt? Where are you hurt, Shep?"

He pounded on the window and the driver stopped his cab. The gleam from the street light showed Shep's face—white as white. Cary's hands were exploring under Shep's white waistcoat.

"Here it is," he said. "He's been stabbed."

"Hospital! Hospital! Hospital!" Bill yelled at the cab driver. The car lurched forward jolting over the cobblestones.

"We'll have to stop the cab," Cary cried, "he's bleeding like anything."

"Nikki," Shep whispered, "could I put my head in your lap."

Very tenderly she lifted his head down into her lap.

"You may not believe it," Shep said, "but this is . . . the best thing . . . that ever happened . . . to me. . . ."

Shepard Lambert died next day in the Hospital de Sao Josè. Cary Lockwood wrote a letter to Shepard's mother in Illinois. Nikki wept like a child when she read it. She said it was the most beautiful letter she'd ever read.

CHAPTER XII

CARY and Nikki were sitting in the garden lounge of the Ritz Hotel in Madrid (exclusively patronized by the highest Spanish and foreign society) at eleven o'clock in the morning drinking cocktails when Bill came in. He was loaded with packages and he was grinning all over the shop. He said he was full of beer. He said he'd found a marvelous place called the Café Vermouth where they served you an anchovy on a toothpick in a clam shell with your beer.

"What have you got there?" Nikki inquired.

"S'prizes," Bill said mysteriously.

"S'prizes? For whom?"

"S'prizes for you, Nikki."

"For Nikki? Why, William Talbot! You went and got s'prizes for Nikki?"

"So that's what you've been up to all morning," Cary said, "buying things for Nikki. We wondered what had become of you."

"And I had a swell time, too. Well, let's see now, Nikki," said Bill, looking over the packages on the seat of the green wicker bench. "Open that one first." It was a flat, important package labelled Parfumeria Gal, Madrid.

With every package Nikki opened, Bill's grin grew broader. Nikki was very excited. In a minute she was surrounded by sheafs of wrapping paper and cardboard boxes and cord, and entrenched behind an array of bottles.

"Bill—you blessed! I've never had any Spanish perfume in my life." She threw her arms about his neck and kissed him. "Why *Bill*—why *Bill*—aren't you sweet! How on earth did you know what to choose—'*Flores de Talavera*,' she read, '*Trini* . . . *Jardines de Espana* . . . *Heno de Pravia*.' Why, Bill!"

"Well," Bill said, "I had a fellow with me and anyway I tried 'em all out myself."

He reached into his waistcoat pocket and brought out a half-dozen flat, brilliant little bottles. "And I made 'em give me the samples, too."

Nikki arranged them in a shining staggered little line on the table.

"Now," said Bill, "am I getting popular?"

"Popular! Bill, you're—you're too wonderful—" Nikki was lost for words.

"All right then—open that."

It turned out to be a color print—a starry night sky, blue—and a narrow, dark street and rich shadows and two lovers in costume standing close to each other.

"Why, Bill, this is perfectly stunning!" Nikki cried, as she rolled it up. "I don't know what to say."

"Well, I had a sharpshooter helping me," Bill said, a little sheepishly. "He said it was the best in the place."

"What's that?" Nikki asked pointing at a large bundle wrapped in yellow paper with the word *Jiminez* printed on it in block lettering.

"Oh that," said Bill, "that's just something I got."

"—not for me?" A vague shadow of disappointment fell across Nikki's face.

"Nikki, you're spoiled," Cary said.

"Oh, Cary, how can you say that! Why, I'm so happy with my s'prizes I can hardly talk."

Bill picked up the bundle and put it in Nikki's lap.

"It's for you, beautiful," he said.

She looked at him in quick disbelief.

"It's for you—I got it for you."

"Do you mean it?"

"I was only teasing you."

"Bill, you're a wretch."

Very carefully she untied the yellow cord. "It's so heavy," she said.

She folded back the wrappings. Then she

sat quite still, looking at the heap of brilliant color in her lap; huge crimson, yellow, and blue blossoms worked onto a brilliant white background. She lifted the fringe delicately with her fingers. It was nearly a half metre long.

For a long time she sat staring at the Spanish shawl in her lap. When she looked up the tears were standing in her eyes. She couldn't speak. Then she buried her face in the shawl and wept.

The tears came to Bill's eyes, too. He put his arm clumsily about her shoulders and said, "Now, now, Nikki—" but he couldn't say anything more either. Cary looked away from them.

After awhile Nikki dried her eyes with her handkerchief. "Aren't I silly," she cried, "I really—" but the tears came to her eyes again and she couldn't speak.

Bill was full of information about the shawl. He'd got it from a very serious house, he said, the Casa Jiminez, at the last price. He'd looked at a green one, and a blue one and a very, very old one, but this was the shawl for Nikki; white with all that splintered sunlight.

Was it too long?

Nikki stood up and swung the shawl about her hips and shoulders. "She's got the figure for it," Bill declared. He was very proud of his idea.

"But this is very expensive," Nikki said doubtfully, examining both sides of the shawl.

"Very expensible," Bill agreed, "obtained at incalculable expense. It took a lot of old Spanish women a lot of time to make that there shawl."

"Hundreds of years," Nikki said, "I bet."

"Real silk," Bill said. "I'll show you how you can tell the difference," he said. "You see now if this was artificial silk," he said, taking a single white silk strand of the fringe and wrapping it around his index finger, "you see, if it's artificial silk when you take a thread in your finger, it breaks." He gave it a convincing tug and the thread did not part. "If it's natural silk, well then you cut your finger instead," he explained.

He insisted that Nikki and Cary both test the threads. "You see," he said triumphantly, "you see."

With all the beautiful crystal bottles in front of her and the Spanish shawl in her lap, Nikki looked as though she might weep again.

"I'll have to go upstairs," she said finally, "you shouldn't take advantage of a poor girl like this."

"I'll send for a page," Bill said, "and he can take them up to your room."

"No, no," said Nikki, "I want to carry them up myself."

When Nikki had gone, Cary looked at Bill. "You old son-of-a-gun," he said. He thought it was a little wicked to play up to Nikki's weakness for gifts.

Bill was full of information when Nikki came back. "This is Thursday and there are jai alai games and a bull-fight. We can see both if we are really nippy. The jai alai begins at 4:15 and the bull-fights at 5:30. We can look in at the courts for a half-hour or so, and then drive to the arena—not five minutes between them—and we wouldn't even miss the paseo at the beginning." Had Cary or Nikki ever seen jai alai? O. K. then, how was this for a program for the afternoon: see the jai alai, see the bull-fights and catch the Sud Express for Paris at 20 hours. O. K.? O. K. Bill sent a waiter into the hotel lobby to look for his sharp-shooter.

He was an impassive little fellow with a greenstone ring and a tie-pin. Bill presented him to Nikki and Cary as Pedro Something or other, Rasilla, perhaps.

"I give you my card," Pedro said quickly.

"We haven't any cards, I'm sorry," Cary said as they looked at his.

"Now listen, Pete," Bill said. "We're going to leave everything to you, because we've got our drinking to attend to. Now, first you better get our rail tickets from the porter and get space for us on the Wagon Lits for Paris —two compartments—then get tickets for the jai alai—include yourself, of course, and then for the bull-fights—and then tell the cashier to get our accounts ready—and then you better steer us onto the train because we may be in a kind of state. You better get a car for us so we can move around."

"Si, si, si," said Pete.

"Do you need any money?"

"No, no. I geeve you my account—after."

"All right, Pete, you do your stuff, and look, we want seats right down in front. Pay premiums if you have to—but we have to be close. Understand? Miss Kansas City here can't see very far."

"I will command the best."

"We'll be right here when you get back," Bill said.

They sat and drank their cocktails. "These sure are beautiful cocktails," Bill said, "let's order a hundred, anyway."

It was curious how they all felt alike now. They had to keep going, going, going. They dared not stop to think. They dreaded a pause in the conversation. Your mind would go back to Shep and the Portuguese shooting gallery and you mustn't think about that. You had to stay as far ahead of your thoughts as you could.

Each detected the same fear in the other; it was behind Cary's eyes, a shiver of dread betrayed Nikki every little while, and Bill's agitation showed in his continued, excited conversation.

The three were in the same state that Shep had once tried to explain: they were swimming naked at night in a lake beneath whose black velvet surface lurked invisible monsters ready to pull you under if you should let your legs down. You had to keep swimming for a far-off invisible shore.

"Would you *like* to see a Spanish bull-fight, Nikki?" Bill asked suddenly. "I never thought to ask you."

"I'd love to see one," Nikki said.

"Good old Nikki! The only thing I guess," said Bill seriously, "is about the horses. When the bull charges the horse. You won't like that."

"Well, I can turn my head."

The garden lounge of the Ritz Hotel in Madrid is a lovely place, sunny and quiet with distant Spanish tango music.

After awhile they all felt very peaceful.

"Do you know," Bill said to Nikki, "I solved the problem of Cary's sardines."

Nikki looked at him inquiringly.

"Well," said Bill, "they make the best tips. I gave a can to the valet this morning and he was practically overcome. Then I gave one to the page and one to the chamber-maid and she curtesied as pretty as anything. And I gave one to the elevator operator——"

"My beautiful skinless, boneless sardines," Cary wailed.

"Did you hear that?" Bill demanded of Nikki in an aggrieved voice. "Here he's been complaining about those sardines all the way from Lisbon. Said how heavy they were and how they smelt up the clothes in his suit-case and how he couldn't offend his Portuguese boy friends by not taking them—and now he's crying."

"Well, all the same——" Cary began.

"All the same, what?"

"All the same they were my sardines and anyway you don't have to tip anybody. The hotel charges you ten per cent for service."

"Well, I'll be good—why, listen to him. You'd think I wasn't doing him a favor——"

"Did you give them all away?"

"Well, no, but I figure to give a couple to

the porter and maybe to Pete—if he turns
out all right——"

"My beautiful sardines. The very first
quality," Cary moaned.

"Well," said Bill, "some people are just
naturally ungrateful. I'll never help him out
again."

After a while Pedro came in.

"Hello, Pete," Bill said dreamily, "what's
the news?"

"Is all arrange'," Pete said.

"Sit down and have a drink with us and a
sandwich or something."

"Thank you."

"Now tell us, have you attended to everything—car, tickets, train, everything?"

"Is all arrange'," Pete repeated steadily.

"Good ole Pete. How soon do we leave?"
Pete looked at his watch. "Ten minoots."

"Ten minoots, hey. Well, drink up, boys
and girls, we've got to get agoing."

The jai alai game they agreed among themselves was a kind of washout. The gambling
was the main idea about jai alai and they
couldn't get into that.

The play was fast enough when they played
—but the best player was kind of stout and
bald headed—and after every point the book-
makers in their red berets swarmed out in front

of the crowd and set up a hell of a clatter, shouting the changes in odds.

They left early for the bull-fights. Bill began to tingle when their car pulled up in front of the Plaza de Toros.

He got down and looked up at the high circling wall of the arena.

"You know how I feel," he said. "Just like I was going into the stadium for the first game of the season. I feel like something's going to happen in there. I'll be all right after the kick-off," he said, "after I tackle somebody or somebody tackles me, I'll be all right. Aren't you excited?" he said.

Nikki said she was all agape.

A little girl came up and pinned a red carnation in Bill's buttonhole. He lifted her up so she could manage it. "I wisht I had a can of your sardines," he said to Cary. "I'm all tangled up in francs, escudos, pesetas and centimos. I don't know what to give her."

"Well, give her a couple of pesetas, anyway," Cary said.

Bill set the girl down and gave her two pesetas.

"Plaza de Toros," he said, looking at the lettering out in stone over the entrance, "Plaza de Toros—I saw that once in Carmen. Oh boy—this is great!"

"Is there a bar or anything inside?" Bill wanted to know.

"Oh, yes," said Pedro.

Bill's face lit up. "Well, let's go in and have a drink."

The bar was not very crowded and they decided to drink beer on account of it was quite hot and the Spanish beer was very refreshing. Only Nikki wouldn't drink beer—she asked for a vermouth *con aperitivo*.

The man standing beside Bill was very soused. He had a tall glass of beer in his hand and he swayed uncertainly. He was talking drunkenly to his friend, and as he gestured with his right hand, he tipped up his glass. The beer poured onto Bill's foot in a golden cascade, filling up his shoe.

"What the hell," said Bill.

The drunk was all apologies.

Bill took off his shoe and emptied it and put it back on. "Certainly feels squishy," he said. "Hope I don't catch cold in my right ear."

They had quite a few more drinks and Bill bought fans for all of them and they went inside. Bill wanted to get the guide tight, but it was hard to do.

Pedro had got fine seats for them; the second row, just above the trench, on the shady side. It was like walking into a bowl of sunshine to come into the arena; all golden light and color. Sixteen thousand people in the bull-ring.

For ten centimos Bill bought a Programa Oficial de Espectaculos printed in bold black type on a single sheet of pink flimsy. Plaza de Toros de Madrid, the program said. Gran Corida extraordinaria. The bulls, it said, came from the acreditada ganaderia de D. Antonio Perez, de San Fernando (Salamanca). There were inked drawings of the bulls, six of them, in two vertical columns of three each, with their names, numbers and colors. The name of the first bull was Capuchino, negro Num. 15. From his picture he was a jet black, fierce looking beast with wide tapering horns.

Joselito, the great bull-fighter, Pedro was explaining to them, had been killed in this ring a season or so before, but there were some promising young novilleros coming up. Marquez, Antonio Posada, and Nino de la Palma.

"Do you know Paolino Uzcudun?" Pedro Rasilla demanded abruptly.

Nobody knew Paolino Uzcudun and Pedro was downcast. Bill wanted to know what about Paolino.

"Boxer," Pedro said. "Some day will be champion. A very strong boy. Strong as a beer."

"Strong as a what?" Bill said.

"Like a tigre. Like a beer. Strong as a beer. Can't hold a lamp chimbly without breaking it. No drink. No smoke. Once at the Lido I saw him. The girls tease him. They pass the drinks right under 'is nose. He don't touch. I was surprise to see his will power. He dance every dance like a beer."

Pedro was of the opinion that Paolino was too strong for anybody. He said he saw him fight a Belgian in the ring and the Belgian hit Paolino on the nose and made his nose bleed and Paolino got mad and gave such a punch to him, he knocked him out of the ring.

Pedro also gave them some of his other opinions while they were waiting for the ring to be cleared.

"The movies tires me a little," he said. "I go to sleep. I am in favor of the theatre."

In the afternoon sunlight the parade seemed more resplendent than the one they had seen at night in Lisbon. The black-and-silver-and-orange uniforms of the bull-fighters glistened in the slanting rays of the sun. The music sounded more bravely. There was a more lively jingle to the bells on the mules. The procession came directly across the ring, the bull-fighters bowed to the King of Spain, seated in an upper box. Nikki studied it all gravely through her glasses.

When the bugle blew for the first bull, Bill,

who was sitting on the aisle seat, began to tremble with excitement.

"Is it so dangerous?" he asked Pedro.

"Sure," said Rasilla, "bull-fighting is dangerous."

"Is it true," Cary wanted to know, "that the bull is blind when he charges. I've heard it somewhere."

The guide said the bull was perhaps a little blind with rage when he charged the cape. He explained further to Bill that bull-fighting wasn't dangerous if you didn't work close and if you ran away when the bull came.

"It takes a little heart to go into the bull-ring," he said. He had seen the knees of novices knock together, he said, in their tight breeches on their first appearance in the Madrid arena.

The leaves of the double wooden gate at the far side of the arena swung open. Capuchino came out with a roar, charging across the arena, a huge black vicious bull, full of fight.

"None of your skinless, boneless Portuguese," Bill said. "Look at that baby."

One of the bull-fighters ran out and pulled the bull back and forth with his cape, vaulting over the fence when the bull charged directly at him.

"Marquez," Pedro said, as a bull-fighter

stepped out and held his cape for the bull. "It's his bull. He must kill the bull."

Marquez played the bull close to him with the cape. At each charge and pivot the crowd shouted. "Close work," Pedro said. "He work close."

Suddenly the bull caught sight of the gray horse against the barrier across the arena. He charged with the speed of an express train. The force of the charge lifted the horse into the air, throwing him on his side, and upsetting the rider. His pic pole flew off into the sand. The next moment the bull was driving into the belly of the fallen horse. Nikki did not say a word. She was very pale and she took her eyes out of the arena and levelled her glasses into the crowd.

Marquez drew the bull away from the horse with his cape and directed him at another picador sitting on his horse next to the barrera. The bull-ring servants helped the fallen gray horse to his feet, all blood and sand and entrails. They led him close to the trenches. An attendant with a short knife stood up over the fence and grasped the horse's right ear firmly in his left hand. He raised the knife shoulder high and brought it down between the back of the horse's ears with a quick, powerful blow. The horse collapsed as if he had been shot. They covered him with canvas. Afterwards the bull-ring servants hooked chains to him and the mules dragged him out.

The bugle sounded again. "This is for the Banderilleros," Pedro said.

A Banderillero holding the two red darts closely together in each hand, skipped across the ring to where the bull stood and as the bull charged, planted the barbs in the bull's shoulder, swerving clear of the horns, and continued running to the barrier, vaulting safely inside.

"Fast on his feet," Bill said, "that guy's pretty fast all right. Ought to do the hundred in about ten two. I bet I could catch him though."

Bill was the most excited about the bull-fight. Nikki was silent and a little unhappy. Cary sat with his chin cupped in his hand, carefully following the movements below.

The dart men planted four pairs of banderillas in the shoulders of the bull.

From far away came the sound of the bugle again. "Now he must kill the bull," said Pedro. Marquez, holding his sword and his cape before him, walked across the ring and came to attention under the King's box. "What's he saying?" Bill demanded.

" 'E dedicate the bull to the King of Spain," Pedro explained.

Marquez turned and with the cape in his

left hand and his slender shining blade in his right, walked out toward Capuchino, standing with lowered head in the center of the ring. He played the bull back and forth with his cape until finally the bull stood still, his head lower than ever, his front feet apart. Four of the bull-fighters came out and stood behind Marquez, holding their capes. Marquez passed his cape experimentally under the muzzle of the bull. Capuchino did not charge. Facing the bull and planting himself directly between the two wide horns, Marquez raised his sword to the level of his eyes, sighted along it, and rising high on his toes, drove the blade between the bull's shoulders. The long white blade disappeared into the body of the bull, right up to where Marquez held it with his hand. Capuchino lunged, went to his knees, shaking his head. Blood poured from his nostrils in a torrent. He raised himself, fell back, rolled over on his side. The crowd applauded wildly.

"Nize work," Pedro said. "Nize going."

"Hell," said Bill Talbot, "that doesn't look so tough."

Pedro smiled patronizingly. "No? Well, it takes skill."

"What the hell," said Bill, "I think I could be a bull-fighter myself. As a matter of fact, I think I'll be one anyway."

"You should have started at twelve years of old," Pedro said.

"I'll bet I could start now."

"Is not for you," said the Spaniard.

"You think I haven't got the nerve or something?"

Pedro held up his hands. No, it was not that. Meestaire Talbot was American, no? Well, bull-fighting was for Spaniards. It took something else. Technique.

"I'll bet he thinks we're ascared," Bill said.

"He tackled a horse once," Cary told Pedro.

"Is not the same," Pedro insisted stubbornly.

The glamour, the thrill, the color, the danger of bull-fighting had communicated itself to Bill Talbot. He wondered why he'd never thought of it before. Why, this was as good as football, or flying, or fighting.

Watching Bill's face, Cary could see that Bill, in his mind had gone through all the steps leading up to his supremacy as the ace bull-fighter in the Madrid arena. Right up to the moment when he was dedicating the bull to Nikki.

Bill was asking Pedro if there were no American bull-fighters. "I think one," Pedro said, "but not here in Spain. He fight in Mexico City." He said he thought the name of the American bull-fighter was Sidney Franklin.

There were six bulls in all to be killed and Bill and Cary and Nikki very soon learned the twenty-minute four part routine in the killing of each bull: the release of the bull into the arena, the preliminary runs with the cape, the encounter with the picadors, the planting of the banderillas, the final dispatch by sword. The skilled graceful technique of the bull-fighters made it appear simple and effortless. Between the second and the third bulls, Bill said he had to go and sharpen his skates and asked to be excused. He was on the aisle seat so he didn't disturb anyone when he went out. But when he came back it was plain to see that he had visited the bar. "Where's your hat?" Cary asked him.

Donoso, a coal black bull, was let into the arena as Bill sat down. The animal came straight across the ring. Bill followed the course of the bull hypnotically. He seized Pedro's arm tightly. "Is the bull blind when he charges?" he whispered.

"I think he see only the cape."

"You sure he's blind when he charges."

Pedro was watching the bull.

Bill reached over and plucked the program out of Cary's hand. Suddenly rising from his seat he slipped into the aisle, ran down the steps, leaped into the trenches and vaulted like a professional over the barrera into the arena itself. Holding the pink flimsy like a cape, he stepped into the path of the bull. The audience, thinking it an unadvertised novelty on the program, cheered and laughed, but Cary and Nikki and Pedro jumped to their feet, white and frightened.

Twice Bill pulled the bull past him with the foolish little sheet of paper. Each time a shout went up from the crowd. Oh! Ah! Hola! Nikki had Cary's arm in a hysterical grip.

Then Nikki saw that Bill was down, down in the white hard packed sand of the bull-ring. The bull was on top of him, driving into his body, hooking left and right, short savage, powerful hooks. Nikki's hand lost its grasp on Cary's arm and she slid silently down between the seats. The matadors ran out from the shadow of the barrier and drew the bull away with their capes. One of them pulled on the bull's tail.

They picked Bill up and carried him across the arena and through the gates and out of sight in the dark passageway under the stands.

Cary held Nikki's head in his left arm and fanned her back to consciousness. Pedro led them around to the infirmary. None of them could talk.

Bill was lying on a table under a low brilliant electric light. He looked up and grinned when Cary and Nikki came in. Two men in white surgical uniforms stood at the head of the table. A third was cutting away Bill's white shirt and zephyr with a pair of scissors. Pedro explained the presence of Nikki and Cary to the doctor.

"I slipped," Bill volunteered.

"Too bad," Cary said. "You were going great. You were a big success . . ."

"Wasn't I though. Oh, Jesus, Doc . . . know why I slipped, Cary? Know why I slipped? On account of that beer in my shoe . . ."

"How do you feel?" Nikki asked.

"I don't hurt—yet," Bill said. "Hey, doctor," Bill said, suddenly raising himself up on the table, "what the hell are you doing down there . . ."

The doctor signaled the man at the head of the table. He placed a gauze cone over Bill's face and opened a can of ether. The doctor jerked his head angrily back at Pedro.

"He wants that we should go right away," the guide said hurriedly.

Nikki caught Bill's hand and pressed it against her cheek.

"I'm glad I wore my new blue shorts," Bill

371

was saying, "I'll be a big success in the hospital . . ."

Two reporters were standing outside the door. They interrogated Pedro rapidly in Spanish. Pedro turned to Cary. "They want to know w'y you' friend descend into the bullring."

Cary regarded them thoughtfully for a moment. "Tell them," he said, "that it seemed like a good idea . . . at the time."

Cary took Nikki back to the Ritz and then came back to the infirmary. It was an hour before train time when he got back. Nikki was anxiously waiting for him downstairs.

"Is he all right? Is he all right?"

"They took him to the Hospital del Nino Jesus," he told Nikki, "where they take all the wounded toreadors," he added smiling. "He won't be out for a month or so. He sent you his extra special love and says not to hang about. He said he needed a good long rest anyhow."

"Is he badly hurt?"

"He's got a couple of horn wounds in his left side."

"We can't go off and leave him," Nikki said.

"There's nothing for it," Cary said. There was nothing they could do for the present for Bill in Madrid. Besides, Cary said, he had to get back. His clocks would be arriving in London.

"I know what I'll do," Nikki said. "I'll give Bill my turtles. Then I'm sure he'll be a big success in the hospital."

"We'll have to leave in a few minutes," Cary warned her.

"I'll be ready for the train," Nikki said.

CHAPTER XIII

THE Sud Express from Madrid arrives in Paris at sixteen hours. Among the passengers who got down from the train in the great shadowy Gare d'Orsay were Cary Lockwood and Nikki. Porters carried their bags through the gates of the station to a cab at the street entrance. It was raining and dark outside and the lights were just coming up. Standing on the curb, waiting to get into the cab, Nikki shivered.

"Carlton," Cary told the driver.

"Carlton, oui m'sieu'."

They were in Paris again. Home in Paris. Once more they recognized the sights and sounds and the smells of Paris; the insistent, ceaseless tooting of the bulb horns. There were the signs again: Suze . . . Orleons . . . Bière de la Comète . . . Dubonnet . . . Costume Cyber . . . Byrrh. Neither spoke on their way across town. The cab slipped and slid on the wet glistening pavement. Nikki clutched Cary's arm, when the back end of the cab slued about.

The doorman at the Carlton was very glad

to see them. He saluted and took their bags
out of the cab while Cary paid off the driver.
Inside the hotel the porter handed Cary the
keys to Nikki's and his own rooms, and an ac-
cumulation of letters. Cary and Nikki went
up in the lift together. They got out on the
fifth floor, turned right along the hall and
stopped before eighty-eight. Cary unlocked
the door and opened it. Nikki entered first
and switched on the light. They were home
again in Nikki's sitting room. There, on the
white marble mantelpiece was the brass Arab
steed with the horseman astride, with a hawk
poised on his wrist. There were the two gilt
candlesticks and the ormolu clock. There was
the colored engraving in the gold frame on the
wall; the gallant in ruffs sitting beside the lady
on her dressing table, "La Toilette." There
was the other engraving of the lady playing
with a Pomeranian over the title "La Consolation de l' Absence, Dedidee a Milady Com-
tesse de Douglas."

Nikki's eyes fell upon the little portable victrola standing on the table next the door. The
mechanism had run down and the needle still
sat upon the record. It was Toselli's "Serenade." Play me out with music, play me out
with music. She turned away and took off her
hat and slipped off her coat. The porters came
up with the bags. Cary gave them five francs

each and they bowed themselves out. The sitting room was beautifully in order, but it had the empty feeling of an unlived-in room. It seemed so lonely and reproachful. Cary walked across the room and opened the French windows. It was raining harder now. Paris was all alight.

Nikki came and stood beside him at the windows, looking out. Close by, on the left loomed the great gray stone mass that was the Arc de Triomphe. Far down the Champs Élysées to the right was the Obelisk. On the buildings across were self-same old familiar signs: Peugeot . . . Citroen . . . Apartment a Louer . . . Nikki shivered at the open window and turned back into the room. Cary closed the windows.

Nikki opened the door to her bedroom, went inside and turned on the lights. Cary picked up her bags and carried them in after her. Nikki had opened the doors of her wardrobe and was standing in front of it staring at the rows of dresses on their hangers, and the tiers of shoes. Dead. All dead, she said and closed the wardrobe.

Cary went to the windows and drew the heavy red drapes together. Nikki turned on the night light and switched off the glassy lights in the chandelier. Once more the bedroom glowed mysteriously in red and gold as when Cary had first seen it. There were the little red mules on the second shelf of the night table with their forlorn little gold pompoms.

Nikki sat down on the edge of the bed. Her shoulders drooped.

"Well," she said, "we're home."

"Yes, Nikki, we're home."

Cary was standing over by the door, against the wall, regarding her somberly.

Nikki picked the telephone up and called a number. After a long while she got an answer. She spoke for a few moments and then replaced the receiver. She looked up at Cary and tears were standing in her eyes. "He said the poor little fellow is dead."

"Who said that?"

"The doctor says Eighty-Eight-Carlton died. Distemper."

"I'm so sorry."

"Cary, do you mind if I go into the bathroom a minute? I want to wash my face."

"Oh, no," Cary said and started back into the sitting room.

"Please don't go away," Nikki begged. "Don't go in the other room. Stay in here, Cary. Please do."

"All right."

Nikki got some things out of her bag and went into the bathroom. "Don't go away, now." Cary heard the water running.

When she came out Cary was standing by the door.

"Well," he said, "I think I'd better ——"

"No! No!" Nikki cried out, running over to him. "No! No! Cary. Don't say it! Don't say you're going!"

"But, Nikki, I'm afraid I——"

"No!" cried Nikki fiercely. "You're not."

"But. . . ."

She flung her arms around Cary's neck. "Oh, Cary, Cary, don't go," she begged, "don't go—don't go——"

Cary stood looking down at her uncertainly.

"Don't leave me, Cary—promise me you won't leave me."

"But Nikki. . . ."

"Don't you see, Cary—don't you understand? You can't leave me alone now. I can't be alone. I'm afraid. You will stay with me, won't you? You won't go. Oh, Cary, Cary, Cary——" Hysteria seized her at the thought of being left alone.

Her knees began to give away and she started to slip through Cary's arms to the floor. Very tenderly he picked her up and carried her over to the bed. She would not release her arms from about his neck.

"Cary, you won't go, will you? I'm—I'm so frightened."

"No, Nikki, I won't go."

She searched his face with timid, frightened eyes.

"Cary——?"

"Yes, Nikki."

"Cary—don't you like Nikki?"

"How can you ask that?"

"Cary—say something to me. Say something nice to me. You've never said anything nice to me—not once. Be nice to me Cary. Say something nice to me."

"Did you really want me to?"

"Oh, I've wanted you to so much. I've waited and waited."

"Poor Nikki."

"Haven't I been pretty good, Cary? Haven't I done better? Don't you think I——"

"Yes, Nikki, you've been splendid."

"Ah, but that's sweet of you, Cary—to say that. You don't know."

She was silent.

"Cary—" she began timidly.

"Yes, Nikki."

"Cary—you won't think I'm bold—or foolish, will you?"

"No, Nikki."

"And you will tell me the truth, won't you?"

"I'll try."

"Cary—Cary," she said, "Cary, do you—don't you love me . . . a little?"

He looked down at her for a long time—at the white face, at her blind frightened eyes.

"Yes, Nikki, I love you."

Nikki closed her eyes and took a deep breath.

"Darling," she whispered, "darling, darling, darling—darling, darling, darling—" She drew him down to her searching for his mouth with her own.

Eighty-eight Carlton was still and dark. The drawn curtains held back the gleams from the street-lights below. The ticking of the red-leather traveling clock on the night table was the only sound in the bedroom. Nikki's breath came so softly there was no sound of her breathing. She was lying on her side, her face toward the wall, her hand beneath her cheek. She was asleep.

Cary lay staring with wide open eyes into the darkness. Suddenly he knew the feeling Nikki had cried out to him—loneliness. He was desperately lonely here in this wide tall dark room. He wanted Shep, he wanted Bill, he wanted Francis, he wanted Johnny Swann. He wanted to hear Shep's excited voice again. He wanted to hear Bill laugh. He wanted the Minnesota farm again and the incense of burning leaves in the autumn. He wanted the

cool waters of Puget Sound. He wanted his
old rooms back at Oxford with the half-moon
of tulips outside and the sound of the Westminster chimes from Cardinal tower. He
wanted the hard, firm turf of the sports fields
beneath his spiked running shoes. He wanted
to hear the rattle of punt poles on the river,
the jingling of push-bike bells. He wanted
his old apartment on the Heumarkt in Vienna.
He wanted back all the times he had been
happy and all the places where he had known
happiness.

He would never be alone again. In the
darkness he could see the outline of the sleeping figure beside him. He could smell the
fragrance of her dishevelled hair. He could
see, above her disarranged clothing, the white
contours of her throat. A gleam of white
flesh showed above the tops of her tightly
drawn stockings. Her garter clasps were
shinning in the darkness. Nikki stirred in
her sleep.

A great wave of tenderness for the sleeping girl swept over Cary. She could not be
left alone; well, she would not be left alone
now. Not ever. He saw her again in forgotten attitudes; seated at her dressing table,
standing with an empty glass in her hand,
peering through her lorgnon. He saw her
again in Claridge's when she had wept and

kissed his hands. He remembered when she took his ring to wash. He heard her low, husky voice.

The catch on the bathroom door let go with a soft click, and the door swung part-way open on its hinges, letting a shaft of light into the room. Cary raised himself on his elbow and looked down at the pale averted face.

"Nikki—Nikki, sweet——"

He took her tight little fist in his hand. The fingers relaxed. He held it up to his lips to kiss. In the palm lay a little stone—a little heart-shaped stone from the tomb of Héloïse and Abélard; the forgotten talisman. Cary felt a terrible tug at his heart. No harm can come to our true love.

"Nikki, Nikki——"

Slowly she turned her face toward his. Her eyes were tranquil as a nun's.

"Nikki," Cary whispered, "Nikki, I'm so sorry."

"About me?"

"Yes, about you. I didn't know . . . about you."

"Aren't you glad?"

"Oh, Nikki," Cary said brokenly, "I'll never leave you. I'll stay with you, Nikki."

"Cary—you're sweet."

"What can I do, Nikki? What can I do for you? Is there anything I can make up to you—Oh, tell me something I can do for you. What do you want? Tell me. Tell me. What do you want, Nikki?"

"Well," said Nikki bravely, "I've always wanted a pair of Spanish ear-rings."

LISBON, PORTUGAL,
  June 15, 1929.

Afterword

by Stephen Longstreet

It was the accepted custom during the High Renaissance for a master of a grand or new style to surround himself in his studio with apprentices and students who assisted the master, laying in backgrounds, painting the unimportant parts of his pictures. When a demand came from some duke or cardinal for a popular madonna or a tasty reclining courtesan, the apprentices, if advanced enough, often copied one of the maestro's works, which the maestro might touch up and deliver to the buyer. It was common practice, and a good one for learning the nuances of one's craft, to grasp a style. Today these products of the *rinascita* are known as of "The School of Rubens," "School of Titian," a product of "The Rembrandt Circle."

If Ernest Hemingway had surrounded himself with apprentices and students of his work, studying under his guidance his revolt against his times, temporal and emotional, *Single Lady*, by John Monk Saunders, could be honestly labeled as "a novel, done in anchored unserenity, from the School of Ernest Hemingway—*The Sun Also Rises* period."

In the 1930s when I was making journeys to the

West Coast to write of film doings (I was soon to
become the motion picture critic of the *Saturday
Review of Literature* under the house name of
"Thomas Burton"), John Monk Saunders was one of
the prominent members of what was spoken of as
"the Paris Crowd," a group fastidious, intelligent,
often given to mischief and paranoia. Although F.
Scott Fitzgerald, then a depressing, low-keyed figure, was attempting a new career as a screenwriter,
the true heroes of the group included William
Wellman, the director of *Wings*; Arthur Hornblow,
the town's concise, rather prissy gourmet and wine
taster; Albert Lewin, who made the film, *Picture of
Dorian Gray*, and other outre works ("The pro-
ducers can't get over the fact I have a university
degree, have lectured at colleges, and pronounce
French correctly"); and Walter Wanger, who also
had been educated to a level above that of Harry
Cohn and Louie (never *Louis* in Hollywood) B.
Mayer. There were in the Saunders circle a few film
actresses, one a friend of H. L. Mencken ("she reads
books"). Also there had been Mabel Normand, the
Mack Sennett comedienne, who testified she was
leafing through a volume of Freud, while shelling
and eating peanuts in her limousine the night the
film director William Desmond Taylor was murdered. A crime never solved.

It was in such an illusionist atmosphere that
Saunders lived, a collection of people in the "industry" (as it was called) who felt themselves by educa-
tion and background to be those few who gave to
Hollywood the gloss of an erudite aspic. Some

sensed they were lowering their standards (Saunders was *the* former Rhodes Scholar) by engaging in the making of the motion pictures that carried their names. They managed to awe the town by their air of ineffable superiority.

I remember there was about Saunders a sense of having been there with the early Hemingway, having met Gertrude Stein, been on great drunks with famous avant-garde names, met Sara and Gerald Murphy at the Ritz.* Saunders did not resent being classed with Fitzgerald's "all the sad young men," or La Stein's "lost generation." Truer than some backgrounds presented to Hollywood: Brooklyn-born Josef Von Sternberg's false claims to be a noble *von*, or Von Stroheim's unproved memoirs as a gay hussar in Alt Wien (translated by one local radio announcer "Old Wine"). John Monk Saunders really had the essentially fortuitous credentials.

He was born in Hinckley, Minnesota, on November 22, 1897. No deep research has been done on his background, but the family must have had some cultural or prosperous background. Not only did Saunders graduate from the University of Washington, but later, as noted, he was a Rhodes Scholar at Magdalen College, Oxford, which in those days meant much more than it does in our decrepit era. Even before that, in 1917, Saunders had trained at the United States Military Aeronautics Department

---

*He certainly was aware of, was on the fringe of the Hemingway-Stein circle in Paris, but his name does not appear in the index of Carlos Baker's *Ernest Hemingway, A Life Story.*

at Berkeley and was commissioned a 2nd Lieutenant in the Air Force. How much flying he did in the war is enmeshed, immersed, in a mass of faint information based on gossip, and stories of men flying the canvas ships—Sopwith Camels, French SPADs over the Western Front. What is known is that Saunders did get back to graduate from the University of Washington in 1919 and returned to Europe as a Rhodes Scholar, *then* to live in that spacious, untranquil European decade of the 1920s, about which many myths and legends were produced. And are still staining the true picture of the expatriate.

Whatever his contacts, or life, in Europe were —their breadth and spaciousness—he was a very presentable young man, seemingly of solid early American stock, very well educated. By 1927 he was in California, having published short stories and worked on the *New York Tribune* and the *Los Angeles Times*. A revolution had taken place in the motion picture world. It had learned to talk (and sing). Actors now had to have words to say. Saunders wrote the original story for *Wings* (1927), the epic of the fliers of World War I. It was Saunders's first major story credit in Hollywood and set him up as one of those men who could "write gutsy, ballsy stories" (Jack Warner). *Wings* was a breakthrough for Saunders; the film industry bases one's standing in the tight-knit community by one's screen credits—not one's abilities, promise, or talents. Writers were suspect, however. One studio head, till the day he died, referred to writers as "schmucks with Underwoods." Saunders's most important film credit came in 1930 with an 11-page story, "The Flight Commander." Howard Hawks turned this into a screenplay called *The Dawn Patrol*, with the help of two other writers and the movie became a classic.*

Saunders became one of the well-known, fully accepted figures of the motion picture world—a world of exotic odalisques, huge tax-free incomes—a world of living gayly and wildly in a montage of drink, beautiful men and women now long gone, giant automobiles. It was the romantic, vulgar fan magazine's idea of life among the annointed screen personalities. If it seems false, banal and callow today, it was actually opulent and full of tenacious enthusiasm, an exciting world of ruined lives, shattered careers, and high-priced serfs bowing to the whims of powerful studio bosses—"If your luck held and you didn't crap out handling the dice" (John Ford).

The pinnacle of success for a male screenwriter was to marry a Hollywood movie star. John Monk Saunders married Fay Wray (his second wife), a charming tiny and graceful film actress who had the knack of presenting illusion and fact as interchangeable. She's remembered today because she was also the love object of King Kong, who, infatuated, carried her in his huge fist to the top of the Empire State Building, to be shot down by Air Force planes.

*Saunders worked in the following films: *Wings, The Legion of the Condemned, The Dockwalloper, Last Flight, I Found Stella Parish, The Finger Points, The Dawn Patrol, A Yank at Oxford,* and *West Point of the Air. Wings* (1927) and *The Legion of the Condemned* (1928) were published as photoplay novels.

Afterword

There were some jests made that former Lieutenant Saunders had led the attacking squadron of fliers.

Single Lady was published in New York by Brewer & Warren in 1931. My copy of the novel is the Grosset & Dunlap "Photoplay Edition," which has on its cover and title page:

THE
LAST FLIGHT
PHOTOPLAY TITLE OF
SINGLE LADY

The back of the title page states:

Copyright, 1930–1931
Liberty Magazine
Copyright, 1931
by
John Monk Saunders
Second Printing before Publication

The novel appeared first as a serial in *Liberty* titled "Nikki and Her War Birds"—and even before publication the book was planned as a film version. Four stills are bound into my copy: *A First National and Vitaphone Production starring Richard Barthelmess as Cary Lockwood and Helen Chandler as Nikki.* *

Reading the novel, it is soon clear that it is certainly a product of a student of the master; an apprentice taking notes in a corner of the studio, and

---

*Saunders wrote the screenplay for *The Last Flight*, which was directed by William Dieterle. The novel was also made into an unsuccessful Broadway musical, *Nikki*.

analyzing the master's strokes, trying for his promiscuity if not his fidelity; hoping for the new and novel approach to figures of speech and landscape. It's all there—Hemingway in photo-copy. The names of the drinks, the crisp choppy dialogue—even in its impotence and stoic mortality. The Paris and Lisbon of the lost romantics; sad, bittersweet in turn. Even the damn bullfights —that unique spectacle of public butchering.

Cary Lockwood is Jake Barnes (his genitalia intact—*Liberty* readers and film fans liked a whole man), and Nikki is, of course, Lady Brett. The novel attempts attitudes and charming toughness, also secret sorrows, parties, booze crawls, and the fringes of sex (as in Hemingway the sex isn't mature, or really very well done or interesting—just hints of traumatic, euphoric experiences). And all in a glow of named brands: Campari, Pernod, and Grand Champagne. The right street names: Rue Notre Dame des Champs, Avenue de L'Observitoire. The right song, "China Lady"; and the bystanders offering the proper chic comeback, "Bravo le negre blanc." All that is needed are the true brush strokes by the master himself, the tighter control of the dialogue, a firmer grip on the story so it doesn't fly off into parody in a paroxism of over-exaltation. But these finishing touches are missing.

Here is the yellow brick road to Hemingway Land, that Ol' Devil Nostalgia even before the mold had set. As Saunders presents it, the novel is like a too-dark version of a motion picture we've seen once before, perhaps in too glorious Technicolor. The

signs insist—yes, this may be the Deux Magots, and
the dark stairs of the Paris–New York Hotel on the
rue Vaugirard, the Boul' Mich and the intake of
croissants and coffee while reading the *Paris Soir*.
Good local color in these E. H. out-take prints, but
somehow it's a dupe print of a dupe print.*

What fails to come through in all the Hemingway
copyists are the true tacky dalliances of those Paris
years, the meanness of the menage a trois, the libid-
ious hopes and petulant endings in tears. A feeling
life is lived at a railroad station buffet, that love ends
in the dank sadness of a rainy afternoon. The early
vintage Hemingway had something true about the
American contact with the Galerie Lafayette, the
hard-nosed gendarmes, even picking up one's check
from home at the Guaranty Trust or the American
Express, or eating caneton a la presse. Hemingway's
students don't catch that at all properly. Their books
are as impotent as shadows.

A Paris novel of Americans in the Paris of the 20s
had to be more than drinking Calvados, or a bock at a
zinc; not just remembering a Paquin gown or an old
Norton-Harjes uniform in a closet; or even a record-
ing of "Dardanella" as "nifty," or "keen" to dance to.
In Saunders's *Single Lady* we do get a carousel of
impressions moving quickly to a very faint tune. But
the master's own enigma is missing. The one true
hand is not there in *Single Lady*. The colors come

---

*An *out-take print* is a scene shot but spoiled by the actors. A
dupe print is a fuzzy pirated version of a movie, illegally made,
not from the negative.

out muddy; the whole tone is like a copying of a Picasso, created by filling in numbered sections on a white surface with the proper already mixed colors.

I must say I enjoyed reading *Single Lady*, for all its delirious, vulnerable excessiveness. One balks only at the added plot, shoved in, one suspects, to make it worth its salt to the magazine and the film studio; something about a great Spanish gold treasure to be recovered. The novel is better than camp. It does have a refractory integrity; is a vision of the way bright young men saw themselves in the 1920s in Europe. Hemingway was the Messiah of American literature, and any hard-working apprentice of writing could catch enough of the obvious stance, the self-indulgent mirror hero, to write his own version of what he now thought life to be for a free-wheeling young man loose in Paris, at a good rate of exchange. The novel Saunders wrote is pure self-delusion, admiration for brusqueness with just enough commercialism to make possible its sea crossing to Hollywood.

Saunders was not the only American writer to try for the brass ring on the Hemingway merry-go-round. The ground in the 20s and 30s was littered with cadavers of writers who had taken on the Hemingway infection and had by either promise or perversity died of it, at least as writers. Saunders came closest to *The Sun Also Rises*; it could almost be called a plagiarism, scene for scene at times, character for character in certain sections, even the E. H. shorthand dialogue is attempted:

"Where are you going?"

"Oh, out—"

"Out where?"

"Out to get a drink."

"I suppose you couldn't arrange that here?"

Close—but no cigar.

Hemingway's greatest contribution to American writing had been a cleaning up of the native prose, bringing with it a stripped lyric grace physical action closer to the reader than any other writer of his time. A genius in his youth, in the Nick Adams stories, in later life in tragic perversity, Papa was always just a few rungs above his apprentices. If E.H. knew of or reacted to John Monk Saunders's novel, I have been unable to find any trace of it.

The Crash of 1929 and its aftermath in the 30s seemed to have lessened the impact of the "lost generation" crowd; the Marxists and "Unfriendly Hollywood Ten" groups were forming. Saunders's marriage to Miss Wray ended in divorce in 1939. With few demands for his services, he drifted away from Hollywood as it swung Left. In 1940 rumor drifted back to the west coast that he had taken his own life. Aged 42, John Monk Saunders hanged himself in Fort Myers, Florida. That last romantic note now seems a dress-rehearsal, anticipating the master himself in his departure from a world a long ways from the 1920s of the master's and the pupil's prime.

TEXTUAL NOTE

The text of *Single Lady* published here is a photo-offset reprint of the first edition, first printing (New York: Brewer & Warren, 1931). No emendations have been made in the text.

M.J.B.

Lost American Fiction Series

published titles, as of October 1976

please write for current list of titles